In
Too
Steep

Also available by Kate Kingsbury

Misty Bay Tea Room Mysteries

In Hot Water

Merry Ghost Inn Mysteries

Be Our Ghost
Doom with a View
Dead and Breakfast

Manor House Mysteries

An Unmentionable Murder
Wedding Rows
Fire When Ready
Berried Alive
Paint by Murder
Dig Deep for Murder
For Whom Death Tolls
Death is in the Air
A Bicycle Built for Murder

Pennyfoot Hotel Mysteries

A Merry Murder
A Perilous Promise
Mulled Murder
The Clue is in the Pudding
Herald of Death
Mistletoe and Mayhem
Decked with Folly
Ringing in Murder

Shrouds of Holly
Slay Bells
No Clue at the Inn
Maid to Murder
Dying Room Only
Death with Reservations
Ring for Tomb Service
Chivalry is Dead
Pay the Piper
Grounds for Murder
Check-Out Time
Eat, Drink, and Be Buried
Service for Two
Do Not Disturb
Room With a Clue

Raven's Nest Bookstore Mysteries
(writing as Allison Kinglsey)

Extra Sensory Deception
Trouble Vision
A Sinister Sense
Mind Over Murder

Belle Haven House Mysteries
(writing as Rebecca Kent)

Murder Has No Class
Finished Off
High Marks for Murder

In Too Steep

A MISTY BAY TEA ROOM MYSTERY

Kate Kingsbury

CROOKED LANE

NEW YORK

Published in the United States by Crooked Lane Books, an imprint of The Quick Brown Fox & Company LLC.

Crooked Lane Books and its logo are trademarks of The Quick Brown Fox & Company LLC.

Library of Congress Catalog-in-Publication data available upon request.

ISBN (hardcover): 978-1-63910-066-8
ISBN (ebook): 978-1-63910-067-5

Cover illustration by Greisbach/Martucci

Printed in the United States.

www.crookedlanebooks.com

Crooked Lane Books
34 West 27th St., 10th Floor
New York, NY 10001

First Edition: August 2022

10 9 8 7 6 5 4 3 2 1

To Bill, for all the years of love
and support. I could not have taken
this journey without you.
I will love you forever.

Chapter One

"**A**nother one? You've got to be kidding." Detective Lieutenant Tony Messina stared at his officer in disbelief. In almost four years of living in the quiet seaside town of Misty Bay, he'd had to deal with only one homicide, and that had been less than a month ago.

"No, sir. I'm not." Police Officer Ken Brady placed a printed report in front of the detective. "He was found by the mailman early this morning."

Messina scanned the brief report. *Name: Lewis Trenton. Age: Sixty-five. Occupation: Beachcomber.* He looked up at the officer. "Beachcomber?"

"Yes, sir. Trenton was apparently a hermit. Lived alone in a cabin in the hills. According to the mailman, the victim spent most of his days looking for stuff on the beach."

"Stuff?"

Brady shrugged. "You know, people leave stuff on the beach or lose stuff in the sand. Or maybe the gift shops bought seashells, pebbles, agates from him. Stuff like that."

Messina eyed his officer with interest. "You seem to know a lot about it."

"Yes sir. My wife collects that stuff."

"Ah." Messina looked down at the report. The phones in the office were quiet that morning. Only one of the four officers with the department sat at his desk, and he was studying his computer with an intensity that made Messina wonder if the guy was fighting a video game battle.

He was still having trouble accepting that this peaceful little town had experienced its second murder in a month. Having spent most of his career in Portland, he was used to the brutal realities of homicide cases. Back then, there were times when he'd dealt with one or more a week.

He thought he'd left all that behind when he transferred to Misty Bay. It was one of the reasons he'd searched for a position in a small town. That, and the need to escape from memories too painful to bear.

Snatching his mind back to the present, he studied the report. "It says here that he was shot."

"Yes, sir. The ME is out there now. He's probably waiting for you."

Messina envisioned the stern-faced medical examiner. He was a man of few words. Stationed in Newport, he acted like Misty Bay was a backwoods community, hardly worth his time. It was probably nothing personal, but the guy always made Messina feel like an intruder instead of someone trying to do his job. "So, what are we waiting for?"

A confused frown flashed across Brady's face. "Sir?"

Messina sighed. "Let's go." Striding over to the door, he hoped that this case would be easier to solve than the last one. That was one he'd like to forget. Not only had he been hampered by small-town witnesses determined to keep their mouths shut, but he'd also had to deal with a group of wannabe detectives.

Those ladies at the Willow Pattern Tearoom were something else. They may have helped solve the case, but they had no business getting mixed up in a police investigation, and it had almost ended in disaster for one of them. At least this time they had no excuse to get involved, which was fortunate. Though he had to admit, meeting Jenna Ramsey made it worthwhile.

Wondering why the memory of the dark-eyed, defensive server at the tearoom persisted in invading his thoughts, he pulled open the door and stepped out into the drizzly sea air.

*   *   *

Two days later, Vivian Wainwright stared at the empty nail sticking out from her kitchen wall. She was certain she'd hung Felix's leash there last night. She always left it there after his evening walk. Now it was gone.

She turned to look at the dog, who sat staring at her, his brown eyes glistening with expectation. "I'm sorry, Felix." She shook her head at him. "We can't go without your leash. I must have left it somewhere, though I can't imagine where that could be. I'm sure I hung it up right there."

She jerked a thumb at the nail, and Felix tilted his head on one side. "Yes, I know. You want to go for your walk. I want to take you. But we can't go without your leash."

Every time she said the word "go" the dog's ears pricked up with expectation. *Look at me,* she thought. *I'm talking out loud to a dog.* Anxiety stabbed at her, and she quickly suppressed it. *Lots of people talk to their dogs, right? After all, dogs are family, like kids.*

3

She'd been talking to dogs all her life. It didn't mean she was losing her mind.

It was just that a lot of weird things had been happening lately. Like misplacing items, forgetting where she'd put them, and finding them in odd places. True, she'd been under a lot of stress. Owning an English tearoom was no picnic, even if it had been her lifetime dream. After all, she was past sixty, and a little old in the tooth to have taken on a business that demanded so much energy.

Aware of the doubts creeping in, she made an effort to pull herself together. "I'm being paranoid again," she told Felix, who immediately leapt to his feet, furiously wagging his tail.

Vivian sighed. "Okay, let's go look for your leash."

On the word "go," Felix made a mad dash for the living room, bounded over to his toy box and started dragging out a ball, a squeaky bear, and the rope snake that had been a gift from Hal.

At the thought of Hal Douglass, Vivian's spirits lifted. Her connection with the owner of the Furry Fun pet supplies store down the street had become solid, fun, and comforting, without all the trappings of an intimate relationship. If what she suspected was true and Hal wanted more, so far, he hadn't pressured her. He was keeping it light, and that was just what she needed right now.

Something caught her eye, and all thoughts of Hal vanished as she stared at the leash in Felix's mouth. "What in the world?" She took the leash from him, her mind straining to recall last night.

True, she had been tired after a busy day in the tearoom. Jenna Ramsey, one of her efficient assistants, had called in to say she had car trouble, and was late getting to work. Which meant that Gracie Jackson, the other helper, had to take on Jenna's duties, leaving Vivian to fill in where she could while still making sandwiches and brewing tea.

By the time she'd been ready to take Felix for his walk, all she'd wanted to do was collapse in front of the TV with a glass of wine and a plate of spaghetti Bolognese. But she could have sworn she'd hung Felix's leash on that nail. In the three weeks since she'd adopted the dog, some things had become habit, and hanging the leash was one of them. Why on earth would she suddenly change course and drop it in his toy box?

Shaking her head, she fastened the leash to Felix's collar. Not an easy task since he wriggled around with excitement at the prospect of his outing. Fresh air, Vivian decided, was exactly what she needed to clear her head.

The walk across the beach, with the sea breeze bathing her face, never failed to restore her energy and enthusiasm. There was nothing more invigorating than the fragrance of sand and seaweed, the pounding of waves breaking along the shoreline and the cries of seagulls diving for food.

In her opinion, the Oregon coast was one of the most beautiful landscapes in the world. With its backdrop of the forested range of mountains, creamy sands, and towering rocks rising from a restless ocean, all that grandeur could revitalize even the most depressed state of mind.

Half an hour later, she arrived back home feeling refreshed and invigorated. Late October weather usually meant rain, but that morning remained dry, though the heavy clouds threatening the ocean promised a wet afternoon.

Exhausted from his explorations of tide pools and seashells, Felix flopped down on the rug in the living room and promptly fell asleep. Vivian glanced at her watch. She just had time for a bowl of cereal before she had to start baking the pastries for afternoon tea.

The Willow Pattern Tearoom had become renowned for its delicious cakes and pastries, all baked by her in the tearoom's kitchen below. Thanks to her British mother, Vivian's recipes were authentic, as was the imported tea from England. Living her lifelong dream, she strove to create as close to the English experience as possible, and judging from the many compliments she received, she succeeded.

Right now, however, she intended to enjoy a quick breakfast and scan the local weekly newspaper before heading for the downstairs kitchen. She was anxious to read the news this morning.

A couple of days ago, a TV news anchor had presented a brief report of a shooting in Misty Bay. As usual, the Portland station had declined to go into details, deeming a small coastal town less than newsworthy compared to the problems and events of the city.

In Misty Bay, however, the news was received with shock and disbelief. The residents had not yet recovered from a previous murder, and the idea of someone being shot to death on the outskirts of their quiet, peaceful town was inconceivable. Since no one seemed to know much more than what they'd heard on TV, Vivian was hoping the local newspaper would relate more of the story.

Seated on her couch in her tiny, uncluttered living room, she settled her reading glasses on her nose and unfolded the paper. As she'd expected, the glaring headlines were dramatic: *Local Beachcomber Brutally Shot to Death in Gruesome Attack*. After eagerly studying the text, however, she was disappointed to find little more than what she'd heard already.

Lewis Trenton, a local recluse, had been attacked in the living room of his hillside cabin in an apparent robbery attempt, though nothing appeared to have been stolen. The victim, who apparently had no family or friends, was found dead at the scene, with his shotgun lying by his side. So far, the police had no suspects.

Staring at the picture provided of the cabin's living room, Vivian had to wonder why a robber would need to shoot an elderly man for what appeared to be nothing but junk in the house. Why waste time on a broken-down shack when there were so many expensive homes nearby?

She was about to lay the paper down when something caught her eye. Standing on a shelf next to a wilted plant, a model of a clock tower looked familiar. She peered at it more closely, then grabbed her laptop from its perch on her bookshelf, and carried it back to the couch.

It took her only a minute or two to find the article on the newspaper's website. Bringing up the photo, she enlarged it, then sat back with a sigh. There was no doubt about it. The model on the dead man's shelf was a replica of London's Big Ben. And she was a hundred percent certain it had been bought from her tearoom less than a month ago.

It would seem that Lewis Trenton had known at least one friend.

* * *

Vivian was still thinking about the murder when Jenna arrived at the tearoom later. By then trays of scones, lemon curd tarts, Eccles cakes, and Bakewell tarts lined the shelves in the kitchen, and the sweet smell of baking filled the room.

The tall, vigorous woman sniffed the air as she shrugged off her jacket and hung it in the closet. "Every time I walk in here, my stomach forgets I ate breakfast."

Vivian laughed. "Well, you're welcome to sample a pastry. I'm always ready for a review of my baking."

Jenna flipped her black hair back from her face. "Thanks, but I have to watch the waistline. I don't have Gracie's metabolism. She could eat a whole cow and not put on weight."

"I heard that." The young woman standing in the doorway looked over at Vivian. "The door was unlocked."

Vivian sighed. "I forgot to lock the door behind Jenna. The last thing we need is customers wandering in here before we're ready."

Gracie had dyed her short hair blue, and Vivian was still trying to get used to the sight of blue spikes sticking up all over her assistant's head. "Well, I locked it again." Gracie bounced over to the rows of shelves. "Ooh, those scones look awesome."

"You can have one after we make the tea. Meanwhile, you can finish cleaning up the counter."

Gracie nodded at the counter. "Looks like you already cleaned it up."

Vivian followed her gaze. "So I did. I'm getting ahead of myself."

Jenna stared at her. "Are you okay? You seem a little out of it."

Vivian sighed. "Sorry. I guess I'm preoccupied. I saw the story about the shooting in the local paper this morning, and I can't stop thinking about it."

"I saw it too." Jenna opened a cabinet and took out a kettle. "Why would anyone want to shoot a helpless old man?"

"I keep asking myself the same thing." Vivian watched Jenna fill the kettle and place it on the stove while Gracie sat down at the dinette table.

"Maybe he stole the guy's girlfriend or something," Gracie said, ever the romantic.

Jenna snorted. "Have you seen the pic of him? He was a raggedy old hermit who looked like he hadn't bathed in a year."

"But he didn't deserve to die that way," Vivian said quietly.

Jenna shot her a look of remorse. "No, of course he didn't."

"Are we going to look for his killer?" Gracie leaned forward, her blue eyes sparkling with excitement. "Like we did with Dean's murder?"

"No, of course not." Aware that she had spoken too harshly, Vivian softened her voice. "That's the job of the police."

"Thank goodness." Mugs rattled in Jenna's hand as she took them down from the cabinet. "I wouldn't want to go through that again. It was a little too close for comfort for me."

"Yeah," Gracie said, sounding a little deflated, "I guess it was, like, bad for you. Especially since you almost died."

"It wasn't much fun."

"But then that hunky Detective Messina rescued you," Gracie rolled her eyes at the ceiling and clasped her hands together at her throat. "Remember when he carried you in his arms to his car? It was so, like, dreamy."

She'd drawled the word out in a throaty voice that brought a frown to Jenna's face.

Seeing her friend's discomfort, Vivian felt compelled to jump in. Gracie was young and could be less than discreet at times. Jenna had been accused of murdering her ex-husband and had almost died at the hands of the true killer. She didn't need to be reminded of the trauma.

"You know quite well, Gracie," she said, "that Jenna was unconscious and doesn't remember any of that. Anyway, it's all over with now, and I'm not going to speculate on this murder. What did intrigue me was the picture of Lewis Trenton's living room. It showed one of my Big Ben models on his shelf."

Jenna lifted a teapot from its shelf and put it on the counter. "Really? You sold one of those?"

"I know. They're so ugly I almost sent them back. I was really surprised when we sold one. Thank goodness I only ordered three of them."

Gracie wriggled around on her chair. She was always bristling with excess energy and found it difficult to sit still for long. "I take care of all the souvenirs, and I don't remember selling one of those."

Vivian smiled. "It was one evening, right after you'd left for the day. The customer showed up at the door just as I was locking it. She said she was from out of town, so I let her in to look at the shelves." She reached into the cabinet and took down a tin box, decorated with scenes of an English village. Her mother had brought the box with her when she'd left England to start a new life with Vivian's father in Oregon.

Her mother had kept her teabags in the tin, and that's where Vivian stashed her personal teabags. Every time she opened the tin, she was reminded of her parents, both of whom had now passed away.

"So, someone bought it for the guy?" Jenna handed her the teapot as the kettle began to whistle.

Taking the teapot from her, Vivian nodded. "Well, she said she was buying it for a friend, so I'm guessing it was Lewis. In which case, our hermit had at least one friend." She took the kettle from the stove and poured a small amount of boiling water into the teapot. After swirling it around for a moment or two, she emptied it into the sink, dropped three teabags into the teapot, then filled it with water from the kettle.

"I wonder if she knows he died." Jenna tipped a small amount of milk into each mug.

"I keep wondering that too." Vivian took three scones from the shelf and put them on a plate. Carrying them over to the table, she added, "I think it's so sad that someone will be buried with no one to mourn him."

Silverware clattered as Jenna picked out a teaspoon from the drawer. "Maybe he liked being alone. Some people prefer it."

Gracie looked at her. "Do you like living alone?"

Jenna shrugged. "Not really, but then I'm not a recluse. Apparently, this guy lived alone by choice. Why else would he live in a cabin in the hills, away from everyone else?"

"Well, I guess we'll never know." Vivian watched Jenna stir the teabags in the teapot, and then pour the dark brown tea into the mugs.

"Well, I'm glad I've got a new roomie," Gracie said, eyeing the scones. "After my last one left, I loathed living alone. Alyssa can be a pain at times, but at least I have someone I can chat with again." She looked back at Jenna. "Better than chatting to a cat."

"Cats can be good company," Vivian said, taking two of the mugs from Jenna. "But I can heartily recommend a dog. I haven't had Felix that long, but already I think I'd be lost without him. I swear he understands every word I say."

Jenna grunted. "And he can't talk back at you. Who needs a husband, right?"

Vivian placed the mugs on the table. "You'll change your mind when you meet the right man. Don't let a bad marriage sour you on all men. There are some good ones out there."

"Like Hal?" Without waiting for an invitation, Gracie grabbed a scone.

Vivian smiled. "Yes, like Hal."

Gracie sent Jenna a sly look. "And Tony Messina?"

Jenna put her mug down on the table so hard, some of the tea slopped over the side. "Once and for all, I'm not interested in Detective Messina—or any man, come to that—so quit fantasizing about something that's not going to happen."

"We'll see." Seemingly unfazed, Gracie took a bite of her scone.

Gracie wasn't the only one who thought there could be a connection between Jenna and the tight-lipped detective. Vivian had seen for herself a spark pass between them, one that could possibly be ignited with a little help.

Right now, however, there were more practical matters to attend to, and time was passing by. They barely had time to drink their tea before she opened the tearoom and the rush began. "We need to start thinking about what to do for Halloween," she said as she sat down at the table. "It's little more than a week away."

Gracie's face lit up. "Ooh, let's decorate with skeletons and witches and a bunch of ghosts."

"Well, I was thinking of something a bit more elegant, like maybe small pumpkins and autumn leaves—that sort of thing."

Gracie pouted. "Boring."

"Well," Vivian said, feeling a need to defend herself, "Halloween wasn't a big deal in England until the 1970s. It's kind of a modern thing over there, and I like to keep the Willow Pattern old-fashioned."

"Sounds great." Jenna sat down at the table. "Don't listen to Modern Millie. Simple and sophisticated—that's the Willow Pattern Tearoom. Right?"

Gracie mumbled something Vivian couldn't hear, but then in the next instant sat up with a grin spreading over her face. "I've got it! How about turning off all the lights and, like, just keep the candles lit. It'll be so cool. Kind of mysterious and creepy."

"Except we do most of our business in the afternoon when it's still daylight," Jenna reminded her.

"Oh yeah." Gracie sounded deflated again.

Seeing her depressed face, Vivian murmured, "Okay, I guess it wouldn't hurt to have a ghost or two hovering over the store shelves."

Gracie lit up again. "Awesome! I'll make a couple of them to hang in there."

"I know where to get decorations at a reasonable price," Jenna said. "Leave it to me."

Vivian smiled. "Thank you both. I don't know what I'd do without you two."

Gracie lifted her mug of tea. "I don't know what I'd do without this job." She looked around at the two large ovens, the metal shelves, and the wooden counter where Vivian mixed, stirred and kneaded her afternoon tea delicacies. "This feels like home to me now, and you guys are like my family."

Vivian felt a lump in her throat and quickly cleared it. "I feel the same way. Now, let's finish our tea and get to work."

Half an hour later, she walked out into the tearoom to conduct her customary check before the first customers arrived. Jenna had done most of the work the night before, as usual, and Vivian was reassured to see each of the eight tables immaculate with their white tablecloths and the new gold napkins. Minutes ago, Jenna had set out the delicate English bone china teacups, saucers, and small plates. Vases of marigolds added a glow of sunshine to each table, soon to be accompanied by milk jugs and teapots, and the tiered cake stands loaded with crustless sandwiches and pastries.

On the other side of the room, Gracie kept the shelves stocked with souvenirs and food products from Britain, and divided her time between serving customers and helping Jenna in the tearoom.

Vivian smiled as she headed back to the kitchen. As always, she could rely on her two assistants to take care of the room while she was busy in the kitchen, making sandwiches and tea and loading up the cake stands.

This afternoon, however, she had trouble focusing on her tasks. For some reason, the image of that Big Ben model kept popping into her mind. She finally admitted to herself that she was still concerned about Lewis Trenton. She might not know the man, but no one should have to meet his maker without someone to mourn his passing.

As the day drew to a close, she could no longer resist the urge to know more about the hermit. There was one way to find out. She could ask the locals if they knew him. Small-town gossip could be very informative.

After pulling off her apron, she hurried out into the tearoom and was pleased to see two of the tables still occupied. Jenna was busy clearing off the empty tables, and Gracie stood by the shelves, talking to a customer.

Noticing customers she hadn't seen before, she walked over to the elderly couple and smiled at them. "I hope you enjoyed your tea and scones?"

The gentleman nodded with such enthusiasm he dislodged his glasses. "Absolutely great," he assured her, as he straightened them. "I'd like to come here every afternoon. My wife doesn't bake, and there's nothing I enjoy more than fresh baked pastries."

His wife gave him a sour look before murmuring, "It was very nice. What kind of tea was it? It tasted a bit strong."

"It's black tea, made from tea plants in Ceylon," Vivian told her. "The growers harvest the top two leaves and bud of the tea plant, which is the highest quality and most flavorful part of the plant. I import it from England. It's their top-selling tea over there."

"Oh." The woman looked unimpressed. "What other teas do you have?"

"That's the only one." Vivian looked her straight in the eye. "It's the only one I need. If it's too strong for you, just add water to your cup from your hot water jug." She tapped the stainless-steel jug with her finger.

The woman looked at the jug as if she'd never seen it before.

"The scones were delicious," her husband said, seeming uncomfortable with his wife's attitude.

"Thank you." Vivian smiled at him. "I'm glad you enjoyed them. Are you visiting the town?

"No," his wife answered for him. "We moved down here six months ago."

"When I retired," her husband added.

Vivian nodded. "It's a wonderful town to retire in. Though we do have our problems now and then. I guess you've heard the news about Lewis Trenton, the beachcomber who was killed a couple of days ago?"

The woman sniffed. "He was a recluse, from what I heard. They say his home was a disgusting mess when they found him."

Her husband shook his head. "I don't know why anyone would want to shoot the poor guy. He never did anyone any harm. I heard he would do anything to help someone out. He spent weeks trying to find a home for a stray dog he found on the beach."

His wife stared at him. "How do you know that?"

"The guys in the barbershop were talking about him this morning."

The gentleman at the next table spoke up. "I knew Lewis," he said. "It's a shame. He didn't deserve to die that way."

Vivian moved over to him. "How well did you know him?"

The man shook his head. "I don't know that anyone knew Lewis that well. He didn't like getting close to people. He was a loner, deeply religious. I own a souvenir shop in Newport, and he brought items in to sell now and then, like shells and agates. I remember he found a Japanese fishing float once and had the devil of a time trying to decide if he wanted to sell it or keep it."

Vivian smiled. "What did he decide?"

Her customer grinned back at her. "He gave it away. To a customer's little girl who seemed fascinated with it."

That told Vivian a lot about the hermit. "Thank you," she said. "He sounds like a good man."

The customer's words stayed with her, and later that night she went down to the storeroom and unpacked one of the two remaining Big Ben models. Much as she disliked it, she told herself, she would keep it on the shelves in memory of Lewis Trenton. May he rest in peace.

Chapter Two

The following morning, Vivian awoke with a start to find Felix standing over her, his nose inches from hers and his warm breath washing her face. Struggling to sit up, she pushed him away from her. "What? Are you sick? Do you need to go potty?"

Hearing one of his favorite words, Felix bounded off the bed and with his tongue hanging out of his mouth, furiously wagged his tail.

Sighing, Vivian turned on the bedside lamp and swung her feet out of bed. There were some drawbacks to owning a dog, she reminded herself, glancing at the clock. Then again, it was close to six AM, the time she normally got up.

She tapped the rug with her toes, feeling for the slippers she had placed there the night before. Her foot contacted nothing but air, and she peered down at the empty floor. She'd left her slippers there last night. She was sure of it. She always left her slippers there.

Frowning, she got up, with Felix dancing around her like an impatient ballerina. A quick search of the bedroom convinced her the slippers were not there. She sat down for a moment on the side of the bed and tried to remember every moment leading up to climbing under the covers.

She'd followed her normal routine—cleaned her teeth, got undressed, turned on the alarm, slid out of her slippers, and climbed into bed. Frowning, she got down on her knees and peered under the bed.

Felix, apparently thinking this was a new game, danced up to her and deposited a wet lick on her face. At the same moment, the alarm clock shrieked its warning. Felix barked, startling her even more.

She scrambled to her feet. Every night, for as long as she could remember, she had left her slippers at the side of the bed. What could she have done with them?

Right now, however, she had to use the bathroom. With Felix at her heels, she crossed the room to the bathroom door and switched on the light. Her gasp of surprise raised the hairs on the dog's neck. Right there, in the center of the floor, lay her slippers.

She stared at them, wondering what had possessed her to leave them there instead of by the bed. This was the second time she'd misplaced something. Could she be having problems with her memory?

She'd been distracted, she reminded herself, thinking about that poor, lonely man facing an intruder and dying from a gunshot wound with no one to help him. Being buried alone with no one to mourn him. Such a sad ending to his life.

Shaking her head, she wondered why the death of Lewis Trenton should haunt her so much. She couldn't worry about all this now. She had a frisky dog to take out to the yard and pastries to bake. The hermit's saga and her lack of concentration would have to wait.

Felix hurtled down the stairs ahead of her and waited for her at the door leading to the backyard. The sun had not yet risen, and the rain clouds darkened the sky even more, yet Felix darted out onto the grass as if it were broad daylight.

He disappeared into the darkness, and she ventured outside to look for him, wrapping her robe more closely around her as the chill, salty air enveloped her. A light, misty rain dampened her hair, and she called to the dog. To her relief, he galloped out of the shadows toward her.

She felt unsettled, out of sorts. Thoughts of the dead hermit and worse, worrying about her recent lapses, were bringing her down. Making a mental note to make an appointment with her doctor to get her memory checked, she followed Felix back up the stairs to her apartment.

She watched the news on TV while she ate a bowl of cereal with Felix at her side, waiting in vain for a crumb to drop. The anchor made no mention of Lewis Trenton, and she resolved to put the hermit out of her mind. She had bigger things to worry about.

As usual, Felix's head drooped when it was time for her to go downstairs. "I'm sorry, buddy," she said, guilt nagging at her. "I know you get lonely, but I can't have you roaming the kitchen while I'm baking. I'll have the OSHA down on my head."

Felix answered with a half-hearted thump of his tail.

She spent the next three hours in the downstairs kitchen, baking her signature scones as well as cherry and almond Bakewell tarts, Chelsea buns, and her specialty—the intricate Battenburg cakes. She had just finished cutting the colorful cakes into slices when the shop doorbell announced a visitor.

Vivian checked her watch. She still had at least an hour before her assistants arrived. The sign on the door notified customers that she opened at noon. Maybe it was Hal at the door. He sometimes stopped by to take Felix for a walk. Dusting her hands on her apron, she hurried across the tearoom to the door.

She pulled it open, delighted to see Hal Douglass's smiling face, his shaggy gray hair ruffled by the wind and his warm brown eyes peering at her through his tortoise-shell glasses. "Hi! Come on in!" She dragged the door open wider and stepped back to let him in.

He stepped inside, and raised his chin. "I smell something good."

"I know. You want a scone?"

"After I take Felix for a walk."

"He'll be forever grateful." She beckoned him with her forefinger. "Come into the kitchen and I'll get my keys."

He followed her into the kitchen, his gaze drawn immediately to the stacked shelves. "What delectable treats have you created today?" His eyed widened as he caught sight of the Battenberg cake with its checkered pink and yellow squares and the yellow border of marzipan. "That looks incredible."

"Thank you." His compliment pleased her more than it should. "I'll give you a slice when you get back from your walk."

"I don't know that I can hold out that long, but I'll give it a shot."

She laughed as she opened a drawer and drew out her keys. "Here." She handed them to him. "Felix will be happy to see you. Thank you."

"No need to thank me. You know how much I enjoy walking with him. He's a great dog."

"He is, indeed. And you're a good man for caring about him." She hadn't meant to say those words out loud, but they apparently pleased Hal, judging by the warm look he gave her.

She watched him leave through the door that led to the stairway, telling herself, as she had so many times, how lucky she was to have a friend like Hal. He was great company, fun to be with, and made no demands on her to make her uncomfortable.

Pushing away the thought that she was more invested in the relationship than she was willing to admit, she piled the slices of cake on a platter and took it over to the shelves.

Her next task was to make fillings for the sandwiches. Opening the fridge door, she studied the contents, trying to decide whether to make egg and cress, or cheese and cucumber along with the roast beef and horseradish sandwiches.

The dinging of the shop doorbell again raised her head. Hal had left by the back door moments ago. He always came back in that way. Frowning, she headed for the shop door again. If it was someone trying to sell her cleaning products or something, she'd point out the "No Solicitors" sign and send him on his way.

This time, when she opened the door, she was surprised to see Natalie Chastain waiting on the doorstep, clutching a bottle of wine. As usual, the woman looked as if she were auditioning for a perfume commercial. She'd tucked a bright red scarf in the neck of her white coat. A white wool cap captured her recently dyed red hair, and thick black mascara framed her green eyes.

Natalie owned the Sophisticated Grape wine shop farther down the street and was a rare visitor to the Willow Pattern Tearoom. Vivian wouldn't exactly call her a friend, but tolerated her as a neighbor. Natalie craved attention and went out of her way to get it. She loved to gossip and was inclined to embellish the stories she passed on. If you didn't want your private life spread all over town, you were careful about what you said to her.

Right now, she was waving the bottle at Vivian. "I brought you some wine."

Vivian narrowed her eyes. There was usually a price for a gift from Natalie. "That's nice of you. Thank you." She hesitated, then reluctantly acknowledging she had time, added, "Would you like to come in?"

"Just for a moment." Natalie stepped inside, and Vivian closed the door behind her. "I left my new assistant in charge, so I don't want to stay too long."

Natalie went through assistants like Felix went through treats. Vivian nodded. "Time for a cup of tea?"

Natalie shuddered. "No, thanks. I only drink coffee in the mornings."

"Oh, right. I forgot." Vivian gave the bottle a meaningful look.

"Oh, here." Natalie shoved the bottle at her. "Actually, I was wondering if you could spare half a dozen of your scones. I have an appointment with a new distributor this morning, and I'd like to offer him a snack or something."

Vivian smiled. "Of course. I'll go get them." Half a dozen scones were a small payment for a bottle of good wine, she told herself, and added a couple more as she bagged the pastries.

When she carried them out into the tearoom, Natalie was standing at the store shelves, apparently absorbed by the array of souvenirs.

Vivian walked over to her and handed her the scones. "I hope your distributor enjoys them."

"Thanks." Natalie looked back at the shelves. "I just saw one of these the other day in a thrift store. They're selling it at half the price you're asking for it."

Vivian stared at the souvenir she'd pointed out. As far as she knew, there were only three models of the Big Ben in town, and two of them were in her shop. "Are you sure? Was it exactly the same as this one?"

"Exactly." Natalie peered more closely at her. "Are you okay?"

Intrigued by the news, Vivian barely heard her. There was a possibility that someone else was importing the same British souvenirs, of course, but it was much more likely that the one in the thrift store had belonged to Lewis Trenton. His belongings had probably been donated there, since he had no one else to claim them.

"I didn't mean to upset you."

Blinking at Natalie, Vivian shook her head. "You didn't. I was just surprised. I'd like to take a look at it. Which thrift store was it?"

"Hidden Treasures. It's the one on Main Street. It's mostly junk, but now and then you can find something nice for a really good price."

"Oh, I know where it is. I've been in there a couple of times. Thanks—and thank you for the wine."

"Sure." Natalie raised the bag of scones. "Thanks for these. I wish I could eat them myself, but I have to watch my waistline."

Vivian was willing to bet that the woman couldn't resist sampling at least one of the scones. She watched Natalie waltz out of the shop, wondering how anyone in their thirties managed to stay so slim.

As for herself, she'd given up the battle decades ago and had settled for being pleasingly plump. She could still look reasonably acceptable, especially if she dressed up. At least, Hal seemed to think so.

Envisioning his warm smile, she sighed. She'd promised herself she would stop worrying about their relationship and just enjoy it, but she had to wonder how long it would be before Hal grew tired of her keeping him at arm's length.

She knew what was holding her back. For one thing, she couldn't quite dismiss the notion that she'd be betraying her late husband. Martin had died more than three years ago, but she could still imagine him looking down on her in disapproval. More likely, however, it was her reluctance to love again and risk having to go through the pain of losing once more.

Sooner or later, she would have to deal with it. Hal was lonely, and he deserved to have someone to share his life. He'd lost his wife years ago and had made it clear he was ready to move on. It wasn't fair of her to keep him dangling with false hope. Yet the thought of him with another woman gave her so much pain she couldn't bear to think about it.

In fact, she told herself, she needed a distraction. She could get her baking done early tomorrow and make time to run along to the thrift store. She could check it out and see if the Big Ben was still there.

Hal arrived back a few minutes later, just as she was placing a bowl of egg salad in the fridge. She heard him talking to Felix as he led the dog upstairs, and for some reason her nerves tingled as she waited for him to come back down.

She had her back to him when he walked into the kitchen, and took a second or two to compose herself before turning to greet him. He looked windswept and robust, with his hair tossed across his forehead and his cheeks warmed by the cold breeze.

Her heart melted. "Hi. How was your walk?"

If her voice sounded a tad strained, he didn't appear to notice. "Great." He swiped his hair back with his hand. "Felix got a little messy. He was chasing a seagull and was ten yards into the ocean before he realized he couldn't fly. I got him cleaned up as well as I could, but you might have some sand on the carpet."

She grinned. "That's okay. I have a vacuum cleaner. Sounds like he had a good time."

"We both did. I wish you could have come with us."

"So do I."

The sudden longing in his eyes shortened her breath. Everything around her seemed to fall quiet and still, and for far too long she found herself unable to look away. With an effort, she gave herself a mental shake and turned back to the fridge. Opening the door, she tried to sound cool and collected when she asked, "Would you like some tea? The girls should be here soon."

"The girls? Are you entertaining a party?"

He sounded normal, and thankful that the moment, whatever it was, had passed, she relaxed. "I meant my assistants. I know I shouldn't call them that. Jenna is almost forty and Gracie is twenty-something. Jenna would kill me if she heard me refer to her as a 'girl.'"

"I think she might be flattered." Hal looked at his watch. "Speaking of assistants, I should get back to the shop. Lord knows what havoc Wilson has created by now."

Vivian smiled. Wilson was still a teenager, working his first job at the pet store. Put him in front of a computer and he was a genius. Put him behind the counter, and he was like a child lost in a maze. He seemed incapable of grasping the most basic procedures of a salesclerk.

Hal had the utmost patience with him, determined that Wilson would not be let go from his first job. Vivian loved that about him, that he was willing to put up with the young man's shortcomings rather than blot his record.

"I hope he hasn't done too much damage," she said, as she pulled out a beef roast from the fridge.

"Me too." For a moment he hesitated, as if he were about to say something else, but at that moment the shop doorbell rang, and he glanced at the tearoom. "That's probably your girls. I'll let them in."

"Thanks." She watched him walk away from her. "And thanks for taking Felix," she called out after him. "I know he loves going out with you."

"My pleasure." He looked back at her. "See you later."

She nodded. "Later."

He went out the door, and for a moment she felt let down, as if she'd let something good slip through her fingers. She was being ridiculous, she told herself. Why couldn't she just relax with him and stop agonizing over their relationship?

Jenna appeared in the doorway just then, and Vivian put her troubling thoughts aside.

"I just saw Hal," Jenna said as she hung her jacket in the closet.

"He just got back from taking Felix for a walk." Vivian carried the beef roast over to the counter and reached for her carving knife. "I think I have a messy dog waiting for me upstairs."

Jenna laughed. "Isn't that part of the fun?"

"I guess." Vivian began carving the roast into thin slices. "Is Gracie here yet?"

"I saw her parking her car down the road." Jenna took a clean apron out of the drawer and tied it around her waist. "She should be here any minute." She opened the cabinet and reached for a large jar of clotted cream, then took down eight small porcelain pots.

26

At that moment, the shop doorbell dinged, and seconds later Gracie rushed in, sounding out of breath. "Sorry I'm late. I locked my keys in the car. I tried to get the door open with a nail file, but it didn't work. I'll have to call the auto shop to open it for me."

Jenna shook her head. "There's always a calamity going on around you."

"I know. That's what makes life fun." Gracie slumped down on a chair and started thumbing her cell phone.

"Speaking of calamity," Vivian said, as she carefully sliced the last of the roast, "Natalie was in here earlier."

"You're right. That's a total disaster," Jenna muttered. She made no secret of the fact that she thoroughly disliked Natalie, though she often shopped for wine in her store.

Vivian sighed. "No, I meant that Natalie saw one of our Big Ben models in a thrift store. I think it might have belonged to Lewis Trenton."

"I need help," Gracie said into her phone. "I locked my keys in the car. Yes, on Main Street. Just down the road from the Willow Pattern Tearoom. It's a red Mazda. Thanks."

"You'd better go wait for them," Vivian said as Gracie slipped the phone in her pocket.

"Okay. I'll be right back." She dashed out of the kitchen, and seconds later the doorbell announced that she'd left.

"You seem awfully hung up on that guy's death," Jenna said as she filled the pots with the clotted cream.

"I am," Vivian admitted, "and I don't really know why. I guess it's because I hate the thought of having no one to mourn him. There has to be someone out there who cares enough to go to his funeral." She suspected that she was also using the hermit's

27

murder as a distraction from her dilemma with Hal, but she wasn't about to admit that.

"How about the woman who bought the replica?" Jenna carried the pots over to the fridge. "You said you thought she bought it for a gift for the guy."

"I did, and I'm thinking about getting in touch with her to see if she knows he died."

"Didn't she say she was from out of town?"

"She said she was staying with a friend in Newport, and lives in Portland. I have her name from her credit card payment. I might be able to track her down."

Jenna closed the fridge door. "Hot on the trail of another mystery, right?"

Vivian sighed. "Am I totally juvenile? You'd think I'd have enough on my plate, with a business and a dog to keep me busy."

"You were married to a prosecuting attorney for over thirty years, and you're a passionate fan of crime novels. It's not surprising that the mere whiff of a mystery sets you off on a chase."

Vivian had to grin. "Well, when you put it like that . . ."

Jenna walked back to the counter, carrying a jar of strawberry jam. "Go for it. You've got me interested in it now."

"I think I will. I'll check out the customer's name later. I'm also thinking of buying back the Big Ben, if it's still there."

Jenna raised her eyebrows. "I thought you didn't like them."

"I don't. But I'd like to keep that one. In memory of Lewis."

"You never met him."

"I know." Vivian shrugged. "But at least he'll have one person to honor his life."

"Well, if you need any help, I'm here."

Vivian smiled. "Thanks. I just might take you up on that." Seconds later the shop doorbell rang again. "That's probably a customer." She glanced at her watch. "Gracie must have left the door unlocked. It's almost noon anyway."

Jenna put down the jar of jam. "I'll take care of it," she said as she headed for the door.

Vivian took a large platter down from the cabinet, then picked up a loaf of bread from the shelves. After spacing the bread slices out on the platter, she spread a light covering of mayonnaise over them, then laid slices of roast beef on each one.

She was about to add a dash of horseradish sauce to each sandwich when Jenna walked back into the kitchen. "Gracie's back," she said, "so I left her with the customer."

"Did she get her car unlocked?"

"She did." Jenna picked up the jar of jam. "She said the guy from the auto shop arrived just as she got back to the car. He must have left right away."

"Well, he doesn't have far to come. They're only four blocks away."

Jenna took down more pots from the cabinet. "That's what I love about this town. Everything's so convenient."

A vision of Hal's pet supplies store popped into Vivian's mind. Impatient with herself, she focused instead on the sandwiches.

Tonight, she promised herself, after she'd taken Felix for his walk, she would try to track down the customer who bought the Big Ben. It would give her something to do and keep her mind off other unsettling matters.

If that were possible.

That evening, with Felix snoozing at her feet, she pulled up the last month's accounts on her computer. It took her only a couple of minutes to find the transaction. The customer's name was Stacey Patel, and she had bought the Big Ben model three weeks earlier.

Since she didn't have an address for the woman, Vivian put a search in her computer. To her delight, there was only one Stacey Patel listed for Portland. It took another two minutes to get the woman's address and phone number.

Vivian considered calling her, but decided against it. If the woman was a relative, or even a friend or acquaintance, being told of Lewis's death over the phone could be devastating. It was unlikely the murder was eventful enough to make the local news in Portland, given the dramatic incidents of everyday life in the city.

She'd rather not take the chance of distressing the woman if she lived alone. This was news better delivered in person. With the tearoom closed all day on Sunday, she could go to Portland to visit Stacey Patel. She would take a chance on her being home. Felix could come with her. He'd enjoy the outing. It would make a nice break for both of them.

For a brief moment she toyed with the idea of asking Hal to come with her, then decided against it. She didn't need any distractions while talking to what could well be a bereaved woman.

With that settled, she sat down on the couch to watch the evening news.

Chapter Three

Felix obligingly woke Vivian up early again the next morning, and for once she thanked him. She took him for a short walk, then instead of lingering over a bowl of cereal while watching the morning news, she grabbed a couple of granola bars and hurried down to the kitchen.

By the time she'd filled the trays with custard tarts, Scottish shortbread, maids of honor, and scones, she had less than an hour before Gracie and Jenna were due to arrive. Warning herself she wouldn't have much time to browse, she hurried upstairs to the apartment, tugged on her coat and scarf, and patted Felix on the head. "I'll be back to take you out in the yard real soon," she told him, then fled down the stairs and out into the street.

A soft mist dampened the air, and she turned up the collar of her coat. This late in the season, there were few visitors in town. A handful of people wandered along the sidewalk, and in front of her an elderly man walked his dog. Unlike Felix, this dog seemed content to trot quietly along at his master's side. Felix would be all over the sidewalk, sniffing at anything that seemed remotely interesting.

Thinking about the dog made her feel guilty at having to leave him locked up in her apartment instead of romping on the beach. Maybe Hal would come by again and take him for a walk. There she went again, thinking about that man. She definitely needed something else to keep her mind occupied.

Reaching the thrift store a few minutes later, she eagerly explored the shelves.

Natalie had been right when she'd said most of the items were junk, but now and then Vivian spotted a treasure, like the vintage glass vase which was priced way too low, and a beautiful gold watch that she could envision gleaming on Hal's wrist.

Hastily switching her thoughts back to her mission, she walked over to an aisle lined with rows of train sets, boxes of Legos, and various model kits. Right at the end of the aisle, she noticed a display of windmills and, standing next to them, the model of Big Ben.

It looked a little shabby, as if it had been tossed around a bit. She hesitated for a moment, reminding herself she was keeping it as a memento, then she took it down from the shelf and carried it over to the counter.

Natalie was right again. The price was half what Vivian had charged for it. Considering its dingy appearance, it should have been a lot lower, but she handed over her card to the friendly salesclerk, again reminding herself that she was doing this for Lewis Trenton. He obviously treasured his meager belongings, and she hoped that he was looking down on her and thanking her for making sure Big Ben didn't end up in the trash.

Hurrying back down the street, she spotted Jenna's car pulling up in front of the tearoom. In the summer months the assistants sometimes had to park blocks away and walk back to the store. Gracie didn't seem to mind. She reveled in the turmoil of crowded streets, packed tables in the tearoom, and customers jostling each other for room at the souvenir shelves.

Jenna, on the other hand, couldn't wait for winter. She worked hard in the tearoom, serving hungry customers, helping make sandwiches, cleaning and replenishing the tables, and vacuuming the floors. The vacation season lasted well into October, and by the time November rolled around, Jenna was more than ready to let up a bit.

As for Vivian, she was happy no matter the season, as she so often assured herself. She was living her dream, made possible by her late husband's generous life insurance policy and her own skill in the kitchen. And, of course, her mother's recipes.

She reached the door of the tearoom seconds behind Jenna, who stood in the doorway impatiently waiting for her to open the door. "Sorry," Vivian sang out, as she stepped up beside her. "I thought I'd be back before you got here. I really need to get extra keys made for you and Gracie."

Jenna swung around in surprise. "What are you doing out here?"

"I went to the thrift store." Vivian swung the package up at her. "I bought Lewis's Big Ben."

Jenna eyed the paper bag with obvious skepticism. "How can you be sure it belonged to Lewis?"

"I don't know. I just am. Who else in town would import something like this?"

Jenna smiled. "I can't argue with that."

"Good. Let's go in and make some tea. I'll take Felix potty out back while we're waiting for the kettle to boil."

"Where are you going to keep that thing?" Jenna asked, as she followed Vivian into the kitchen.

I haven't decided yet." Vivian laid the package down on the kitchen table. "I don't have room in my apartment for it." She drew the model out of the paper bag. The salesclerk had lovingly wrapped it in white tissue paper, and Vivian unwound the sheets, carefully flattening out each one to use again later.

As she pulled the last sheet from the Big Ben, Jenna gasped. "Look at it. It looks like you dug it out of the local dump site."

Vivian frowned. "It doesn't look that bad." She had to admit, now that she was taking a closer look at it, the thing definitely was the worse for wear.

"Well, you can't display it in the tearoom," Jenna said, as she carried a kettle over to the sink. "If our customers see that, they won't even look at the rest of the souvenirs. They'll think they're all junk, like that one."

"It wasn't junk when Stacey Patel bought it," Vivian said, trying not to feel offended. Jenna meant well, and she was only repeating what was in Vivian's own mind.

Jenna swung around so sharply, she spilled water from the kettle onto the floor. "You found her name?"

"I did. And her address."

"How did you do that?"

"You can find pretty much anything you want to know about anyone on the internet. Martin showed me how." Vivian gathered up the sheets of tissue paper. "I'm going to see her on Sunday. She needs to hear of Lewis's death in person."

Jenna's face registered doubt. "She might already know about it."

"Then I'll sympathize with her." A sudden idea hit Vivian and she sent Jenna a triumphant look. "I'll take this to her." She held up the Big Ben. "She can keep it as a memento. It will mean more to her than to me."

At that moment the shop doorbell chimed, and Jenna glanced across the room. "That's Gracie. I'll go let her in."

Left alone, Vivian took a closer look at the Big Ben. Maybe she could clean it up a bit before taking it to Stacey. A little spit and polish, and it could look almost like new. Meanwhile, she decided, she would put it up on a shelf in the kitchen until Sunday.

She carried it over to the shelves and reached up with it to the top shelf. As she raised it above her head, she uttered a sharp cry of disappointment. The entire base of the model was missing. She couldn't believe she hadn't noticed that in the thrift store. Whatever had happened to the thing for it to have that much damage?

She lowered it again just as Gracie sailed into the kitchen, followed more slowly by Jenna. "Sorry I'm late," Gracie said as she shrugged off her jacket. "I overslept."

Vivian raised her head. "You're not that late. I haven't taken Felix potty yet."

Gracie walked over to her, staring at the model in Vivian's hands. "Is that one of ours? It's a mess. What happened to it?"

"I'd like to know that myself," Vivian said with a touch of bitterness. "I just bought it back from the thrift store. I think it's the one that belonged to Lewis Trenton."

Jenna walked over to the counter and picked up the kettle. "It looks like a bunch of guys used it for a football."

"It's not that bad." Gracie peered more closely at it. "It just needs cleaning up."

"No, it's more than that." Vivian turned the model upside down. "See? The whole base is missing."

Jenna set the kettle on the stove. "Well, that's a bummer. Are you still going to take it to Stacey?"

"Who's Stacey?" Gracie walked over to the shelves. "I've gotta have one of these scones. The awesome smell in here is making me hungry."

Vivian barely heard her. Something down inside the model had caught her eye. Just a faint glitter, but enough for her to take a second look. Poking a finger deep inside, she wiggled it around until she felt something sharp against her skin.

The object was stuck in a crevice, and it took some prodding and scraping before she finally pried it loose. Something fell into her hand, and she opened her palm to examine it.

Jenna had apparently been watching her, as she moved closer to take a look. "What is it? Did you find something?"

Vivian peered at the small item in her hand. The sparkle of the white stone took her breath away. "I think," she said faintly, "that it's a diamond."

"What?" Jenna laughed. "How the heck could a diamond end up in one of our souvenirs?"

"Let me see!" Gracie rushed over to Vivian to peer at the stone. "It sure looks like a diamond."

Vivian raised her head and met two pairs of disbelieving eyes. "There's one way to find out. I'll take it to a jeweler and get it appraised."

"You'll have to pay for that," Jenna reminded her. "It might be more than what the stone is worth."

Vivian shrugged. "Maybe, but at least it will satisfy my curiosity."

"There's a jeweler on Birch Street," Gracie said. "I went in there once to look at engagement rings."

Jenna gaped at her. "You were engaged? When was that?"

Gracie shrugged. "Oh, I never got engaged. I thought my boyfriend was going to propose. He invited me to dinner and said he had something important to talk about. So I went looking at rings, so I could, like, get an idea what he paid for the one he was giving me."

Vivian saw the gleam in Jenna's eye and hastily intervened before her friend could say something she'd regret. "So, what happened?"

Gracie walked back to the shelves. "Well, he didn't propose. He invited me to dinner so's he could tell me he'd met someone else and was dumping me."

"Oh no!" Vivian stared at her in dismay. "I'm so sorry. That must have been so painful."

"Yeah, it was." Gracie turned to look at her. "But then I heard he broke up with the new girl, so I guess he just wasn't ready to get married."

"How old were you?" Jenna asked, reaching for the kettle as its whistle screamed at her.

"Eighteen."

"Then I guess you both had a lucky escape." Jenna poured boiling water onto the teabags in the teapot.

"Yeah, right? Gracie looked at Vivian. "Can I have one of these scones now?"

"Sure. Go ahead." Vivian looked back at the stone sparkling in her hand. "I have to take Felix out to go potty. I'll take this to the jeweler tomorrow."

"I could run down there with it now, if you want," Jenna offered as she poured a small amount of milk into three cups.

"No, it can wait." Vivian carefully wrapped the gem in a sheet of the tissue paper and tucked it into her purse. "I'm dying for a cup of tea. But first, I have to let Felix out to go potty."

After having settled the dog back in the apartment, she returned to the kitchen. For the next half hour, she listened to

Jenna and Gracie discussing the pros and cons of marriage, with Jenna weighing in heavily on the drawbacks. Vivian paid little attention. She was trying to figure out how a precious stone got wedged inside the model clock.

The fact that the base was missing probably meant that someone had pried it off to put the jewel in there. That raised a bunch of questions. Why leave it in such an odd place? The fact that it was hidden in there must mean it was valuable to someone. Why wasn't the base replaced to secure it? Had Lewis tucked it away in there? If so, it was unlikely to be worth much, or he would almost certainly have sold it.

"Don't you think, Vivian?"

Vivian blinked at Jenna, feeling guilty for having ignored the conversation. "I'm sorry. I wasn't paying attention. What were you saying?"

Jenna narrowed her eyes. "You were thinking about that diamond, right?"

Vivian sighed. "Right. I can't imagine Lewis keeping something so valuable, so it's either not worth much, or someone else put it there."

"Maybe Stacey what's her name?"

"Patel." Vivian frowned. "But then why would she give it to Lewis? None of this makes sense."

"Maybe Lewis found it somewhere and didn't realize it was valuable," Gracie suggested.

"That's possible." Vivian drained the last of her tea and put down the cup. "And maybe, as I said, it's not valuable at all. I guess I'll find out tomorrow when I take it in to the jewelers. Meanwhile, I have an anxious dog waiting for me to take him potty." She rose from her chair and carried her cup and saucer over to the counter.

She wasn't sure what she would do with the stone if it turned out to be a real diamond. She couldn't give it back to Lewis. Any decision would have to wait until after her visit to the jewelers, she told herself. Right now, she had more important things to do.

When she opened her apartment door a few minutes late, Felix greeted her with leaps and bounds, his tail whipping back and forth in a frenzy of excitement. He leapt down the steps, ahead of her, to the back door, and the moment she tugged it open, he shot through it to the grass patch.

Watching him sniff around the yard, Vivian wondered if he still missed Barry, his previous owner. Hal had told her about the young man, explaining that he was moving to France and couldn't take Felix with him, so he was looking for a home for the dog. Hal took her over there to meet Felix and she immediately fell in love with the dog.

It had been almost a month since she'd brought the dog home, and he seemed to have settled down. She would even say he was happy in his new home. Still, he must miss his former master. Troubled by the thought, she called out, "Felix! Time to come in."

The dog turned his head to look at her, but made no move to run toward her.

Vivian sighed. She could hardly blame him. Being shut up in the apartment all day couldn't be much fun. That's why she was always so grateful when Hal stopped by sometimes to take him for a walk. "I'm sorry, baby." She bent down to scratch his neck. "I have to go back to work. I'll give you a cookie before I leave."

That was an offer the dog couldn't refuse. His ears pricked up, then he leapt past her through the door, and bounded up the stairs.

After giving him the promised cookie, she closed the apartment door, trying not to notice the dejected drooping of his head. She'd make up for all of it on Sunday, she silently assured herself. He would enjoy the drive to Portland, and she could take him for a long walk in the park where she used to take her dogs when she lived there.

Having consoled herself a little, she hurried back downstairs.

Kept busy all afternoon, Vivian had little time to think about Felix or the mystery of the Big Ben model, now sitting on a high shelf in the kitchen. Although most of the out-of-town visitors had gone, her regular customers now filled the tables. Many of them stayed away in the summer months, reluctant to share their favorite rendezvous with "loud-mouthed intruders," as one of her less gracious customers once complained.

Vivian spent most of the afternoon filling sandwiches and making tea while Jenna sped back and forth between the tearoom and the kitchen, carrying layered cake stands loaded with the sandwiches as well as scones and pastries. In between trips, she filled small china pots with strawberry jam and Devonshire cream for the scones, and milk jugs for the tea.

Gracie, meanwhile, watched over the shelves stocked with British candy, pickled onions, various sauces and mixes, and boxes of British tea. Other shelves held English cups and saucers, models of famous UK landmarks, tea towels with prints of English villages on them, and other keepsakes from across the pond.

It was past six PM when Vivian finally closed the door behind the last customer. By then she was more than ready to take Felix for a walk, then relax in front of the TV. She went to bed early that night, with the prospect of another early rising looming in her mind.

Arriving at the jewelers late the next morning, she was greeted by an eager young woman behind the counter, who seemed disappointed when Vivian told her she had come for an appraisal. "I'll have to call Alistair," she said. "He's our jewelry expert. You can leave your gem with me, and we'll call you when the appraisal is ready."

"How long will it take?" Vivian glanced at her watch. "I don't mind waiting if it's not too long."

"Alistair can usually appraise a jewel within an hour," the clerk told her, "but it will take him a couple of days to write up the report."

"Oh." Vivian sighed. "Then I guess I'll have to wait for your call." She handed over the stone, still wrapped in tissue paper.

"There's a fifty-dollar charge for the appraisal." The clerk took the package and unwrapped it. "This is a nice stone," she said, holding it up to the light.

Watching the sparkles shooting from the jewel, Vivian caught her breath. It certainly looked like the real thing. Then again, a cubic zirconia looked very much like a diamond and was considerably less valuable.

She hesitated for a moment, then opened her purse. Fifty dollars was a bit pricey but worth it to know if the stone was genuine. It was a gamble she was willing to take. Otherwise, she would drive herself nuts wondering about it.

She left the store, still trying to convince herself that she was doing the right thing. *Hal would probably think I'm crazy,* she thought, as she walked briskly back down Main Street to the tearoom.

She had to pass the Furry Fun pet store on her way, and struggled with the temptation to go inside. Pausing at the window, she could see Wilson behind the counter, but no sign of the owner.

The urge to see him was too strong to resist, and after a moment or two of hesitation, she pushed the door open and walked into the shop. Wilson greeted her with a nod, then went back to arranging a display of dog collars on the counter.

Vivian quickly checked out the store, but Hal was nowhere to be found. Wandering back to the counter, she wondered if he was at the tearoom, waiting to take Felix for a walk.

Wilson looked up as she approached the counter. He stared pointedly at her empty hands, before asking, "Can I help you?"

"I'm looking for Hal." Vivian gave him a smile. "Is he around, or did he go out?"

"He didn't go out." Wilson went back to hanging the collars onto a hook.

Vivian tried again. "Then where is he?"

Wilson had a "mind-your-own-business" expression on his face when he turned his head toward her. "Upstairs."

"Did he say how long he'd be up there?"

"Uh-uh."

She wasn't sure why she felt uneasy. "How long has he been up there?"

Wilson looked at the clock on the wall behind him. "About an hour, I guess."

Now Vivian felt a flicker of alarm. "Is he okay?"

Wilson shrugged. "He's resting."

The flicker became a flame. Hal would never leave the store in Wilson's hands just to rest up. Something was wrong. She pulled her phone out of her purse, then dropped it back in. Knowing Hal, he would tell her he was fine and to get back to the tearoom.

She glanced at her watch. She had time to check up on him. "I'm going up to see him," she told Wilson, who paid no attention to her as she hurried behind the counter and through the door that led to the stairs.

Climbing as fast as she could, she reached the top of the stairs, breathless and heart pounding with anxiety. She practically ran down the narrow hallway to Hal's apartment door and rapped on it with her knuckles. Getting no answer, she rapped again, louder this time.

His gruff voice answered her. "You can come in, Wilson. The door's unlocked."

"It's not Wilson." Vivian opened the door and peered inside. "It's me."

To her relief, Hal looked reasonably well, though maybe a little pale. He sat on the couch, a book on his lap and an odd expression on his face. "What are you doing here?"

"That's not very gracious, considering I'm taking the time to check on your well-being." Vivian closed the door behind her and walked over to him.

"Sorry." He gave her a sheepish grin. "I was surprised to see you."

He started to get up, but she held up her hand. "Stay right there. Are you coming down with something? Can I get you something from the pharmacy?"

His brown eyes glinted at her through his glasses. "Aren't you afraid I'm contagious?"

"I'm not coming that close."

"Too bad."

Under any other circumstances, she would have reacted to that remark, but now that she was closer to him, she could see his drawn cheeks and the circles under his eyes. She had seen that same look on her late husband's face, and her stomach sharply contracted. "Are you in pain?"

"Just tired." He dropped his gaze to his hands. "I'm fine, Vivian. Go back to the tearoom. You have customers waiting for you."

Vivian looked at her watch. "I don't open for another twenty minutes. And you're not fine. I'm not leaving here until you tell me the truth. Do you have chest pains?"

He seemed startled when he looked up at her. "Why would you think that?"

"I can tell something is wrong. Please, Hal. This is important. It's no time to be macho or stubborn. Do you have chest pains?"

He sighed. "Maybe."

"Where?"

He laid his hand high on his chest.

"Pain in your arm?"

"No."

"Out of breath?"

"A bit."

She dragged her phone from her purse. "What's the number of your doctor?"

"I'm not calling my doctor."

"No. I am." She glared at him. "Either you give me his number or I call 911."

A smile played around his mouth. "I had no idea you could be so bossy."

"There's a lot you don't know about me."

"Not for want of trying."

She didn't know whether to yell at him or hug him. "Your doctor's number?"

He sighed again. "Okay. I'll call. I promise."

"Do it now."

She had put enough threat in her voice to finally get through to him.

"Okay, okay." He leaned over to reach for his phone on the table next to him and winced.

"It's bad, isn't it?"

He straightened and puffed out his breath. "No, it's getting better."

"Liar."

He gave her a look that would have rocked her if she hadn't been so worried. "Thanks for caring."

The lump in her throat wouldn't let her speak. She did care. She knew that now. She really cared. It was way too soon to acknowledge it right then, and definitely not the right time. She needed some space to analyze her feelings. And Hal needed to see his doctor. The sooner, the better.

She watched him dial the number on his phone, and waited until he had explained everything to the receptionist, then again to the doctor's nurse. After answering a bunch of questions, the nurse was apparently satisfied that he could wait until the next day for his appointment.

Vivian was finally able to relax a little. "I have to get back to the tearoom now," she said as he laid the phone down next to him. "Stay there and please, don't do anything strenuous. I'll leave Wilson my number, and he can call me if he needs anything. If you don't feel like driving to the doctor's tomorrow, please call me so I can take you. The girls can take care of the tearoom until I get back."

His smile went a long way toward making her feel better. "Yes, ma'am."

She wagged a finger at him. "I mean it. I don't want you to drive yourself if you're having chest pains. If the pains get worse, promise me you'll call 911."

"I promise."

She hated leaving him like that, but there wasn't much else she could do except worry about him. "Can I get you anything before I go? Have you eaten?"

"Yes, and no, I don't need anything. The pain is going away already. It's probably just indigestion."

He did look a little less pale and drawn, and somewhat reassured, she nodded. "Call me when you get back from the doctor's office?"

"I will." He grinned at her. "Now go—before your able assistants send out a search warrant."

"Okay. I'll talk to you tomorrow."

"And don't worry about me. I'm fine."

"Right." After a last long look at him, she turned and headed for the door.

Wilson was at the register when she arrived back downstairs. He was frowning in concentration, pressing each key as if it would set off an explosion. His customer, a young woman with flaming red hair, stood fidgeting at the counter with a look of impatience on her freckled face.

Vivian could never understand how someone who was so brilliant with a computer could be so intimidated by a cash register. According to Hal, Wilson's technical knowledge was beyond belief, yet he seemed terrified of making a mistake when ringing up a sale.

Vivian waited while he handed the woman her card and the bagged items she had bought. Finally, the customer left, and

Vivian moved closer to the counter. "Hal says he's feeling a little better," she told Wilson, "but I don't think he should be doing anything too strenuous." She dug in her purse for her business cards and handed him one. "You can call me if you need help or if you think Hal needs help, okay?"

Wilson took the card with the tips of his fingers and stared at it. "Okay."

She had to be satisfied with that, and she left the shop wishing Hal had a more reliable assistant to lean on. Not that he liked leaning on people. He'd lived alone and taken good care of himself since his wife died, and he could be stubborn about accepting help. That was something else they had in common.

For a second or two, she touched on the revelation she'd experienced in his apartment minutes ago. It had shaken her to realize just how much she cared for him. She would have to deal with that sooner or later, but right now, she had a tearoom, two assistants, and hopefully a bunch of customers needing her attention. Her relationship with Hal would have to wait, though she had a feeling that the anticipation of where this could lead would occupy her thoughts for the rest of the day.

Chapter Four

Vivian barely slept that night, her mind buzzing with worry over Hal, and what she should do about her newly discovered feelings for him. She had to admit to herself that the emotions had been there for some time. She had simply refused to acknowledge them.

Was she actually falling in love with the man? If so, how could she be sure he felt the same way? The sensible side of her brain warned her she was too old to indulge in such fantasies and could end up getting badly hurt. The enterprising side, however, welcomed this new adventure with unadulterated excitement.

She had met Martin in college, and their relationship had grown slowly over three years before he had finally proposed. She had loved her husband, and she had never doubted that he loved her, but her marriage had been more of a partnership than a companionship. Martin was uncomfortable about showing affection, and his work often put him behind a wall that she found difficult to penetrate.

She assumed it was his way of protecting her from the more gruesome aspects of his profession. Prosecuting criminals wasn't pretty at times. In all other aspects, he was a kind, respectful, and faithful husband. How many women could say that of their own husbands?

Hal, on the other hand, was unpredictable, demonstrative, and fun to be with, and she found that incredibly exciting. So far, she had kept him at arm's length, wary of sending him the wrong message. Now, it seemed, she was ready to get on board with whatever this was turning out to be. It was both scary and exhilarating.

She spent the entire next morning fighting the urge to go and check on him. Instead, she tried to focus on the baking and was relieved when she heard the shop doorbell announcing the arrival of at least one of her assistants.

This time it was Gracie who stood in the doorway, trying to duck out of the steady rain that washed the dust from the street outside. "I made two ghosts," she said, thrusting a tote bag at Vivian as she lunged into the tearoom. "I'm going to hang them over the shelves."

Vivian took the bag from her. "I guess we should start decorating today."

"Yeah. Jenna's bringing her decorations in today, so I thought we could stay over tonight and put them up?"

"Good idea." Vivian turned back to the door again as the bell rang once more.

"It's pouring out here," Jenna said when Vivian let her in. She shook her long, dark hair, sending drops of water flying into the air.

Hal would have to drive through the rain, Vivian thought, then gave herself a mental shake. He was going to be fine. She had to stop worrying about him. If he was in trouble, either he or Wilson would have called her.

She did her best to hold onto that thought as the afternoon dragged by, despite the usual rush of customers. Hal's appointment was for two PM, and she kept looking at her watch every five minutes after that, until finally, her cell phone in her pocket buzzed.

Gracie was out at the shelves, taking care of a customer, while Jenna was in the kitchen, loading up yet another cake stand with sandwiches and pastries.

Vivian snatched the phone from her pocket and stabbed it at her ear. "Hal?" Hearing his voice on the end of the line, her nerves tightened. "How did it go?"

"It went fine. I'm on my way to the hospital to get X-rays."

Her stomach seemed to drop. "Should you be driving? Why don't you let me drive you there?"

"I'm okay, Vivian. I've got something to take for the pain, if it comes back, and my doctor doesn't think I'm going to drop dead any time soon, so please quit worrying about me or you'll give yourself a heart attack."

"It's not my heart I'm worried about," Vivian said, her voice grim with concern.

"Really? Well, you don't have to worry about mine. I'll keep it safe for you."

Her breath caught in her throat. "Just be careful, okay?"

His sigh echoed down the line. "Will do. I'll call you later."

"Please do." She slipped the phone in her pocket, and turned to see Jenna staring at her with a quizzical expression. "That was Hal," she said, for some ridiculous reason fighting tears. "His doctor has sent him to the hospital to get X-rayed."

Jenna's face registered concern. "What's wrong with him?"

"Chest pains." Vivian drew a shaky breath. "He swears he's okay, but I'm worried about him."

"Of course you are." Jenna moved closer to her. "Try not to get too upset. His doctor wouldn't have let him drive if he thought Hal was in danger of having a heart attack."

Vivian nodded. "You're right. I know you're right and Hal is right, but I can't help being scared for him."

"I'm sure he'll be fine." Jenna took the knife Vivian was holding out of her hand. "Why don't you let me finish filling those sandwiches. Go take Felix for a walk. You'll feel better."

Vivian squared her shoulders. "No. Thanks, but I'm fine." She took the knife back. "You have enough to do. Keeping busy will take my mind off things."

"Okay, if you're sure."

"I'm sure." She turned back to the counter, where slices of bread waited for her to layer on the ham, brie, and cress. It wasn't only the worry of Hal's health that kept her stomach in knots for the rest of the afternoon. It was the memory of his words: *"I'll keep it safe for you."*

She was out of practice, she told herself. It had been forty years since she had been this juvenile about someone. She couldn't let doubts drive away what could be a magical experience. She wanted a relationship with Hal Douglass, and she might as well go for it. You only live once.

That evening, after Vivian had closed and locked the shop door, Gracie and Jenna brought out their Halloween decorations. Gracie hung two ghosts and a gruesome-looking skeleton over the souvenir shelves while Jenna placed miniature pumpkins, all holding a candle, in the middle of each table, then circled them with a display of orange, red, and brown blossoms and leaves.

Gracie had brought a large pumpkin that lit up inside, which Vivian put on the front porch, and Jenna hung a wreath of autumn leaves on the door. As a finishing touch, they hung garlands of orange and black pumpkin faces along the wall behind the tables and around the windows.

Vivian had to admit, the room looked very festive and classy, though she could have done without the skeleton. She had to remind herself that it was tucked down between the shelves, out of sight of the tables. "It looks wonderful," she told her assistants. "You did an amazing job. Thank you both."

"That was fun," Gracie said as she tugged on her jacket. "Now I can't wait for Christmas."

"It'll be here soon enough." Vivian opened the door to let them out into the street. "Take care, both of you. I'll see you in the morning."

She watched them leave, telling herself, as she so often did, that she was lucky to have such wonderful women working for her.

Hal's call to her that evening was brief. He sounded tired, and her heart ached for him.

"How did things go?" she asked, knowing he wouldn't have any answers yet.

"Okay, I guess. I should get a call tomorrow with the results."

"You'll call me?"

"You'll be the first to know."

She had to be content with that, and after wishing him a restful night of sleep, she hung up. She badly wanted to be there, watching over him to make sure nothing bad happened during the night. She barely slept, tossing around in the bed, making Felix grunt with irritation at being disturbed.

The alarm clock woke her up before Felix could the next morning. He lay at her feet, his head between his paws, oblivious to her sliding out of bed and into her slippers. When she came out of the bathroom, however, he was sitting up, waiting for her, his ears pricked in expectation.

"I know. You want to go potty."

He uttered a little yip and charged off the bed, nearly knocking her over in his haste to get to the door.

After letting him out in the yard, she checked out the downstairs kitchen to make sure she had enough supplies for the morning baking, then called Felix in to go back upstairs for breakfast.

She was putting her cereal bowl in the dishwasher when her phone buzzed. She immediately thought of Hal. Heart racing in anticipation, she snatched it up. A quick glance at the screen dashed her eagerness when she saw the name of the jewelers.

Holding the phone to her ear, she greeted the caller, who sounded like the young woman she'd spoken to in the shop.

"Alistair has your report ready," she told Vivian. "You can pick it up whenever you like."

"I'll stop by this morning," Vivian promised her. She put the phone back in her pocket and looked at Felix, who was standing over his empty food dish, staring at her as if willing her to fill it again.

"You've had your breakfast," she told him. "You'll have to wait for dinner now."

His head drooped, and she knew he was preparing for her to leave him alone. "I'm sorry, baby," she said softly. "I wish I could take you downstairs with me. I'm afraid even Hal won't be able to take you out today. I'll come up at lunchtime and let you out in the yard for a bit, okay?"

The dog lifted his head and gave her a mournful look that increased her guilt. Maybe she could take him to the jewelers with her, she thought, though she'd have to tie him up outside the store.

Leaving that decision until later, she left the apartment and was halfway down the stairs when her phone buzzed again. This time she was delighted to see Hal's name on the screen.

"I got the results," he told her in answer to her breathless greeting.

She halted at the foot of the stairs; her stomach clenched in anxiety. "And?"

"I need a couple of stents in my arteries."

The ice-cold feeling crept over her. "Oh? When?"

"Next week."

She struggled to relax. Obviously, it wasn't an emergency.

"Okay. What will you do about the shop?"

"It's a minor procedure. If all goes well, I'll be home that night. Wilson can manage for one day without me."

He didn't seem too worried about it at all. Relief made her weak. "He can call me if he has a problem." She paused, then added, "I'll drive you back and forth to the hospital."

Knowing how independent he could be, she half expected him to insist on driving himself. She was surprised when he answered, "Thanks. I was hoping you'd offer."

"You could always ask me, you know."

"I know."

There was such warmth in those two words she could feel them heating her ears. "Meanwhile, you'd better take it easy."

"I will. I figure I'd stop by later and take Felix onto the beach."

She frowned. "That's not exactly taking it easy."

"It's relaxing, and that's what I need right now. No stress."

Sighing, she gave in. "Okay. Felix will be ecstatic."

"Me too."

A thought struck her, and she hesitated for a moment, wondering if she should ask him the favor.

He must have sensed something, as his voice sharpened. "Are you okay?"

"Yes, I was just thinking . . ." Again, she paused.

"Thinking what?"

Deciding that it wasn't that big a deal, she said quickly, "You pass by Birch Street on the way to the beach, right?"

"Right. I take the shortcut through the parking lot."

"I thought so. I'm supposed to stop by the jewelers to pick up an appraisal. Would you mind picking it up for me? You'd have to tie Felix up while you're in there."

"No problem. I know the place. It's called Alistair's Jewelry, I believe."

"That's the one. Thanks so much."

"Sure. See you later."

She smiled as she stuffed the phone back in her pocket. She was feeling a little less paranoid about Hal's health problems, though she'd be very glad when it was all over and he was safely back home again.

Having been freed from having to go to the jewelers, she spent a relaxing morning doing what she loved, baking the delectable British cakes and pastries that kept customers filling the tearoom tables.

Her mother's recipes had served her well, most of them dating back to the Victorian age. As she baked, Vivian loved to imagine the ladies in their crinolines, meeting in an elegant drawing room for afternoon tea and gossip about the aristocrats and their extravagant lives.

She was trying to envision herself in a crinoline when the shop doorbell advised her that Hal had arrived. Dusting the flour from her hands onto her apron, she hurried across the tearoom to open the door for him.

He greeted her with his usual grin and stepped inside. "Wow, I see you're ready for Halloween."

Following his gaze to where Gracie's ghosts hovered over the shelves, Vivian murmured, "Too much?"

"No! It all looks very festive." He raised his chin and closed his eyes.

Alarmed, she quickly closed the door. "What is it? "Do you have a pain? Have you got your meds with you?"

"What?" He opened his eyes again and looked at her. "No, I'm fine. I was just enjoying that incredible aroma of fresh baking. It's mind-blowing."

She laughed. "Come on in. I'll give you a slice of sponge cake."

"When I get back with Felix." He followed her into the kitchen, where she handed him her keys. "I should get a key made for you," she said, then immediately realized how risqué that sounded. "I mean so you can let yourself in to get Felix."

He smiled. "I know what you meant. I don't mind picking up your key. It gives me an excuse to bug you."

"You never bug me." She hesitated for a moment before throwing caution to the wind and adding, "I'm always happy to see you. You brighten my whole day."

He looked pleasantly surprised. "I'm very glad to know that."

"I thought you might be."

For a long moment their gazes locked. Then he nodded, turned, and left through the door to the stairs.

She tried to ignore the quivers in her fingers as she reached for her mixing bowl on the counter. She had a distinct feeling that a line had been crossed, and now it was too late to turn back. And she couldn't be happier or more excited about it.

Jenna and Gracie arrived shortly after that, and Jenna immediately asked how Hal's visit to the hospital had gone.

"He has to have two stents put into his arteries," Vivian told her.

"Ew!" Gracie screwed up her face. "That sounds gross."

"Hal said it was a minor procedure, so I'm trying not to worry."

"I'm sure Hal is right," Jenna said as she filled a kettle with water. "He'll be fine."

"I hope you're both right." Vivian put the last tray of scones on the shelf and took out a teapot from the cabinet. "But I'm still going to worry."

By the time Hal returned with Felix, Jenna was in the tearoom, laying out pots of strawberry jam while Gracie arranged tins of British candy on the shelves. Vivian had just finished mixing egg salad for the sandwiches and was placing the bowl in the fridge when Hal walked into the kitchen.

"Felix had an exciting morning," he said, handing her an envelope. "Some kid threw him a ball, and the two of them chased up and down the beach until they were both exhausted. He'll probably sleep all afternoon."

"Good." Vivian smiled at him. "Thanks for taking him and for picking up this." She waved the envelope at him.

"No problem. I passed right by the jewelers, and Felix patiently sat outside and waited for me."

"Well, I appreciate it." She dug in her purse for her reading glasses and perched them on her nose. Deciding that he needed an explanation, she told him about finding the Big Ben in the thrift store and her discovery of the jewel. "It's probably worth nothing," she said, as she slit open the envelope with her thumb, "but I thought it was worth finding out for sure. I really don't think Lewis Trenton would be hiding diamonds in a model but—" She broke off with a gasp.

"I take it the thing is real."

Looking up, she met Hal's questioning gaze.

"I don't believe it," she said faintly. "It says here that the diamond is worth three thousand dollars."

"Oh, wow." Hal shook his head. "Looks like you hit the jackpot."

"But I can't keep it. It's not mine."

"You bought the model it was found in, so I'd say it was yours."

She scanned the appraisal again. "Lewis must not have known how much it was worth. He probably found it somewhere. But then, why would he hide it away where no one can see it? It doesn't make sense."

"It does seem a little far-fetched. The only reason I can see for him to hide it would be if he knew it was valuable. But the guy was destitute. You'd think he'd sell it."

"Exactly." She uttered another gasp. "This could be the reason he was killed. Maybe the owner of the diamond knew Lewis had it, and wanted it back."

Hal raised his eyebrows. "Uh-oh. You're not going to go chasing after another killer, I hope."

"What? No!" She shook her head to emphasize her words. "I won't be doing that again." She studied the appraisal again before saying, "I guess I can take the diamond to Detective Messina and let him deal with it."

"Good. I'm glad to hear it. I'd hate to go through all that worrying about you again."

She gave him a remorseful smile. "Sorry. I didn't mean to worry you."

"I know. But I'm going to worry about you any time I think you're in danger." He looked at his watch. "I'd better get back to the store, if Wilson hasn't burnt it down by now."

"You're not working, are you?"

"No, I'm not. I'm sitting behind the counter, giving Wilson orders."

"Good." She sighed. "I worry about you too."

"That's very comforting to know."

"I'm glad."

Once more their gazes locked. She could almost hear her heart beating as she sought frantically for something sensible to say.

Then Jenna walked into the kitchen, breaking the spell.

"I'll talk to you later," Hal said as he headed for the door. "Let me know what Messina says."

"I will." She watched him leave, then turned to find Jenna staring at her. "You're going to talk to Messina?"

"I am." Feeling suddenly tired, Vivian sat down at the table. "I just had the diamond appraised. It's worth three thousand dollars."

"What?" Jenna's eyes widened. "That's a lot of money."

"Yes, it is. I'd love to know how it got hidden in that model."

"You still don't think Lewis put it there?"

"If he did, I'm sure he didn't know how valuable it is."

"Then why would he hide it away?"

"Exactly what Hal asked." Vivian sighed. "I think it might have something to do with Lewis's death. So, I've decided to take it to Messina and let him sort it all out."

"You're not going to keep it?"

"No, I'm not. I don't want some criminal hunting me down for it."

"Good point. What does Hal think about it?"

"He's relieved I'm not chasing after a killer again."

Jenna gave her a sharp look. "You sound disappointed about that."

"Disappointed?" Vivian shrugged. "No, just curious. You have to admit, this whole thing is kind of weird."

"And you're dying to know what's behind it all."

"Well, hopefully we'll find out from Messina eventually."

Jenna puffed out her breath. "I doubt you'll find out anything from that man. He's a tight-lipped smart-ass with an attitude."

"And you like him."

"Huh?" Jenna's cheeks turned pink. "What gives you that idea? I can't stand the man."

"Keep telling yourself that." Vivian reached up into a cabinet and took down a loaf of bread. "Eventually you might believe it."

Jenna stared at her for a moment longer. Then, shaking her head, she pulled a cake stand toward her and started filling it with pastries.

Vivian smiled as she opened a bottle of fish paste. She and Jenna were having the same problem—fighting an irresistible urge to trust their hearts again. Except now, she at least, had pretty much decided to go for it. Life was always going to be full of the unknowns, and taking risks was part of the adventure.

She was excited about the possibilities now. Glancing at her friend, she hoped that Jenna would soon reach that point and decide that taking a chance on love was better than looking back in regret and wondering what might have been. A cliché, perhaps, but oh so true.

Chapter Five

Messina sat at his desk and stared at his computer in disgust. Only the second murder in the three years or so he'd transferred to Misty Bay, and he had nothing to go on. No fingerprints, no DNA, no nothing.

Lewis Trenton had been a hermit, locked away in his lonely cabin in the woods, with no neighbors, passersby, or security cameras to help find the creep who killed him. According to the little information Messina had to go on, Trenton had no relatives and no friends, and few people knew he existed. Brady had described him as a beachcomber, wandering along the seashore, hunting for seashells and agates and the occasional lost treasure buried in the sand.

His killer could have been another vagrant, roaming through the woods, looking for something to eat. From what Messina had heard, if that were so, Trenton would have likely offered the guy some food.

But a shotgun had been found lying next to Trenton's body, which meant he'd been gunning for someone he saw as a threat. Only the killer got to him first.

Messina rubbed away the beginning of a headache with his fingers. It was his job to find the thug who had prematurely ended the life of a human being. Maybe Trenton had no one who cared whether he lived or died, but the fact remained that someone out there deserved to rot in jail for what he'd done. Somehow, somewhere, there had to be a place to start.

"Hey, you okay?

Messina jerked up his head to find Brady staring down at him, his eyes half closed in concern. "Yeah, I'm fine. What's up?"

"You've got a visitor." A grin spread over Brady's face. "One of them women from the Willow Pattern tearoom."

Messina's headache vanished. He didn't know what it was about Jenna Ramsey that kept him in a tailspin. He hadn't thought he'd ever feel that way again after his wife and daughter died. It had taken him a long time to climb out of the dark place they'd left behind, and it had been Jenna who had opened up the door to new opportunities.

He didn't even know her all that well. He'd made the mistake of accusing her of murdering her ex-husband. Understandably, she hadn't exactly been thrilled by that. Despite their bad start, however, he'd felt something stir inside him the first time he'd come into contact with her. Something that had finally begun to heal the hole in his heart.

He didn't have a clue if she felt the same way, or if she knew what he was feeling, or if she even cared. He didn't know if she would ever forgive him for bringing her in for questioning and making things awkward for her with her customers.

He wasn't really sure if what he was feeling was real attraction or just a need to end the loneliness, and that's what gnawed at him whenever he thought about her, which was way too often.

He sat up straight and smoothed back his hair. "Show her in."

"Yessir!" Still smiling, Brady strolled back out of the office.

Messina shook his head. His officer was a good cop but could be totally crass at times. Knowing that Brady was aware of his attraction to Jenna made him uncomfortable, and he could only hope and pray that his officer wouldn't say something to embarrass him in front of her. If he did, Messina told himself, he'd slaughter the bastard.

Sitting back, he tried to relax as he waited for his visitor.

* * *

"I'm going to run over to the police station," Vivian announced as the last of the afternoon tea customers left the tearoom. "I'll be back in time to lock up. You two won't mind if I leave you to finish up here, right?"

"Well, we'll miss you dreadfully," Gracie said with a mock frown, "but I guess we can struggle on without you. Right, Jenna?"

Jenna rolled her eyes. "You're such a clown." She nodded at Vivian. "Go ahead. We'll be fine."

"Are you sure you don't want to go with her?" Gracie's smile was mischievous as she gazed up at Jenna. "You could say hello to that dishy detective."

Jenna grunted, turned, and headed for the kitchen.

Vivian sighed. Gracie loved to tease and was serenely oblivious as to how it was received. "I won't be long," she said. "Try and stay out of trouble until I get back."

"I'll try, but it won't be much fun." With a wave of her hand, Gracie danced across the floor to the kitchen.

The morning rain had stopped when Vivian stepped outside. A few people were strolling along the sidewalks, peering in the windows of the antique stores, the souvenir shops, the bookstore, the candy store, the bakery and, farther down the street, the Furry Fun pet store.

Hal had seemed well enough, Vivian thought, as she walked down to the side street where she parked her car. Yet she couldn't stop worrying about him. She'd be glad when the procedure was over and he was safely home again.

She envisioned herself greeting him at the hospital and bringing him home, and felt a warm glow of satisfaction that she could be there to take care of him. A sudden gust of wind from the ocean blew her hair into her face, and she ducked into her car and closed the door.

Minutes later she arrived at the police station, where the fresh-faced Officer Brady greeted her with a friendly smile and a wink.

"Wait here," he told her. "I'll see if he's free to talk to you."

He seemed to be enjoying some kind of private joke, and Vivian had a feeling it had to do with Jenna as she waited for him to return. He was back within seconds, still wearing a grin as he led her to a door behind the reception counter.

The second Vivian entered the office, she knew why Brady was smiling. Messina sat at one of the five desks, and he was staring at her with disappointment written all over his face. Obviously, he had expected Jenna to walk through that door. The resolute detective was smitten, and she couldn't be happier about it.

By the time she reached his desk, his expression had mellowed as he asked, "How can I help you, Mrs. Wainwright?"

"It's Vivian, remember?" She smiled at him. "I found something valuable, and I thought I should give it to you." She opened her purse and took out the small box where she'd stowed the diamond. "I had it appraised," she said as she handed it to him, "and the jeweler said it's worth three thousand dollars."

Messina raised his eyebrows at that.

She studied him while he opened the box. He wasn't exactly handsome, but there was a rugged, earthy aura about him that was appealing. His slightly hooked nose and firm jaw gave him a warrior look, yet she remembered his face warm with tenderness as he held Jenna in his arms right after he'd rescued her from a murderous villain.

At the moment, she realized he was staring at her, his dark brown eyes boring into her head like laser beams. "Where did you get this?"

Suddenly uncomfortable, she squirmed on her chair. "It was stuck inside one of my models."

His face registered confusion. "What?"

Taking a deep breath, she told him the whole story: how she'd sold the model to a customer, then had seen it in the photo of Lewis Trenton's living room. She explained how she'd found it in the thrift store and discovered the diamond. "So, I was flabbergasted when the jeweler told me how much it was worth," she said when she was done. "I thought the best thing I could do was to bring it to you."

Staring down at the jewel, Messina pursed his lips. "I commend you on your honesty, Vivian."

"Of course." Vivian rose from her chair.

"I'll need to see the model too."

Vivian nodded. "I'll drop it by here tomorrow."

He looked down at the box again. "No, that's okay. I'll stop by the tearoom and pick it up."

"Oh." She had trouble hiding her smile. "Then we'll see you later." She was dying to add that Jenna would be happy to see him, but wisely kept her mouth shut.

Driving back to the tearoom, however, she had to wonder how things would work out between the detective and her friend. Jenna's marriage had been disastrous, and she swore many times that she wanted nothing more to do with any man.

Then again, Jenna was very good at hiding her feelings behind a wall of indifference. Vivian had seen for herself the spark that lit between those two when they met. Was Messina interested enough to break through Jenna's barricade?

Vivian hoped with all her heart that he was at least willing to try. Jenna deserved to be happy after everything she had gone through. After a childhood with an abusive father and then her bad marriage, she was due for some happiness and stability in her life.

Vivian considered herself extremely fortunate in that she'd had two loving parents. As an only child, growing up had been lonely sometimes, but she wouldn't have traded her life for anyone else's. She had adored her English mother, who had taught her to bake, introduced her to mystery novels, and shared so many wonderful stories about her life in England.

Her father had taught her to ride a bike and drive a car, and most important of all, the values of honesty and kindness. *"If you have both those qualities,"* he'd told her, *"you will live a long and fruitful life."*

It was those attributes that had attracted her to Martin. He hadn't been openly affectionate, but he was a kind man, and honest to a fault. She'd always felt protected and loved by him, even if he couldn't put it into words.

Now they were all gone. But the lessons they had taught her would stay with her forever. Smiling, she climbed out of the car and locked the door. She had Hal now, with his gentle teasing and all his emotions shining in his eyes. She had no doubt that once she let him know she had finally let her guard down, he would have no problem telling her how he felt. And she couldn't wait.

Both Jenna and Gracie greeted her with the same question when she walked into the tearoom. "Well? How did it go?"

"Did he say you could keep the diamond?" Gracie was jumping up and down in her excitement.

Vivian laughed. "No, he didn't."

Jenna grunted. "Doesn't surprise me."

"Well, his hands are tied right now. Actually, the law on finders keepers is a bit confusing, but basically, if the owner can't be located, then eventually the finder keeps the item. If the diamond did belong to Lewis, which I sincerely doubt, I guess it would eventually come back to me. But if the diamond belonged to someone else, then they are the rightful owner and will get it back."

"Oh, crap." Gracie shook her head. "I was hoping for a celebration dinner at The Bellemer."

Jenna rolled her eyes. "You've got rich tastes. That's one of the most expensive restaurants on the West Coast."

Gracie grinned. "I know. I'm dying to go there. I just wish they'd picked a better name for it. Something glamorous, like The Grand Pavilion or the Purple Palace."

"Bellemer is French for 'beautiful sea,'" Vivian said, as she headed for the kitchen.

"Oh." Trailing behind her, Gracie thought about that, then added, "Well, then, I guess the name's okay."

"I wouldn't worry about it," Jenna said, following them both into the kitchen. "It's unlikely you'll be dining there."

"You never know." Gracie took off her apron and tossed it in the laundry basket, then grabbed her jacket from the closet.

"I could, like, meet a rich dude someday, and we could go there when he proposes."

Jenna snorted. "Dream on, honey. Trust me, no man is worth the time. Even if he is stinking rich."

"That reminds me," Vivian said, "Detective Messina will be stopping by to pick up the Big Ben model. He didn't say when, but I'm guessing it will be soon."

Jenna turned away and pretended to be tidying up the counter while Gracie's grin spread across her face. "Can't wait to see the dishy detective again. Better freshen up your makeup, Jenna."

Jenna swung around to glare at her. "And you'd better leave before I tape your mouth shut."

"Hey!" Vivian protested, but Gracie just laughed.

"I'm going." She gave Jenna a light punch on the shoulder. "One day you'll look back and be sorry you didn't hook him while you had the chance." She raced out of the kitchen, and seconds later the doorbell chimed as she left the tearoom.

Vivian sighed. "Don't let her get to you," she said softly. "She's young. She doesn't understand."

To her surprise, she saw a tear glistening in Jenna's eye when she answered. "She's right. I probably will regret it. Part of me wants to grab whatever he's offering, yet a bigger part of me is screaming at me not to be a fool again."

"Not all men are like Dean Ramsey." Vivian pulled out a chair from the table and sat down. "Sometimes you have to take chances to be happy."

Jenna sat down opposite her. "Like you and Hal?"

"Yes, like me and Hal. I was reluctant too, and it wasn't until the possibility occurred to me that I could lose him that I realized how stupid I was to resist what could be an incredible experience."

"You're not still worried about his surgery, are you?"

"Not as much as I was." Vivian stared down at her hands. "But when he first told me he had chest pains, the thought did enter my mind that he could be having a heart attack and might not survive. It was that moment that made me realize how much I cared about him."

"Well, you've known Hal for more than two years. I only met Messina a month ago. I know nothing about him, except that he's a cop and his wife died."

"You know you're attracted to him, right? Why not acknowledge that and see where it goes? Isn't it worth taking a chance to find out rather than looking back in regret? It might not be everlasting, but isn't it time you had some fun in your life?"

Jenna shrugged. "Maybe. I'm just not sure I'm ready for it."

"Well, don't wait too long." Vivian got up from her chair. "He's an attractive man, and he must meet plenty of women who would be eager to grab whatever he's offering, as you so delicately put it."

Jenna smiled. "I'll think about it. Right now, I have to get home and feed Misty. That cat meows like a banshee when she's hungry."

"And I have to take Felix for a walk." Vivian followed Jenna to the tearoom door. "I'll see you tomorrow." She locked the door behind her friend, thinking about the conversation she'd just had with her.

Relationships, she told herself as she climbed the stairs to her apartment, get more complicated as people get older. The young and inexperienced don't always stop to weigh the pros and cons. They mostly follow their hearts. It's life's challenges that can make people analyze and mistrust their feelings until they risk destroying all chances of a successful partnership with someone.

That wasn't going to happen to her, Vivian vowed as she opened the door to her apartment. She fervently hoped it wouldn't happened to Jenna either.

In the next instant, all her convoluted thoughts vanished as Felix leapt at her, thrilled to have her home. This was what it was all about, she thought, as the dog smothered wet kisses all over her face. This unconditional love given so freely and completely. To have that kind of adoration from a man and to give it back in return would be heaven. And Hal just might be the man to make that dream come true.

* * *

Messina stared down at the diamond nestled in its box. Hidden inside a tacky landmark model. That was an odd place to hide a valuable jewel. He pinched his lips together. Experience had taught him never to take anything for granted. His gut told him there had been more than one diamond. There were safer and more practical places to hide a single jewel, and he doubted Lewis Trenton's death shortly after finding the model was coincidence. There was probably a bigger prize at stake to commit murder.

Turning to his computer, he brought up the latest police reports. It didn't take him long to find it. A robbery from a jewelry store in Portland three weeks ago. Over half a million dollars in diamonds stolen. The police had no leads, and the jewels had not been recovered.

Half a million dollars. That would be incentive enough to kill someone.

Messina reached for the phone. The pleasant voice that answered put him through to the leading detective on the case.

At first, the guy seemed reluctant to talk to him. Messina knew why. He'd felt the same way about small-town cops, at times, when he was on the Portland force. Their problems were often petty compared to the big-city crimes.

When Messina suggested that he could have a diamond involved in the heist, however, the detective's tone changed. "What makes you think it's from the robbery?"

"I figure it's from some robbery. I don't know if it's yours. But it does seem like a coincidence, finding it around the same time. It was hidden inside a model of Big Ben."

There was silence on the end of the line for a moment until the detective asked warily, "Is this a joke?"

"No joke. The model is about a foot tall. Plenty of room to stash a bag of diamonds. I couldn't see someone keeping just one in there. What I'm thinking is that the robbers brought the jewels down to a fence, probably in Newport, and he hid them in the model until he could deliver them to his client. Then he takes them out again without realizing he's left one behind."

"I guess that's possible. Where did you find this Big Ben thing?"

"One of our citizens bought the model from a thrift store. She recognized it from when she sold it to a customer a month earlier. She discovered the diamond, had it appraised, and then brought it to me."

"Do you have the customer's name?"

Messina hesitated, wondering how much he wanted to tell the detective. Reluctantly deciding he needed to give him what information he could, he answered, "No, but I do know the last person to own it. His name was Lewis Trenton."

The pause that followed told Messina that the detective recognized the name. "Isn't that the recluse that was shot down there last week?"

"Yes, it is."

"Then he was most likely the fence."

Messina shook his head. Just what he'd expected them to say. "I doubt that. Trenton lived in poverty."

"That was probably a cover. Looks like the guy got greedy, tried to rip off the robbers, and they killed him to get the diamonds back." The detective paused, apparently considering the information. "Okay. Can you bring the diamond up to me?"

"Sure. I'll have Brady take it up there. He's my second in command."

"I'll need the . . . er . . . Big Ben thing as well."

"Copy that. Keep me informed, okay?"

"Will do." The call ended abruptly, and Messina hung up. The Portland cop had made it sound cut and dried, but there was more to this case that anyone knew right then. Trenton just didn't fit the image of a jewel fence, which could mean someone else was operating as one locally and was probably responsible for the hermit's death.

Messina didn't like that. He couldn't interfere in the jewel heist because that was out of his jurisdiction, but a local resident had been murdered, and he was going to find the sleazebag who did it and toss his sorry ass in jail.

He leaned back in his chair, his anger evaporating as he thought about picking up the Big Ben model from the tearoom. He would see Jenna again. Hopefully, he'd be able to have a word with her. He needed to know if his initial attraction to her was a passing flash of interest, or something deeper that needed to be explored.

One thing he did know. In the past few weeks, thoughts of her had helped him put the past behind him and take a tentative step to moving forward. He'd never thought, in the weeks, months, and years that passed after his wife and daughter were killed by a vengeful inmate, that he would ever be able to let go of the memories.

For far too long he'd close his eyes at night, only to see in his mind the flames eating up his house with his precious family inside while he'd been forced to stand by, helpless to rescue them. Time and time again he had wished he'd died with them. The visions had eventually faded, but the pain remained.

Now, for the first time since then, he felt his heart healing and his mind at peace. Maybe this interest in Jenna Ramsey was simply an indication that he was ready to move on, and welcome new adventures. Or maybe it was something deeper; a promise of a meaningful relationship that would forever change his existence.

He wasn't sure which it was, but he was ready and eager to find out. Now he couldn't wait until tomorrow, when he would stop by and pick up the Big Ben, and perhaps start a new chapter in his life.

*　　*　　*

Messina arrived at the tearoom shortly before noon the next morning. Vivian had just finished making the sandwich fillings while Jenna spooned strawberry jam into the small china jars and Gracie unpacked the new shipment of souvenirs in the storeroom.

Hearing the shop doorbell, Vivian dropped her fork into the sink. "I'll get it," she said, as she crossed the kitchen to the door. "It's probably Hal come to take Felix for a walk."

Her rush of pleasure at the prospect of seeing Hal again faded when she saw the detective standing on the porch. Hiding her disappointment with a smile, she opened the door wider. "Come in. The model is in the kitchen. I'll get it for you."

He gave her a brief nod and stepped inside the tearoom. As always, he seemed to dominate the room. She wasn't sure if it was his impressive height or his air of being in complete command of every situation. Except when it came to Jenna. She was anxious to see her friend's face when she let him into the kitchen.

"We have a visitor," she announced as she walked in.

Jenna swung around from the counter, warmth flooding her cheeks when she caught sight of the detective. She mumbled something, then went back to slapping jam into the jars.

"Good morning to you too," Messina said, then looked at Vivian. "You have the model?"

"Yes, I do." Vivian glanced up at the shelf where the Big Ben replica stood. "Jenna? Would you mind getting it for me?"

"Sure." Jenna dropped her spoon onto a plate and reached up for the model. She brought it down, then appeared to take a deep breath as she turned to face the detective. Her smile was a little strained as she handed it him. "Here you go."

"Thanks." He held it up to take a good look at the replica of London's famous clock.

"It's kind of ugly," Jenna said. "We have smaller models on the shelves that are beautiful, more like the real Big Ben."

"Uh-huh." Messina tipped the model upside down. "Is this where you found the diamond?"

"Yes." Vivian nudged a finger at the base. "It was stuck in a crevice deep inside."

"Okay. I'll need to take this with me. I doubt we'll get prints or DNA, since it's been handled by so many people, but we can give it a shot."

Vivian nodded. "I hope you find out who owns the diamond."

"Well, all we know right now is that it could be part of a robbery that took place in Portland a few weeks ago." Messina shifted the model to a more secure position under his arm. "The Portland Bureau believe the diamonds were brought to a fence here at the coast."

Jenna made a soft sound of surprise. "Why would they bring stolen diamonds down here?"

Messina turned to her, his stern features relaxing. "Robbers often bring stolen property to a fence in another town. Less chance of them being caught. The fence then takes the jewels to one of the big cities to sell. Like San Francisco or L.A. The PPD believe Lewis Trenton was the fence and got greedy. They think he hid the diamonds, and the thieves killed him to get them back. I guess in their hurry, they left one behind when they took them out of the model."

Vivian frowned. "Don't fences usually get a cut from the robbers?"

"Yeah, they do." Messina shifted the model more securely under his arm. "But nowhere near as much as the amount Trenton would have scored from selling the jewels himself."

Vivian shook her head. "My point is, if Lewis was a fence, I'm assuming he would have been making a pretty decent living. Why would he spend his time combing the beach for items to sell?"

Messina gave her a brief glance before looking back at the model. "That's a question you'd have to ask the Portland guys. They think it could have been a cover, to hide what he was really doing. Thanks for passing this along." He jiggled the Big Ben. "I'll see myself out."

It was all she was going to get from him, Vivian realized.

Jenna looked disappointed and turned back to her task of filling the jam jars.

On impulse, Vivian smiled at the detective. "Would you like a cup of tea? We were just going to make a pot."

Messina's dark gaze swept over her face. "Thanks, but I have to get back to the station." He glanced at Jenna, who now had her back to him. "Maybe another time?"

"Absolutely." Vivian glared at her friend's back. "Right, Jenna?"

Jenna swung around, her cheeks on fire. "What? Oh, sure! We'd like that."

Messina studied her for a brief moment, and the electric charge between them Vivian had witnessed earlier zinged between them once more. Then Messina nodded, swung around, and marched out of the kitchen.

Jenna's shoulders slumped, and she puffed out a breath. "Whew! That was intense."

Vivian smiled. "You've got to give him more encouragement. I think he's trying to figure out if you're interested."

Jenna shook her head. "I don't know what's the matter with me. I've never had any problem making up my mind about doing something. Most of the time I just charge ahead and get it done. But this is different. I feel like I'm walking a tightrope, and one wrong step will send me crashing to my death."

"Whoa—that's not exactly romantic." Vivian laughed. "It's a sure sign you're interested in the man."

A slow smile spread across Jenna's face. "I am, aren't I?"

"Yep. Now go charge ahead and do something about it."

"I will. Next time I see him. I promise."

"Great. I can't wait to see that."

Jenna turned back to the counter and screwed the cap back on the jar of jam. "So, what did you think about all that stuff on Lewis Trenton?"

"I don't, for one moment, believe that he was a fence. What's more, I'm pretty sure that Messina doesn't think so either."

At that moment, Gracie sailed into the kitchen, carrying an armful of packages. "These boxes of chocolates look so yummy. Our customers are going to clean them out in a week."

Vivian turned to her. "You got all those cases unpacked already?"

"I did." Gracie beamed. "I just love the new tea towels. They have pictures of the Royal Family on them. There's one pic of the queen that's awesome. I'm going to buy one of those myself."

Vivian smiled. "That was a quick sale."

Gracie headed for the door. "I'll get these out on the shelves. I thought I heard the doorbell just now. Do we have a customer?"

"I don't think so. That was probably Messina you heard leaving."

Gracie frowned. "He was here? And I missed him?"

"Yeah, you did." Jenna started placing the jam jars onto a tray. "He was only here a couple of minutes."

"Oh, crap. I was looking forward to seeing him."

Gracie looked dejected, and Vivian hurried to reassure her. "He said he'd be back for a cup of tea sometime."

The young woman brightened at that. "Awesome."

She disappeared out the door, and Jenna sighed. "I'm never going to have a conversation with Messina if Gracie is hanging around."

"Then we have to figure out a way you two can meet outside the tearoom."

Jenna laughed. "I don't think that's going to happen."

Vivian frowned. There had to be some way to get those two together, she told herself. She just had to come up with a brilliant idea.

She was still thinking about it minutes later when Gracie walked back into the kitchen. "No customers yet," she announced, as she sat down at the table. "Tell me about Messina. What did he want? Did he talk about the diamond? What did he say?"

"He thinks Lewis Trenton was a fence for jewel robbers," Jenna said.

Gracie stared at her. "What? No. Really? That's a shocker."

"I don't believe it, though," Vivian said. "Messina didn't look too convinced either when he was telling us about it."

"I guess you won't be taking the model to that woman in Portland now," Jenna said as she took down more of the small pots from the cabinet.

"No, but I'm still going to see her." Vivian walked over to the fridge. "I can't rest my mind until I've let her know that Lewis died."

"You want some company? I haven't been to Portland in ages."

Vivian swung around to look at her. "I'd love that."

Gracie brightened. "Cool! Can I come too? I love going to Portland."

"Good. You can sit in the back with Felix. He'll be thrilled."

"Awesome!" Gracie headed for the stockroom. "I need some more of those fridge magnets. I just sold a bunch of them to a customer."

She disappeared through the door, and Jenna laughed. "I knew she would be more than ready to join us."

Vivian turned back to the fridge. "It should be interesting, that's for sure. Maybe we'll get to learn some more about Lewis Trenton."

"What if we find out he really was a fence for jewel thieves?"

Vivian felt a tingling in the back of her neck. She still couldn't bring herself to believe that Lewis Trenton was a criminal. It just didn't make sense. Was it possible they were heading into another risky situation? She wasn't sure how she felt about that. The last one had nearly cost Jenna her life.

On the other hand, she never had been able to resist a mystery, and finding a valuable diamond hidden in something belonging to a penniless recluse was definitely mystifying. Maybe they would find out more from Stacey Patel. If not, she would let Messina do his job and stay out of it.

Hopefully.

Chapter Six

A thick haze blanketed the town as Vivian drove onto the coast road on Sunday morning. Fog hid the forested peaks of the Coast Range on one side of her. On the other side, a shadowy silhouette of rocks rose from an almost invisible ocean. The seagulls swooped low over the deserted beach, and she could hear their mournful cries echoing in the damp mist.

Excited by this unexpected outing, Felix trampled all over Gracie in the back seat, ignoring Vivian's commands to behave. Gracie didn't seem to mind and laughed every time the dog's tail smacked her in the face.

By the time they had left the coast and were making the slow climb up to the mountain pass, Felix had settled down and seemed content to sit gazing out of the window. Thick forests of evergreens mostly hid the view, though now and then Vivian caught a glimpse of gentle slopes and the occasional river glimmering in the faint sunlight peeking through the mist.

As they neared the summit of the pass, they came upon a vast stretch of the mountain that had been ravaged by wildfire decades ago. Over the course of eighteen years, four large fires had destroyed three hundred and fifty-five acres of trees.

Then, in the seventies, one of the biggest replanting campaigns in history restored much of the forest. It never failed to impress Vivian every time she saw it, how such a great achievement had been made possible by human hands determined to appease Mother Nature.

They arrived in Portland more than an hour later and pulled up at the address Vivian had found on the internet.

"Are you going to call her first?" Gracie asked as she struggled to stop Felix from jumping at the window.

"I think it's better if we just surprise her." Vivian shut off the engine. "If she gets a call from a stranger asking to see her, she could just refuse to open the door. I'm hoping she'll recognize me when she sees me, and feel comfortable talking to me."

Jenna gave her a meaningful look. "You're really eager to talk to this woman."

"Yes, I am." Vivian opened the car door. "Once I know that at least one person is mourning Lewis's death, then I can stop worrying about it."

"Why is it so important to you?"

Vivian paused on her way out of the car. "I don't know. It just is. I don't think there's anything sadder than people dying with no one there to care about them. It happens a lot to the homeless, and it's heartbreaking."

"What happens if no one turns up to claim his body?" Gracie asked, one arm holding Felix down.

"Then the state will bury him." Vivian sighed. "Probably without a funeral. We have about two weeks before that happens."

"Okay." Jenna opened the door. "Then let's go."

"I'll wait here in the car with Felix," Gracie said, putting her arm around the dog, who immediately licked her face. "I don't want to leave him alone."

"He'll be fine," Vivian said. "He's used to being alone."

"That doesn't mean he likes it." Gracie scratched his ear. "I'd like to stay here with him."

Vivian smiled. "Okay. Whatever makes you both happy." She got out of the car and closed the door.

"I hope Stacey is home," Jenna said, as she led the way into the apartment complex.

"If she isn't, then we'll have a nice day out in the city and we'll call back later." Vivian paused in front of the apartment door. "Well, here goes." She raised her hand and pressed the doorbell.

Seconds later, the door opened, and a dark-eyed woman with sleek black hair frowned at them. "Can I help you?"

Vivian gave Stacey her best smile. "Hi! I don't know if you remember me. We met in Misty Bay a couple of weeks ago. I own the Willow Pattern Tearoom, and I sold you a copy of London's Big Ben."

Stacey's frown deepened. "Oh yes, I remember you. But why are you here? Is something wrong?"

"Would you mind if we come in?" Vivian waved her hand at her assistant. "This is Jenna. She works with me in the tearoom. We have some news I think you would want to hear."

Alarm flashed across Stacey's face. "What's happened?"

Vivian sighed. "It's about Lewis Trenton. I'm afraid it's bad news."

Stacey stared at her for a few seconds, then shook her head. "Lewis who?"

"Trenton." Vivian was beginning to feel uncomfortable. "I believe you bought the Big Ben for him? You said you were buying it for a friend."

"Oh." Stacey's brow cleared. "I'm sorry, but I've never heard of this Lewis person. I bought the model for the friend I was staying with in Newport."

"Oh." Fighting her disappointment, Vivian made an effort to smile. "Would you mind telling us the name of your friend? The Big Ben was found in Lewis's house shortly after he died. We're trying to find whoever gave it to him so we can inform them of his death."

Stacy's expression grew wary. "I don't think I want to do that."

"Please." Vivian moved closer to the door. "If we don't find the friend who gave him the Big Ben, he'll be buried without anyone to mourn him. I'm determined to find that person, and if you would give us the name of your friend, maybe she can help me."

Stacey seemed to spend an interminable amount of time making up her mind, but eventually she nodded. "Wait there a minute. I'll get her address and phone number for you."

She closed the door, and Vivian looked up at Jenna. "Thanks for stepping in. I think having both of us persuade her really helped."

"I hope so." Jenna glanced at the door. "That's if she doesn't just ignore us and hope we go away."

"Oh, drat. I didn't think of that."

The next minute or so dragged by while Vivian stared anxiously at the door. Finally it opened, and Stacey held out a slip of paper. "I just hope she's not mad at me for giving this to you," she said, looking as if she might take it back at any moment.

Vivian snatched the slip before it vanished and tucked it in her purse. "We'll tell her we insisted until you had no choice."

"Okay. Thanks." Stacey shut the door before Vivian could say goodbye.

"She's not too sociable," Jenna said as they made her way back to the car. "She really didn't want us talking to her friend."

"Well, she doesn't really know us, and she's sending a couple of strangers to her friend's home." Vivian reached the car and opened the door. "I can understand her being hesitant."

"Did you see her?" Gracie asked as Vivian climbed onto her seat. "What did she say? Was she upset? Did she cry? I'm glad I didn't go with you. I hate it when people cry."

"She didn't cry," Jenna said, sliding into the car, "because she didn't know Lewis Trenton. She bought the model for a friend."

"Oh, bummer." Gracie sat back against the seat, one hand on Felix's neck. "It was a wasted trip, then."

"Not entirely." Vivian slid her key into the ignition. "She gave us the name of her friend, so we can follow up with her."

"So, what is her name?" Jenna asked as she fastened her seat belt.

"I don't know." Vivian reached for her purse, sitting next to her, and opened it. She had to hunt for the scrap of paper but finally came up with it. "Ah, here it is." She unfolded it, then announced, "Her name is Brita Stewart and she lives in Newport." She read out the address.

"I don't know where that is," Gracie said.

Jenna shook her head. "Me neither."

"Don't worry. My GPS will find it. Now we have the rest of the day to enjoy the city. First, I suggest we make it to the doggy park so Felix can relieve himself."

"Good idea." Gracie sounded excited. "Then we can eat."

Jenna grunted. "Always thinking of your stomach."

"Actually, I'm ready for some food," Vivian said, turning the ignition key. "The bowl of cereal I had this morning is now a distant memory. I know a wonderful restaurant right on the river. You'll love it."

"Does it have vegan stuff on the menu?" Gracie asked.

"It does." Vivian pulled out into the street and headed for the traffic light. "And the best desserts in town."

Gracie heaved a sigh of pure pleasure. "Cool. I can't wait."

Lunch was everything Vivian had promised. Gracie enjoyed a salad with candied walnuts, Jenna chose the crab cakes, and Vivian treated herself to the grilled salmon. The hot fudge sundae and bananas foster they shared between them finished off the meal, and Jenna sat back with a sigh as she laid down her spoon.

"That was fantastic." She glanced out the window at the people strolling by. "But now I have to walk it off or I'll be five pounds heavier."

Vivian laughed. "You're skin and bones as it is. You don't need to lose anything."

"I'd like to walk as well," Gracie said. "Are there any shops near here?"

"There are," Vivian promised her. "All along the riverfront. We'll take a look at them."

After leaving the restaurant, they walked alongside the water's edge, peeking in the windows of gift shops and admiring the boats docked in the marina, then returned to the car.

Felix greeted them with unbounded joy, and they took him back to the doggy park for another run before settling him in the car again.

"How about we visit Powell's Books while we're here?" Vivian said as she drove into downtown. "I'm ready to pick up some mysteries."

"I've heard of it," Jenna said, "but I've never been there."

"Me neither," Gracie said, her voice muffled by Felix's attempts to lick her face. "It's famous, isn't it?"

"It's the largest independent bookstore in the world and takes up an entire block." Vivian steered the car into a parking lot. "It takes hours to explore it all. If you love books, it's the most fascinating place. You can't leave there without buying at least one or two."

She made good on her comments by buying three new mysteries, then suggested a tour of the Japanese Gardens before making the trip home.

"That was an awesome day," Gracie said later, sounding tired as she cuddled with Felix in the back of the car. "Thanks for letting me come along."

"Sure." Vivian glanced at her in the rearview mirror. "You both made it a fun trip for me. So, thanks for joining me."

"I enjoyed it too." Jenna smothered a yawn. "So when are you going to visit Stacey's friend?"

"Tomorrow." Vivian pulled out into the freeway traffic. "I have to go into Newport anyway, to pick up supplies from my specialty store. It's the only place I can find some of the ingredients I use in my baking."

"Newton's Groceries," Gracie said. "You've talked about them before. The owner is English. Right?"

Vivian smiled. "Right. A London Cockney who's lived here forty years and still talks like he never left England. He's hard to understand sometimes, but he imports baking ingredients a lot cheaper than I can, because he buys in bulk. Even with his markup, he saves me a lot of money."

"So," Jenna said, "you're going to drop in on Brita Stewart while you're there?"

"Right." Vivian glanced in her side mirror and pulled over to pass a slow-moving truck. "It's the same thing again with me. I'd rather deliver bad news in person."

Jenna didn't answer, and Vivian was content to sit in silence as she reached the off ramp that led to the highway. Soon they had left the city behind and traveled through farmland and isolated neighborhoods until they entered the forest and began the climb once more to the mountain pass.

It seemed no time at all before they drove down the mountain to the coast road, and finally pulled into the side street next to the tearoom.

"I'll sleep like a dog tonight," Gracie said, climbing out of the car.

"Me too." Jenna raised her shoulders and dropped them again. "I feel like I've worked a double shift at the tearoom. Must be the fresh air."

"And the soothing ride. Even Felix is falling asleep." Vivian looked down at the dog, who sat patiently waiting to go home. "Come on, buddy. Let's go get you some dinner."

Felix's ears pricked up, and he barked in agreement.

Gracie laughed and bent down to scratch his ear. "Goodnight, Felix. Thanks for making it a fun day."

Felix turned his head and licked her hand.

"You should get yourself a dog," Vivian said.

"No thanks." Gracie started to walk away, calling out over her shoulder, "I can barely take care of myself."

"She's got that right," Jenna muttered, watching Gracie walk down to where her car was parked.

Vivian sighed. "She's a good kid, and she works hard."

"Yes, she is and she does." Jenna shoved her hand in her jacket pocket and pulled out her car keys. "But sometimes I worry about her. She's not too bright when it comes to relationships. Like Alyssa, this new roommate of hers. Some of the things Gracie's told me about her would turn your hair gray."

Vivian frowned. "She's not dangerous, is she? I mean, she's not going to hurt Gracie?"

"No, I don't think so." Jenna pulled up the zipper of her jacket. "But I wouldn't trust that woman an inch. Just saying. See you tomorrow."

She took off, leaving Vivian totally unsettled and concerned. Maybe she should have a word with Gracie, she thought, as she unlocked the tearoom door. Just to find out if there was really something to worry about.

Not that she didn't have other things to worry about. Thoughts about Hal had been popping into her head all day. She had checked her phone more than once in case he'd tried to get in touch with her, even though she knew the ring tone would have alerted her if he had called.

Once inside her apartment, she decided to give him a call. She'd sleep better, she told herself, if she knew he was okay. He sounded tired when he answered, and once more, concern pricked at her as she asked, "How are you doing? Are you in pain?"

"No, I'm fine. Is everything okay with you?"

"Yes! I just got back from Portland." She hesitated, then decided this was not the time to tell him about her mission. Instead, she described Felix's antics in the park and the visit to Powell's Books, leaving out her visit with Stacey Patel. "Now that I've bored the socks off you, how was your day?"

Hal laughed. "Mine was restful and uneventful. I like yours a lot better, and I'm not in the least bored. But you've had a long day, and I'm sure you're tired."

"I am," she admitted. "I'm going to find something light to eat and take one of my new books to bed."

"Sounds like a plan."

She wished him goodnight and hung up. Two more days, she reminded herself. Then his surgery would be over, and she could stop worrying about him.

*　*　*

After getting up early the following morning, she skipped her usual routine of checking her email and watching the news while she ate her bowl of cereal. Instead, she took Felix out to the yard, then went to work baking a batch of scones, jam tarts, Eccles cakes, and cream horns. She'd chosen her simplest recipes and was done well before eleven.

Felix jumped out of his bed the moment she opened the door of her apartment. "We're going for a ride," she told him as she walked over to the closet. "But first you have to go potty."

Hearing one of his favorite phrases, Felix chased his tail around and around in his excitement. He settled down once he was in the car, however, and sat looking out the window as she drove into Newport and parked outside the grocery store.

For once the sky was clear, and in spite of a fresh breeze from the ocean, the sun warmed her face as she crossed the parking lot.

The friendly owner greeted her the moment she walked through the door. "Hallo, Vivian! I haven't seen you in a while. What can we get for you today?"

Smiling, she handed him the list. "It's good to see you, Sid. How's the business going?"

"Good. Though it's slowed down since the summer, like it always does. How about you?"

"Same. I hope you've got some self-rising flour in stock. I'm pretty much out of it."

Sid studied the list. "I do, and the black treacle and the desiccated coconut. Your customers are in for a treat."

"I hope so. I tell them all my recipes are originally from Britain, so I try to use British ingredients as much as possible."

"Can't beat the genuine stuff for Brit baking."

"That's what my mother used to say."

"She taught you well."

Vivian sighed. "She did. I still miss her. And my father."

"I'm sure you do, luv." Sid beckoned to an elderly man wearing a white apron, and handed him the list. "Here you go, mate. Grab those for me, okay?"

The clerk shuffled off, and Sid turned back to Vivian. "I'll have to pop into your tearoom sometime. It's been a while since I've tasted genuine British goodies."

Vivian sighed. "You say that every time I come in here."

"I know, luv. One day, I'll surprise you. I promise."

"I look forward to it." She watched him hurry over to the counter to where another customer stood waiting. There didn't seem to be many customers in the store. The off season could be a struggle for most shop owners at the coast. Then again, the holiday season was fast approaching, and things would speed up again until the next lull, waiting for the spring.

Minutes later she left the store, pushing the cart loaded with supplies that she hoped would last her through the holidays. Felix greeted her with his usual yelps of joy and thrashing tail as she raised the hatch of her car and stacked the groceries into the trunk.

"Okay, Felix," she said as she slid in behind the wheel. "Let's go find this Brita person."

Felix whined in agreement.

Minutes later the GPS led her into a narrow street of elegant condos. After parking in a visitors' space, Vivian assured Felix she would not be long and climbed out of the car. Looking up at the impressive building with its wide windows overlooking the ocean, Vivian wished now that she'd called Brita before calling on her. This being Monday morning, it was doubtful the woman would be home.

Still, it was worth a shot, and squaring her shoulders, she marched into the lobby. A man in a gray uniform ushered her to a desk, behind which sat a young woman with tightly coiled blond hair and thick makeup.

The woman gave Vivian a sour look as she asked, "Can I help you?"

"I'm looking for Brita Stewart."

"Your name?"

Vivian held onto her smile. "It's Vivian Wainwright. Brita doesn't know me. A friend of hers gave me her address."

The receptionist reached for the phone. "Someone named Vivian Wainwright is here to see you," she said after a pause. "She says a friend of yours gave her your address." She looked back at Vivian. "What's the friend's name?"

"Stacey Patel. I talked to her yesterday."

The receptionist repeated the name into the phone, then replaced the receiver. "You can go on up." She nodded at the row of elevators. "Third floor."

"Thank you." Vivian hurried over to the elevators, anxious to get away from the disapproving eyes of the blond custodian.

The young woman who opened the door of apartment 3B was also blond, but a lot more friendly. "You're a friend of Stacey's?" she asked after inviting Vivian into the sumptuous living room.

Vivian had trouble keeping her mouth closed as she gazed at the elegant white couch with its purple cushions, the enormous flat screen TV that covered an entire wall, and the wide windows with an expansive view of the rocky shoreline. "Er . . . not exactly." She made an effort to recover her composure. "Stacey is a customer. I own the Willow Pattern Tearoom in Misty Bay, and Stacey bought a model of Big Ben from me."

"Oh." Brita frowned in confusion. "Yes, she told me. Actually, she gave it to me."

"Which is why I'm here. Do you know Lewis Trenton?"

Brita's frown deepened. "Who?"

Vivian sighed. "He was a hermit who lived in the hills above Misty Bay. The model was found in his living room. I thought you might have given it to him."

"Me? No! I've never heard of him. I didn't like the model. It didn't go with my decor, so I took it to the thrift store."

Glancing at the purple and gold vases on a white sideboard, Vivian could hardly blame her. "Can you tell me the name of the thrift store? Maybe they can tell me who bought it."

"It's called Abundance of Treasures. It's just a couple of blocks from here and—" She broke off as a young man with long brown hair and a thick stubble covering his jaw limped into the room.

"I heard about that Trenton guy on the news," he said as he sank onto the couch. "He lived by himself in the woods, and someone shot him, right?"

"Oh!" Brita looked shocked. "That's horrible! I'm so sorry." She jerked her thumb at the young man. "This is my boyfriend, Chris."

Looking at him, Vivian had to wonder what it was about a scruffy stubbled chin that women found so attractive. Personally, she preferred a clean-shaven man. Hastily dismissing a vision of Hal, she said, "I'm trying to find out who gave Lewis the Big Ben model. That person was probably the only friend he had, and they might not know that he died."

Chris shrugged. "The guy on the news said that the dead guy didn't have no friends nor relatives. He went looking for junk on the beach to sell. He was like the pioneers, didn't even have a bathroom in his house. He used a shack out back. A guy like that wouldn't have no friends."

"Well, he must have had at least one friend who gave him the Big Ben." Vivian turned back to Brita. "That friend could be the only one who cared enough about him to mourn his passing. I'm going to keep looking for them, and at least let them know he died."

"I hope you find them," Brita said. I'm sorry I couldn't help you."

"Yeah," Chris chimed in. "Good luck with finding the guy's friend."

Following Brita to the door, Vivian murmured, "You have a beautiful home."

Brita smiled. "Thanks. My parents left me the condo in their will after they died in an avalanche, skiing in Switzerland."

"Oh, I'm so sorry." Vivian shook her head. "That must have been a terrible shock for you."

Brita started to choke up. "It was. I was going to sell the place, but I knew they would have wanted me to live here. It took me a while to get used to it, but I like it now."

"Well, I think it's lovely." Reaching the door, Vivian stepped outside into the hallway. "It must make you feel closer to your parents."

"It does." Brita's smile returned. "I really hope you find that poor man's friend."

"Thank you. So do I." Vivian raised her hand in farewell and walked slowly back to the elevators.

Next stop, she told herself, was the Abundance of Treasures thrift store. She could only hope that someone could tell her who had bought the model. If not, she would have to give up the search, and that would break her heart.

Chapter Seven

Arriving back in the parking lot minutes later, Vivian checked her phone for the address of Abundance of Treasures. Brita was right—it was two and half blocks away. She peeked into the back window of her car to check on Felix. He was curled up with his head on his paws, sound asleep.

Having satisfied herself that he'd be fine waiting a bit longer for her, she set off for the thrift store. As she turned the corner, the wind hit her in the face, ruffling her hair. Clouds had gathered over the ocean, and tiny white caps rode the waves. A strong aroma of seaweed and sand suggested an incoming storm, and she guessed it would be raining before long. Hoping she would arrive back at the tearoom before that happened, she hurried up to the store.

The entire row of shops looked as if they might have been residential houses at one time, now turned into commercial venues. The small lattice bay windows, the ornate front doors, and the porches reminded Vivian of her tearoom.

The thrift store was comprised of two of these houses, making it the largest store on the block. Behind the windows, the shelves were crammed with an assortment of kitchen utensils, figurines, books, shoes, clocks, lamps, and vases. Inside the store, numerous racks held clothing of all kinds, from jogging shorts to wedding dresses.

Spotting a worried-looking woman in a flower print dress and blue cardigan stocking one of the racks, Vivian walked over to her. "Hi. I was wondering if you sold a model of Big Ben this month."

The woman stared at her. "Big Ben?"

"Yes. You know, the clock in Westminster, London. A friend of mine had it in his living room, and I was wondering who gave it to him. I'd like to know to whom it was sold."

The woman shook her head. "I never saw anything like that." She nodded at a counter where a man with a stiff back and a crew cut was serving a teenager. "Ask Jeremy," she said. "He knows everything that goes out of here."

Vivian thanked her and walked over to the counter. The teenager was examining a pair of earrings with all the intensity of a forensic technician. It was taking her forever to decide if she wanted to buy them, and Vivian glanced at her watch. Jenna and Gracie were probably at the tearoom by now, waiting for her to open the door.

She had just about made up her mind to leave and come back another time, when the young woman thrust the earrings at the clerk. "I'll give you thirty dollars for them," she announced.

"The price is forty-five," the clerk told her. "We don't give discounts here. This is a thrift store."

"Then I don't want them." The customer dropped the earrings on the counter and walked away.

The clerk picked up the earrings, stashed them behind the register, then turned to Vivian. Scowling at her empty hands, he barked, "Can I help you?"

"I hope so." She tried to smile at him, but the resentment on his face was a little intimidating. "I was wondering if you sold a model of Big Ben recently."

Instead of answering, he kept glowering at her as if waiting for her to say more.

She pulled in a breath. "Big Ben? The London clock in Westminster?"

"I know what it is."

"Oh." She paused, then asked, "So, do you know who bought it?"

His mouth tightened. "We don't give out that information here."

"Oh, well, it's just that a friend of mine died, and I was wondering who gave the model to him so I could let them know."

"I'm sorry. I can't help you."

He didn't look sorry at all. If anything, he looked anxious to be rid of her.

Sighing, she turned away. It seemed her quest had come to an abrupt halt. She was almost at the door when a young woman darted up to her.

"Excuse me?" The woman tossed a glance over her shoulder at the counter and looked back at Vivian. "I heard what you said to Jeremy. I know who bought your model."

Vivian felt like hugging her. "You do? I'd really appreciate it if you would tell me who it was."

Again the woman shot a look at the man behind the counter. "I don't know her last name, but she comes in here a lot. Her first name is Connie and she lives in the Cozy Nest Retirement Home on the other side of town. That's all I know about her. I saw her carrying the model out of the store a couple of weeks ago."

"Thank you so much." Vivian glanced at the surly clerk, who was serving another customer. "I hope you won't get into trouble over this."

The clerk shrugged. "Nah. Jeremy's all talk and no action. I just ignore him."

"Well, thank you. I really appreciate your help."

"Sure. And I'm sorry about your friend." She darted away before Vivian realized she was talking about Lewis.

It was true, she thought, as she walked back to the car. Although she'd never met Lewis Trenton, she'd become so involved in finding someone to mourn him, she now considered him a friend. Which made her all the more determined to continue her search. Thanks to a compassionate salesclerk, she now had another lead.

Once more Felix did his dance of joy when she opened the car door. "Okay, buddy," she told him. "We're going home."

Felix whined in agreement, and she drove back along the coast road to Misty Bay, a little faster than normal.

As she expected, Jenna and Gracie were standing on the porch when she arrived back at the tearoom. "I'm so sorry," she told them, as she unlocked the door. "It took longer than I realized. I hope you didn't have to turn away any customers."

"Nope." Jenna paused in the doorway and looked back at her. "But we were on the point of sending out a search party."

"I should have called you." Vivian waited for Gracie to dart inside before following her with Felix on his leash.

"I keep meaning to give you both a key to the place," she said as she closed the door. "I promise I'll get that done tomorrow on my way back from the hospital."

"I wouldn't mind driving Hal to the hospital tomorrow," Jenna said, "so you can get on with your baking."

Vivian smiled. "Thanks, but Hal has to be there at six AM, which gives me plenty of time to get back to the tearoom and do the baking."

"Six AM?" Gracie's eyes were wide with horror. "What time will you have to get up?"

Vivian shrugged. "I figure four thirty. That will give me time to shower and take Felix out before I pick up Hal."

"Four thirty?" Gracie's voice was a squeak. "That's insane! Why does he have to be there so early?"

"So he can come home that evening. He has to stay there for several hours for observation before the doctor will let him leave."

"Well, that makes sense. I guess."

Gracie marched into the kitchen, and Jenna laughed. "I can't see her getting up that early for anyone."

"She would if it was someone she really cared about."

Jenna's smile widened. "It's so good to hear you finally admitting it."

"Admitting what?"

"How you feel about Hal."

Vivian sighed. "It's still so new. I'm not sure how to go on from here."

"Just be yourself. The rest will follow."

"You're right." Vivian started across the room to the kitchen, tugging on Felix's leash for him to follow. "And I hope you'll take your own advice."

Jenna didn't answer, and Vivian led Felix over to the back door, unfastened his leash, and opened the door to let him out into the yard.

"So," Jenna said as she took down a kettle from a cabinet, "did the woman you went to see give the model to Lewis?"

"No." Vivian pulled off her coat and scarf and draped them over the back of a chair. "She said she's never heard of him. She didn't like the Big Ben, so she gave it to the thrift store in Newport. You should see her condo. It was pure luxury. I felt like I was in a fashion shoot or a movie."

"I'm sorry." Jenna filled the kettle with water. "About the model, I mean. That must have been a disappointment."

"Yeah," Gracie said, tying on her apron. "After, like, getting up early and having to do all the baking before you left." She looked at the shelves. "Everything looks so good. My stomach is rumbling."

"Yes," Vivian said. "You may have a scone."

"Great. I'm starving."

"When are you not?" Jenna put the kettle on the stove and opened another cabinet door. She took down three cups and saucers and set them on the counter.

Hearing a scratching on the back door, Vivian opened it to let Felix bound inside. Bending down to pat him, her fingers met damp fur. "Oh, it must be raining." She straightened. "I'll take him upstairs and dry him off, then I'll be back down for a cup of tea."

"And a scone," Gracie said.

Vivian smiled. "And a scone."

Upstairs in her apartment, she hung her coat and scarf in the closet, then dried off the dog with a worn towel. "Now be a good boy," she told him, handing him a couple of treats. "I'll see you tonight."

Felix lifted his head and gave her the mournful look that never failed to make her feel guilty about leaving him.

Arriving back in the downstairs kitchen, she found Gracie and Jenna already seated at the table with a cup and saucer in front of them. Gracie, as usual, was munching on a scone. Jenna jumped up to pour Vivian a cup of tea.

Vivian sank down onto a chair, smiling at Jenna when she placed the steaming hot tea in front of her. "Thanks. I need this. It's been a long morning."

"I'm sorry it was such a waste of time," Jenna said as she sat down. "That's frustrating."

"Well, it wasn't a total waste of time." Vivian raised the cup to her lips and took a cautious sip of the hot tea. She put the cup down and met two pairs of questioning eyes.

"Well," Jenna said, "are you going to tell us what that meant?"

Vivian leaned back. "I went to the thrift store where Brita had taken the model."

"And?" Gracie looked impatient. "What did they say?"

Vivian recounted the conversation with Jeremy and the salesclerk. "So," she finished, "I guess my next step is a visit to the retirement home to find Connie."

"She didn't know her last name?" Gracie brushed crumbs from her mouth with the back of her hand.

"No, but there can't be that many people named Connie there." Vivian picked up her cup again. "She shouldn't be too hard to find."

"So, when are you planning on going there?" Jenna asked, plucking a napkin from the holder. She handed it over to Gracie, who took it with a roll of her eyes.

"I thought I'd go this evening." Vivian sighed. "I need something to occupy my mind."

Jenna nodded in sympathy. "I could come with you. I'll drive you over there, if you like."

"That would be great." Vivian hesitated, then added, "Except I was thinking of taking Felix along for the ride."

"That's okay." Jenna drained her cup and put it back in its saucer. "He can ride in the back of my car."

Vivian smiled. "Thanks. You're a good friend."

"Happy to help." She looked at Gracie. "How about you? Want to come along?"

"I'd like to," Gracie said, "but I promised Alyssa I'd, like, help her with something tonight."

Jenna cocked an eyebrow at her. "Not illegal, I hope?"

A flush spread across Gracie's cheeks. "Why would you say that?"

Jenna shrugged. "Just a thought."

"Well, unthink it. Alyssa might be a pain, but she's not a criminal."

"Sorry," Jenna said, looking totally unapologetic. "I'm just looking out for you, that's all."

Watching Gracie's face, Vivian promised herself she'd get the full story about Gracie's roommate from Jenna as soon as possible.

The sound of the shop doorbell, warning of a customer, brought both assistants to their feet. "I'll go," Gracie said, and darted out of the kitchen without waiting for an answer.

Jenna sat down again with a shake of her head. "Me and my big mouth."

"You're just being protective," Vivian assured her. "We both do a little too much of that where Gracie is concerned."

"Well, she doesn't have a mother to watch out for her," Jenna mumbled. "I know what that's like."

"I know you do." Vivian felt bad for her, remembering her own loving family life that was so different from either Jenna's or Gracie's upbringing. "But Gracie is past twenty-one and considered an adult. We can't run her life for her. She's doing pretty well at that on her own."

"You're right." Jenna stared moodily at her cup. "It's just that . . . I would hate to see her make some of the mistakes that I did."

"We all make mistakes." Vivian sighed. "Heaven knows I made enough of them. But that's how we learn." She paused, then added more quietly, "Though I would like to know the story behind Gracie's roommate."

Jenna's lips tightened. "Well, Gracie told me—" She broke off as Gracie appeared in the doorway.

"We have a couple of walk-ins who want afternoon tea," Gracie announced. "Do we have a free table?"

"We do." Vivian stood up. "Table eight. I'll make the sandwiches. Jenna, go and seat them, please?"

"Sure." Jenna jumped up and reached for her empty cup and saucer.

"I'll get that." Gracie rushed over to the table. "You go take care of the customers."

"Thanks." Jenna turned to leave, then turned back to Gracie. "Sorry about, you know . . . earlier."

Gracie shook her head. "It's okay. I know you meant well."

"I did." Jenna started for the door. "But sometimes I don't know when to quit."

She left, and Gracie picked up the cups and carried them to the dishwasher.

"She was just looking out for you," Vivian said as she hurried over to the fridge. "I know that's not what you want, but Jenna's a caretaker. She's going to worry about you."

"I know." Gracie placed the cups gently into the dishwasher. "Actually, I'm not totally sure she's wrong about Alyssa. I don't think she's, like, doing anything bad, but she does act weird at times."

The shop doorbell interrupted them once more, and Gracie headed for the tearoom, leaving Vivian to wonder just what it was about this Alyssa that had both her assistants worried.

*   *   *

There were times when a detective's job could be incredibly frustrating. Messina studied his computer, his face creased in irritation. He was no closer to finding out who killed Lewis Trenton, and the way things were going, it seemed that the case would go cold.

There were no witnesses to the crime, no clues to follow, no fingerprints or DNA, and it didn't help that Trenton had no friends or even acquaintances who might have been able to help discover what happened that day.

He was at a dead end, and Messina did not like to fail. According to the latest report from Portland, the cops there were still hunting down the jewel thieves. They were convinced that Lewis Trenton was the fence, and since he was now dead and out of their district, they had pretty much written off that part of the case. They were more interested in finding the robbery gang and recovering the jewels.

Not that he could blame them. Half a million dollars was a lot of money. What he needed to do, he decided, was to interfere after all, and do his own investigating into the robbery. Starting with finding out the name of the customer who bought the Big Ben from Vivian. It would give him an excuse to see Jenna again.

As an image of her face floated into his mind, he cursed himself for his dithering. How long was he going to drum up excuses to see her? How was he ever going to know if this was something meaningful if he didn't make a move?

That evening, he promised himself, the minute he got home he'd call her and ask her out to dinner. If she turned him down, then he'd know where he stood. He wasn't sure if he would keep trying after that point, but that decision could wait. Right then he had to decide where he would take her if she agreed to go out with him. That was something he'd enjoy doing.

He turned back to the computer and started researching restaurants.

*   *   *

That evening Jenna drove Vivian and a restless Felix to the Cozy Nest Retirement Home in Newport. Entering the vast lobby with Jenna close behind her, Vivian took a moment to admire the soft pale blue carpeting, the floor to ceiling windows with a view of the mountains, and the gleaming walnut reception desk curving around a corner.

The peaceful, welcoming atmosphere impressed her. If she had to move to a retirement home, she thought, as she crossed the room, she'd put this one near the top of her list.

The sleepy-eyed woman who greeted her reminded Vivian of her mother. "I'm looking for a friend of a friend," she explained, meeting the woman's steady gaze. "I don't know her last name, but her first name is Connie."

The woman frowned. "I don't think—"

"It's important," Jenna cut in. "A friend of ours has died, and we're trying to locate his friends to let them know."

"Oh." The woman's face cleared. "Well, we have two Connie's living here. Can you tell me more about her?"

"I know she shops often at the Abundance of Treasures," Vivian said. "She bought a model of London's Big Ben from there a couple of weeks ago."

The woman smiled. "That would be Connie Murphy. I saw her carry that in here. Connie used to travel a lot. She's been all over the world. London was one of her favorite places. That and Ireland. That's where her family comes from."

Vivian nodded politely and wondered if the woman talked this much about all the residents. "Would it be possible to talk to her?"

"Of course." The woman glanced up at a large clock on the wall behind her. "She's most likely in the lounge, playing cards. Around the corner and to your right. Anyone in there should be able to point her out."

"Thank you." Vivian nodded at Jenna, and the two of them walked around the corner to the lounge.

This room also had floor-to-ceiling windows that looked out over elegant gardens with fir trees, a pond, a waterfall, and a beautiful weeping willow. All so tranquil it was making Vivian feel sleepy. Though she did wonder how much it cost to keep those windows clean.

Tables and chairs were scattered all over the room, which was also carpeted in the same pale blue as the lobby. People sat at the tables or relaxed in roomy armchairs while a silver-haired lady sat a piano, quietly playing a melody.

Vivian spotted an elderly gentleman reading in an armchair, his glasses perched on his prominent nose. She approached him, followed by Jenna, and halted in front of him. "Excuse me, I'm looking for Connie Murphy. Is she in here?"

The man looked up over the top of his glasses. "Who?"

Vivian spoke louder. "Connie Murphy."

A woman passing by with a pile of books paused next to her. "Connie is over there." She nodded at a table in the corner of the room, where three woman and a man sat studying a handful of playing cards. "She's the one with the ribbon in her hair."

"Thank you." Vivian beckoned to Jenna to follow her and walked over to the table.

All four people sitting there looked up when Vivian reached them. "I'm sorry to bother you," Vivian said, smiling at Connie, "but I was hoping to have a minute to talk to you."

Connie frowned. "Do I know you?"

"Actually, no, but there's something important I need to discuss with you."

"Good evening, fair lady." The man seated next to Connie stretched his mouth wide beneath a thick white mustache as he leaned a little too closely toward Vivian. "How may we help you?"

Vivian recognized the type immediately. She'd met enough of them in her time. Men who thought they were God's gift to women. This one, with his wavy white hair and knowing eyes, appeared to have taken good care of himself over the years. He must have been good-looking when he was younger, she thought, though he hadn't aged as well as Hal.

Hastily switching her mind to the matter at hand, she told him, "I'm here to speak with Connie. It's a personal matter."

Connie made a small sound of distress. "How do you know my name? Who are you?"

She sounded scared, and the other two women snatched up their cards and handed them to Connie. "We'll leave you to talk," one of them said.

"I'm sorry," Vivian said, dismayed that she had spoiled their game. "I'm not here to threaten anyone. I won't be more than a minute or two, and you can go back to playing."

"No, thanks." The woman gave her an anxious smile. "I've had enough. It's past my bedtime."

"And mine," her companion put in. "I'm ready to doze off."

The man leered at them as they stood up. "Goodnight, ladies," he purred. "Don't forget we have that trivia match at eleven tomorrow."

The two women treated him to a brief nod and left.

Vivian sat down on one of the vacated chairs, waiting for Jenna to sit before turning to Connie. "My name is Vivian Wainwright," she said, "and I own the Willow Pattern Tearoom in Misty Bay." She glanced at Jenna. "This is one of my assistants, Jenna."

"Hi," Jenna murmured. "Pleased to meet you."

"Oh!" Connie's face brightened. "I know that place. Curtis and I had afternoon tea there."

Vivian smiled. "I hope you enjoyed it."

"I did." Connie clasped her hands together. "The pastries there are divine."

"A memorable experience," the man assured her.

"This is Curtis Rodgers," Connie murmured. "He's a good friend of mine."

"A very *good* friend," Curtis said softly, making Vivian's stomach squirm.

"How nice for you," she lied, turning back to Connie. "Actually, I'm here because I'm hoping you can tell me about the Big Ben Model you bought from the thrift store."

Connie looked surprised. "How do you know about that?"

"A salesclerk told me you bought it and gave me your name. I was wondering if you gave it to Lewis Trenton."

Connie frowned. "Who?"

Vivian's spirits sank. "Lewis Trenton? He lived in a cabin in the hills above Misty Bay."

"Never heard of him," Curtis said, raising his voice.

Connie shook her head. "Me neither. I gave the model to my grandson, Noah, for his birthday."

Vivian sighed. "Would you mind giving me his address? I'm trying to find whoever gave the Big Ben to Lewis. He's passed away, and I need to locate his friends to let them know."

"I think it's time we retired for the night." Curtis rose and took hold of Connie's arm. "Come, my love. I've heard enough of this Big Ben subject."

Connie allowed Curtis to pull her to her feet. "I'm sorry we couldn't help you," she said as she unhooked her purse from the chair.

"If you could just give me the address of your grandson?" Vivian asked again, getting up from her chair.

As Curtis pulled her away from the table, Connie called out over her shoulder. "Noah Russell. He lives here in Newport. On Larch Street. Number 320."

Watching them disappear, Jenna uttered an explosive, "Ugh! What does she see in that creep?"

"Loneliness can make you blind," Vivian said, gathering up her purse.

"Yeah, I know." Jenna got up from the table. "I just hope I never get that lonely again."

Vivian gave her a sharp look. "That doesn't mean you should turn your back on every opportunity."

"I'm not." Jenna slung her purse over her shoulder. "As a matter of fact, Messina called me this evening just as I was leaving to come pick you up."

"He did?" A few heads turned in her direction, alerting Vivian she'd spoken way too loud in her excitement. "Let's get out of here," she said, giving Jenna a light push. "I want to know every word he said."

Jenna laughed and led the way back to the lobby.

Vivian called out, "Thank you!" to the woman at the desk and followed Jenna out into the chilly night air.

Once inside the car, Jenna switched on the engine and turned up the heat. Vivian waited until they were out of the parking lot and driving down the well-lit street before asking, "So? Tell me what Messina had to say."

"He asked me to call him Tony."

Vivian blinked. "Well, that's a good start."

"Then he asked me out to dinner."

"No way!"

Jenna glanced at her. "Why are you so surprised? You've been telling me for weeks that he was interested."

"I know. But I wasn't sure if he would do anything about it. After all, you haven't been exactly enthusiastic in giving him signals."

"Signals?"

"You know, letting him know you're interested too."

Jenna laughed. "Well, he must have picked up something. He was very charming on the phone."

"He was? What did he say?"

"He said he'd been thinking about me and would like to get to know me better."

"Oh, heaven." Vivian settled back on her seat with a sigh of pleasure. "I'm so happy for you."

"It's just dinner. We might not hit it off and we'll go our separate ways."

"You don't really believe that, do you?"

"No." Jenna sighed. "To be honest, I'm scared to death that I'll develop strong feelings for him, and he won't feel the same way."

"I think you've already got strong feelings for him," Vivian said, smiling at the thought. "And I'm pretty sure they're reciprocated."

"Well, I guess time will tell."

"So, when are you going to dinner?

"I don't know. Tony said he'd make reservations and call me later."

"Well, let me know. You know I'll be dying to hear every detail."

"Yeah, I figured that."

Vivian glanced at her watch. "Heavens, it's nine thirty. I was going to go to bed early. I have to get up at four thirty in the morning."

"Are you sure you wouldn't like me to take Hal to the hospital?"

Vivian gave her a grateful look. "I'm sure. This is something I want to do."

"But you have to come back home and do all that baking, then work all day, and go back to get him that evening. You're going to be on your knees."

"And it will be worth every minute of it." Vivian unhooked her seat belt as Jenna parked in front of the tearoom. "You'll understand when you and Tony get together."

"I'm not sure I can ever be that devoted."

Vivian laughed and opened the door. "Just wait and see. Thanks for the ride. And for coming with me." Without waiting for Jenna to drive off, she hurried across to the door and unlocked it. She just had to take Felix down to the yard; then she could go to bed and try to sleep before the alarm woke her up in the morning.

Then she could be with Hal again. She would have preferred better circumstances, but hey, she'd take any chance she could get to be with him. Even if it was a ride to the hospital.

As she dealt with Felix's exuberant greeting, she thought of Jenna and her upcoming date with Messina. She prayed that things would go well for them. They were both good people and deserved to find happiness. She couldn't wait to find out how it would all turn out.

Chapter Eight

Vivian awoke the next morning with the alarm buzzing in her ear and Felix's hot breath on her face. He was standing over her, obviously anxious about the unexpected noise in the middle of the night.

"It's okay, buddy," she said as she sleepily patted his head. "We're just a bit early this morning, that's all."

Yawning, she slid out of bed and felt for her slippers. Her feet met bare carpet, and she frowned. *Not again.* Surely she hadn't left her slippers in the bathroom again? When had she developed that habit?

Padding into the bathroom on bare feet, she switched on the light. She could see nothing but shiny, vinyl floor. Frowning, she tried to think where she was when she'd taken off her slippers.

She had dressed in the bedroom, and changed into her shoes, so she assumed she had left her slippers in their usual spot by the bed. Maybe she had kicked them underneath without noticing.

She knelt down to look, fending off Felix's wet tongue on her face. "Wait a minute," she told him. "I'll take you down to the yard when I find my slippers."

After a thorough inspection of the bedroom and bathroom again, she decided she couldn't waste any more time on the hunt. She slipped her feet into a pair of flats, wrapped herself in her robe and walked into the living room with Felix bouncing along in front of her.

As she crossed the room to the door, a flash of white beside the couch caught her eye. There were her slippers, sitting side by side.

She was losing her mind. There could be no other explanation. Why on earth would she take off her slippers and leave them by the couch? Why didn't she remember doing that?

Standing at the door, Felix uttered a quiet bark of impatience, and she made an effort to control her fears. Everyone got forgetful when they got older, right? Or maybe it was the stress—running the business, her relationship with Hal, this thing with Lewis, taking care of Felix.

At the thought of Felix, she started toward him. "Okay, buddy. Let's go downstairs." She opened the door, and the dog shot out ahead of her. She had things to do, and getting Hal to the hospital on time was the important thing right now. Her state of mind could wait.

Less than an hour later, she parked in front of the pet store and rang the doorbell. She waited, shivering in the dark, for a minute or two before Hal finally opened the door.

"Sorry," he said, "I was writing a note to Wilson. I have to give him detailed instructions for any possible situation."

Vivian nodded in sympathy. "We'll keep an eye on him throughout the day. Just get through this and come back home."

"Yes, ma'am." Hal closed and locked the door, then followed her to the car. "I don't want you guys agonizing over my shop," he said, fastening his seat belt. "You have enough to keep you occupied with your own business."

"There are three of us." Vivian pulled out of the parking lot and headed down the empty street. "One of us can check on Wilson during a lull. I don't want you to worry about anything."

"Thanks." He sat back with a sigh. "I don't know what I'd do without you."

Her heart skipped a beat, and she hesitated before murmuring, "I hope you never have to."

"I heartily second that."

She didn't know if she was relieved or disappointed when he didn't enlarge on that. Instead, he was silent for a few moments before asking, "So, did you take the diamond to Messina?"

"I did." She paused, wondering how much she wanted to tell him. Right now, with his health in jeopardy, Hal didn't need to worry about her. Although she hadn't admitted it before now, she knew she was probably flirting with danger in her search for Lewis's mysterious friend. After all, he was suspected of being a fence for a gang of thieves.

She badly wanted to give the man the benefit of the doubt, but after witnessing some of her late husband's more lurid cases, she knew that when it came to crime, you couldn't rule anyone out, no matter how innocent they might appear.

Realizing that she'd taken far too long to fully answer him, she glanced at him to find him studying her with his forehead creased in a frown.

"Sorry," she said quickly. "I got distracted."

"Uh-huh."

"I did take the diamond to Messina. He's looking into it."

There was an awkward pause, then Hal leaned toward her. "So, what are you not telling me?"

Keeping her gaze fixed on the road ahead, Vivian chose her words carefully. "Messina checked with the Portland police. They say the diamond was part of a jewel robbery that took place in Portland a while ago."

"And?"

He was not going to give up until he'd heard the rest of it. Reluctantly, she told him, "They believe that Lewis Trenton was the fence, that he tried to steal the jewels from the robbers and hid them in the Big Ben, and that they shot him while recovering them. Except they missed one."

"No kidding. I hadn't heard anything about that." Hal sounded shocked. "Why isn't this all over the news?"

"I guess because it's part of Portland's case, and so far they don't know for sure that Lewis is a fence."

"And you don't think he is."

She sent him a quick glance. "What makes you say that?"

"I know you."

She laughed. "Yeah, I guess you do."

"But you don't know Lewis Trenton. What makes you believe he's innocent?"

"If he was a fence, he'd be making a ton of money. Would he really need to go beachcombing for a living?"

"That could just be his cover."

"Maybe, but I can't see him living in poverty like a pioneer, as Chris said."

"Chris?"

She sighed. Her and her runaway mouth. "I've been looking for whoever gave the Big Ben to Lewis. I believe it was a gift from a friend, and I want to let that friend know that he died. I hate thinking of Lewis leaving this earth without at least someone caring about him."

Hal was silent for so long she thought she'd upset him. But then he said, "So how did that go?"

"Well, at first I thought it was the woman who bought the Big Ben from me, since she said it was for a friend, but she gave it to her friend in Newport, who didn't like it, so *she* gave it to a thrift store, and then Connie bought it but gave it to her grandson and—"

"Whoa! You're losing me. Who's Connie?"

Again she shot him a look. "We're almost at the hospital. Why don't we leave this conversation until tomorrow? I promise you I'll tell you every detail then, okay?"

Hal slumped back on his seat. "Okay. But I'm holding you to that promise."

"Deal." She pulled into the parking lot and parked in front of the hospital entrance. "Wait here while I park, then I'll go inside with you."

"You don't have to come in with me. You need to get back to the tearoom."

"What I need," she said firmly as she turned to look at him, "is to make sure you're all set before I leave you alone in there."

He smiled, making her forget everything except how much she cared for him. "Okay. Thanks. But I can walk. Let's park the car and we'll walk back together."

Deciding this wasn't the time to argue, Vivian found a parking space and shut off the engine. "Okay. You ready?"

"Ready for anything." Hal sounded unconcerned as he scrambled out of the car.

Walking along beside him toward the hospital, Vivian wished she felt the same way. Their footsteps echoed in the near-empty parking lot, though she did see a couple of people heading for the entrance.

The night was clear and cold, with dawn still an hour or two away. She pulled in a deep breath of salty air and detected the fragrant aroma of pine. She wished they were taking a stroll along the beach instead of entering a hospital where Hal would be undergoing surgery with no one at his side.

She wanted so much to stay with him all day, until she could take him home again, but she knew he wouldn't allow that, and he was right. There was nothing she could do for him except be with him, and she needed to be back at the tearoom, baking the day's batch of pastries.

"Are you going to tell me what that fierce frown is all about?"

Startled, she turned to look at him. "I was just wishing I could stay with you today."

He halted just steps from the entrance, reached out, and pulled her up close to him. "I appreciate the thought, but I promise you, it's not necessary. I told you, it's a minor procedure that the doctors have done thousands of times. I'm not worried, so you shouldn't be either, okay?"

Her heart was beating so fast she could barely speak. This was the closest she'd ever been to him, and it was . . . exhilarating. "Okay."

"Good." He leaned toward her and before she fully realized what was happening, he planted a brief kiss on her mouth. "Now, let's go inside and get this over with."

She was floating in a daze of shock and pleasure and a dozen other things she didn't have time to explore right now. Following him to the reception counter, she struggled to compose herself. This wasn't the time to analyze what had just happened. She needed to act as though it were the most natural thing in the world and meant nothing more than a grateful response to a kind gesture.

And if she believed that, she told herself, she was more a fool than she'd thought.

She gave herself a mental shake and waited while Hal checked in. It took all her willpower to act naturally when he turned to her.

"I'll text you as soon as I can," he said while an aide waited for him to follow her.

"Right." Vivian's lips felt stiff as she smiled at him. "Good luck."

"Thanks. See you soon."

She watched him walk away and, for some ridiculous reason, felt like crying. Annoyed with herself, she hurried outside into the still dark morning and waited until she got into the car before letting the tears flow.

She didn't know why she was crying. She only knew now what she had resisted for so long. She was in love with the guy. And she had no way of knowing if what he felt for her was love or simply affection and a need for companionship.

What she needed right then, she told herself, was a hot cup of tea and a furry dog to hug. With that in mind, she pulled out of the parking lot and headed for home.

Dealing with Felix's boisterous greeting on her return went a long way toward soothing her rattled nerves. She took him for a brief walk just as the sun was rising behind the Coast Range. Felix trotted ahead of her down the sidewalk, stopping now and then to sniff at something that caught his attention.

She didn't have time to take him on the beach, but paused long enough at the gap to take in the clean, salty air from the ocean breeze before walking back home.

After settling Felix with a treat and his favorite toy, she was about to leave the apartment and go downstairs to the kitchen when her phone buzzed. Anxiety leapt in her stomach when she saw Hal's name on the screen. Pressing the phone to her ear, she tried to sound calm. "Hi! Is everything okay?"

His warm, calm voice reassured her. "Everything's fine. I've just gone through all the checks and balances, and now I'm waiting to go up to surgery. There's something that's been bothering me, though, and I need to straighten it out."

Her mind flashed back to the kiss. He was regretting it already. "Okay," she said cautiously. "What is it?"

He hesitated for a moment, and she felt as if she were sinking into a dark pit. She had to sound unconcerned, like it hadn't meant anything to her either. She wasn't sure she could do that.

"I hope I didn't offend you earlier," Hal said at last. Now he sounded uneasy.

She wasn't sure how to answer that. While she was still struggling for the right words, Hal spoke again.

"With that kiss, I mean."

As if he could have meant anything else.

She formed her lips to assure him she was totally unaffected by it when he added, "You were standing there, right in front of me, and you were just too captivating to resist."

Her mind reeled in the pleasant shock of his words, and she uttered a soft murmur of pleasure. Felix stared up at her, his ears on alert. Making a supreme effort to sound normal, she said softly, "I wasn't offended. As a matter of fact, I liked it."

"Well, good." Now he sounded relieved. "Then you wouldn't mind if I did it again?"

She briefly closed her eyes. "I'd look forward to it."

"Now I can't wait to get out of here."

"Me too."

His voice rose. "Uh-oh. They're coming for me. I gotta go."

Still glowing from the exchange, she clutched the phone tighter. "Good luck. Call me when you can."

"The second I get a chance. Bye."

She lowered the phone and looked into Felix's anxious eyes. "He's going to be alright," she said, leaning down to scratch behind his ear. "He'll be back to take you for a walk soon."

Felix whined, and she squatted down to hug him. "I know. I'm worried about him too. But he's going to be alright. He has to be."

She quickly shut out the threatening memories of Martin's heart attack that had taken him from her so suddenly. One minute he'd been sitting opposite her, commenting on the case he was prosecuting, and the next he had slumped in his chair, his face paper white and lifeless.

It had taken weeks before she stopped waiting for him to call or walk through the door, and months before she stopped waking up in the mornings expecting him to be lying beside her.

She would not think about that now. Hal had assured her his heart was fine. She had to keep those fears at bay, or they could destroy what promised to be an exciting, satisfying relationship. She needed to dive into this with all the exuberance that Felix displayed when she arrived home.

Well, maybe not quite like that, she thought, as Felix landed a wet tongue on her cheek. Standing up, she looked down at him.

"Be a good boy. I have to go to work now, but I'll be back soon to take you potty. Okay?"

Felix's head drooped, and she sighed. "I know. You hate being alone. So do I."

Surprised at herself, she closed the apartment door behind her and started down the stairs. She'd never admitted to herself before that she was lonely. She hadn't fully realized it until now. Maybe she wouldn't have to be alone for long. Heedless of her stiff knees, she practically ran down the stairs to the kitchen.

For the next two or three hours, she forced herself to focus on her baking, trying to block out the thought of Hal, helpless on a hospital bed while doctors threaded foreign objects into his arteries.

She placed the final tray of scones onto the shelves, with time to spare, and climbed the stairs to her apartment, beginning to feel the effects of her early morning rise. Watching Felix bound all over the room when she opened the door made her wish she had some of his energy.

She fastened his leash and let him tug her back down the stairs. He started to pull her toward the back door, but she resisted, telling him, "We have time to go for a walk."

The words had barely left her lips when he bolted out of the kitchen and dragged her across the tearoom to the door. Once outside, he settled to a contented trot, his nose an inch above the ground as he followed a tantalizing aroma.

The air was chilly, and Vivian was thankful for her warm coat as she walked to the side street that led to the gap. There were just a handful of people wandering along the shoreline or chasing after a playful dog.

Once on the beach, she unhooked Felix's leash and watched him race toward the water. He pulled up short at the edge of the oncoming waves and stuck his nose close to the sand, sniffing furiously until he finally lifted his head and bounded off down the beach.

Vivian called out to him, and he slowed down to look back at her, then reluctantly turned around and charged back to her, sand flying from under his feet.

Just then she felt her phone vibrating in her pocket. She pulled it out, her breath catching when she saw Hal's name. She took a second to calm herself before asking a bright, "Hi! How did it go?"

"The doc said it went just fine."

He sounded tired, and she frowned. "Are you okay?"

"Just a little out of it. They doped me up pretty good."

"Well, get some sleep. Did they say when you can come home?"

"I have to stay here for a few hours to make sure there are no complications. I should be able to leave around five or so."

"I'll be there before that. The girls can close up for me."

"Okay. Thanks." He paused, then added, "Where are you? I can hear the gulls."

"I'm on the beach with Felix. I'm going to check on Wilson on my way back."

"I already called him. He's doing okay."

"I'll stop by there anyway, just to make sure."

"Remind me to repay you when I get out of here."

She grinned. "I'll do that. Now get some rest. I'll see you this afternoon."

"Yes, ma'am."

123

She slipped the phone back into her pocket, the grin still on her face. Felix had wandered off again, and she followed him for a few minutes before calling to him. "Time to go home, buddy," she said as she fastened his leash again. "Looks like I'll have some cleaning up to do when we get back."

As if to agree with her, Felix shook himself, spraying sand all over her pants.

Wilson greeted her with a wave when she poked her head inside the door on the way home. "I can't come in," she called out to him. "I have Felix with me."

Nodding his head, he finished stocking a shelf with pet food and sauntered over to her.

"I just stopped by to see how you're doing," she said when he reached her.

"I'm okay." He waved a hand at the empty store. "It's a slow day."

"Well, if you need help, you know who to call."

Wilson stepped outside to pet Felix. "Hal called me a while ago. He said he's okay."

"Yes, I talked to him too. I should be able to bring him home around five."

"Good. I miss him."

So do I, Vivian thought, but she wasn't going to say it out loud.

Just then a woman paused in front of the window, to peer at the assortment of pet supplies.

"I'd better get going," Vivian said, holding onto Felix's leash as he tried to greet the woman. "Call me if you need me."

Wilson nodded. "Thanks." He turned around and strolled back into the store.

The woman at the window followed him inside, and Vivian left, happy that Wilson had at least one customer to keep him occupied.

By the time Jenna and Gracie arrived at the tearoom, Vivian had cleaned up after Felix and left him snoozing in his bed. She was finishing up the sandwich fillings when Jenna rang the shop doorbell.

"I forgot about the keys again," Vivian said when she opened the door. "I think my memory's going."

Jenna laughed as she headed for the kitchen. "There's nothing wrong with your memory. I heard you telling a customer about something that happened when you were growing up, and you even remembered the date."

"Well, it's the short-term memory that goes first." Vivian followed her into the kitchen and crossed the room to the counter. Reaching up into a cabinet for a kettle, she added, "I'm serious. I really do think I have a problem." She took the kettle down and turned to find Jenna staring at her, concern written all over her face.

"A problem? Like what?"

Vivian filled the kettle, struggling to keep the anxiety at bay. "I keep losing things."

"Losing things?"

"Well, not *losing*. Misplacing. I think I've left things in one place, and then I find them in another."

Jenna took the kettle from her and placed it on the stove. "I do that all the time, and I'm thirty-nine."

"No, it's more than that." Vivian told her about the slippers and Felix's leash. "It's other things. A scarf I thought I'd left on the dresser. I found it on the couch. My watch, which I leave on the bedside table every night when I go to bed. That was on the coffee table one morning. I can't imagine why I would take off my watch in the living room. I never do that."

"Stress." Jenna took down three cups and saucers from the cabinet. "It makes you do weird stuff. Like parking your car and then forgetting where you parked it."

In spite of her worry, Vivian had to smile. "I do that too. More often than I want to admit."

Hearing the shop doorbell, Jenna raised her head. "That's Gracie. I'll get it."

She disappeared out the door, and Vivian let out her breath. Maybe Jenna was right. Maybe it was just stress, like she'd told herself earlier.

She'd feel a lot better once Hal was safely home and resting.

Gracie bounced into the kitchen, with Jenna following more slowly behind her. "I just saw the most gruesome skeleton that would have looked perfect in our window."

Vivian shook her head. "Wonderful. Halloween is tomorrow, and I completely forgot about it." She looked at Jenna. "See what I mean?"

"You're worried about Hal." Jenna pulled the tea caddy from the cabinet. "Have you heard how he's doing?"

"He called a little while ago. Everything went fine. That's all he told me. I guess I'll get the full story later."

"He's probably still woozy from the surgery," Jenna said. "It takes some people hours to wake up after that."

"He said I could pick him up around five. I'd like to be there by four." Vivian sat down at the table. "Would it be okay with you guys if—"

Jenna interrupted her. "Of course. You leave when you want to." She took a closer look at Vivian. "In fact, why don't you go now? You look tired. You should be sitting by Hal's bed, watching over him. Gracie and I can handle things here. Right, Gracie?"

"Sure, we can." Gracie peered at Vivian. "You must be bushed. You've been up half the night."

Vivian gave her a weary smile. "Not quite, but it does feel like that." She so badly wanted to get to the hospital and reassure herself that Hal was doing okay. Yet guilt held her back. Her place was at her tearoom, taking care of business. "I'll be fine once I've had a cup of tea."

"No, you won't." Jenna took hold of her arm and pulled her up on her feet. "You're going to the hospital. There's nothing happening here that Gracie and I can't handle."

"But I promised Hal we'd look in on Wilson too."

"I can do that." Gracie took her other arm. "Go pretty yourself up, and then go and take care of your man."

Together they propelled her to the door leading to her apartment.

She went willingly, too tired to resist.

Felix's excitement was soon dashed as Vivian changed into a pink sweater, dabbed on some lipstick, combed her hair, and pulled on her coat. "I'll be back later to give you dinner," she promised him, her own excitement mounting at the thought of seeing Hal again.

She drove carefully to the hospital, aware that fatigue could cause her to make mistakes. The moment she walked into the hospital entrance, however, she forgot about her weariness. All she could think about was greeting Hal and watching his face light up when he saw her.

A helpful nurse directed her to his room, and her steps quickened as she drew closer. She reached the door, which stood ajar, and looked in.

Hal was asleep, his face turned away from her. Her joyful reunion would have to wait.

Happy just to be by his side, she sank onto a chair and dropped her purse to the floor. She was content to wait until he was ready to wake up. Envisioning his smile, she leaned back and closed her eyes.

Chapter Nine

S he was walking along the beach, holding hands with Hal.
Felix was leaping around in front of them, trying to catch a
persistent butterfly, making them laugh. She could feel the cool
breeze on her face, though the sun was warm and . . .

She opened her eyes, confused for a moment in the bright light
of the room. Then she saw Hal. He was awake, his head sideways
on the pillow, watching her.

She struggled to sit up, wondering if she'd been snoring or
sleeping with her mouth open. "Hi." She felt vulnerable, caught in
an embarrassing moment.

"Hi yourself." He grinned at her. "What are you doing here?
It's only a little past one."

"Well, I came to check on you, but you were asleep, and then
I guess I dozed off."

"Yeah, you did."

"Was I snoring?'

He laughed. "No. You were sleeping peacefully. I'm sorry you
had to get up so early."

She smiled back at him. "It was worth it. How are you feeling?"

"Great. I just want to get out of here."

She glanced at her watch. "You have a few hours to go yet."

"Yeah, I know."

He struggled to pull himself upright, and she jumped up to help adjust his pillows. "Is that better?"

"Much better, thanks."

He watched her sit down again, making her feel a little self-conscious. "Since we have so much time on our hands," he said, "we can finish the conversation we started this morning."

She frowned, trying to remember. "What conversation?"

"About your hunt for Lewis Trenton's friend."

"Oh, that." She began telling him about her visits to Stacey, Brita, and the thrift store, and had just reached the bit about her and Jenna's trip to the retirement home when a nurse appeared in the doorway to check on Hal.

"I'm going to run down to the cafeteria," Vivian said, getting up from her chair. "I haven't eaten since early this morning. Can I get you something?"

"I've already had lunch," Hal assured her. "Go eat."

She left him with the nurse and made her way to the cafeteria, where she bought an egg salad sandwich and a cup of coffee to keep her awake and alert. Sitting at a table next to the wall, she ate her lunch, swallowed down the coffee, then hurried back to Hal's room.

The nurse had left, and Hal greeted her with another of his warm smiles. "How was your lunch?"

"Fine. It's amazing how good things taste when you're really hungry."

"Your pastries taste incredible, no matter if you're hungry or not."

"Thank you, kind sir." She smiled at him, and for a second or two their eyes met, and another of those electric moments passed between them; then she dropped her gaze. "I do my best," she murmured.

"You sure do." He settled himself more comfortably against the pillows. "Now finish your story. What happened at the retirement home?"

"Well, we found Connie. She was playing cards with a couple of women and this really, smarmy man named Curtis—"

"Smarmy?"

"Yeah, you know"—she lowered her voice to imitate Curtis,— "'I'm Connie's friend. A very *good* friend,' wink, wink."

Hal laughed out loud. "I get the picture."

"Well, anyway, Connie wasn't a friend of Lewis's. She gave the Big Ben to her grandson, Noah."

Hal shook his head. "I'm sorry. So that's the end of your hunt."

"What? No!" Vivian leaned forward. "I've got Noah's address. I'm going to talk to him. Maybe his parents knew Lewis."

Hal frowned. "And you think they could be his friends?"

Vivian sighed. "I know it's a long shot, but that model landed up in Lewis's hands somehow, and now I've come this far, I'm not going to give up on it until I find out who gave it to him."

"All this makes me uneasy." Hal leaned back against the pillows. "Look what happened the last time you got involved in a murder investigation."

"That was different. I was chasing a killer. This time I'm simply chasing a mystery. I just want answers, that's all."

"Someone shot Lewis Trenton. I'd say there's a killer involved in this somewhere."

Vivian dropped her gaze to the floor. "Okay, so maybe, in the back of my mind, I'm hoping that what I find out might help solve the murder, but that's not why I'm doing this."

"Are you sure about that?"

She looked up at him. "Yes. No. I don't know. All I know is that this whole thing is bugging me, and I can't rest until I find out how Lewis ended up with the Big Ben."

"And if he is the fence for the jewel thieves, they will probably do everything they can to stop you."

Vivian shook her head. "No, I can't believe that Lewis was a fence. I think he got caught up in this somehow as an innocent bystander."

"I hope you're right." Hal struggled to sit upright. "Just promise me one thing."

"What's that?"

"That at the first sign of danger, you'll give up the search and let the cops handle it."

"Of course." She smiled at him, intent on reassuring him. "I may be a bit bullheaded, but I'm not stupid."

He smiled back. "I think that just about sums you up."

"Thank you. Now, can we talk about something else? I called in on Wilson. He wasn't that busy and seemed to be doing just fine in the shop. Jenna said she'd check on him this afternoon."

To her relief, he accepted her change of subject and began telling her a story about how Wilson misunderstood a customer when she asked for catnip. He'd assured her that they only sold baseball caps for dogs, and none of them were knitted. It took a few minutes for Hal to educate Wilson and soothe the irritated customer.

The afternoon passed swiftly, with Hal recounting stories of his past as a firefighter, and Vivian sharing memories of growing up with an English mother, whose odd superstitions and traditions made life stimulating.

Shortly before five PM, Hal's nurse came to tell him he could go home. Vivian left the room while he dressed, and returned to find him waiting for her in a wheelchair. The attentive nurse wheeled him out to the elevator and then out the doors to the fresh sea air.

"Take care of yourself," the nurse said when Hal thanked her.

"I'll see that he does," Vivian assured her. Catching the look Hal sent her, she worried for a moment that she might have sounded a little too controlling. In the next instant, she chided herself. She loved him, and she was going to protect him, no matter what. He would just have to get used to it.

"How are you feeling?" she asked as she settled him in the car. "You're probably exhausted. It's been a long day."

"For both of us. I spent most of mine resting in bed," he reminded her. "How are you doing?"

"Me?" She looked at him in surprise. "I'm fine."

"Tired?"

"A little. But I'd do it all over again without missing a beat."

She closed the door before he could answer and walked around the car to the driver's side. After seating herself behind the wheel, she reached for her seat belt.

"Thank you," Hal said, his voice soft with emotion. "You made this day very pleasant for me."

"Good." She switched on the ignition. "I enjoyed it too."

"I'd say let's do it again, but I can think of better ways to spend the time."

She laughed. "How about dinner when you've recovered?"

"Sounds good. How about Friday?"

She glanced at him. "Will you feel like going out by then?"

"I'll be roaring to go by tomorrow. The doc said I can go back to work as long as I feel okay."

Vivian shook her head. "The miracles of modern science. Speaking of tomorrow, it's Halloween. Are you doing anything special for it in the store?"

"Nah. Wilson ordered a few orange and black pet toys, but that's about it. Dogs don't care about Halloween."

Vivian laughed. "No, I guess not. I'm going to put orange icing on my scones, but other than that, the decorations will have to be enough. We close before the trick-or-treaters are out, but they don't usually come into town anyway. When I was living in Portland, I bought a ton of candy for them. Mostly stuff that Martin and I liked, so we could enjoy the leftovers."

"Yeah, I went that route too. Spent the next two months putting on weight and the next ten trying to get it off again."

"I know what you mean."

He was quiet for a moment, then said softly, "You miss him, don't you?"

"Who?" She shot him a look. "Martin? I did, for a long time. I still think of him now and then, but the pain has faded. How about you?"

"Same. Like I've told you, I'll always love Terry, and I'll never forget her. But I'm ready to move on. I'm kind of hoping you are too."

Her fingers tightened on the wheel. "I am. It has taken me a while, but I am."

"Good to know."

This wasn't a conversation she wanted to have while driving. She needed her full attention on the road.

To her relief, Hal changed the subject. "In another week, it'll be dark by now."

"I know. I can't make up my mind if I would rather keep daylight savings time or abolish it altogether."

They were still discussing the merits and disadvantages of both scenarios by the time they arrived back at the pet store.

"Will you be okay going up the stairs?" Vivian asked as she cut the engine. "I can come in with you, if you'd like."

"Thanks, but I'll be fine. You've spent enough of your time with me today. You need to get back to Felix."

Hal seemed nimble enough as he climbed out of the car, and she relaxed. "Okay, then. You know where to find me if you need me."

He leaned in to smile at her. "I do, indeed. Goodnight, Vivian. Thanks for taking such good care of me."

She smiled back. "Always."

He gazed at her for a long moment, and she wondered what he was going to say, but then he nodded and closed the door.

She waited until he had disappeared inside the store before driving down to the side street and her parking spot.

Felix went berserk when she unlocked the door to the apartment. He got so carried away he leapt onto the couch and over the back of it, fortunately landing on all four feet.

Fighting her guilt, Vivian grabbed his leash and clipped it onto his collar. "Come on, buddy," she said as she opened the door. "Let's go on the beach before it gets dark."

Minutes later, her feet dragged as she trudged across the sand. An early night was what she needed, she told herself. Something light to eat, maybe a sip of wine while she watched *Jeopardy*, then bed.

Felix romped around with his usual boundless energy, stopping now and then to sniff at anything that wasn't sand. He finally exhausted himself and trotted over to her, his tongue hanging out the side of his mouth.

"Hungry, baby?" She fastened his leash again and led him back up the slope to the street. Both of them should sleep well that night, she thought as she reached the door of the tearoom.

She wasn't mistaken. Shortly after eight she fell fast asleep and woke up the next morning once more to the alarm buzzing and Felix's hot breath on her face.

It took her an hour or so to fully wake up, but once she started on her baking, she felt refreshed and invigorated. Hal was apparently out of danger and recovering, and all was well with her world.

She called him once she had her shelves stocked with the pastries, and was reassured to hear him sounding more robust.

"I'm feeling great," he told her when she asked about his health. "No more pain, no more out of breath. I'm doing just fine."

"Oh, I'm so glad. You will take it easy, though, right? At least for today."

"I will. I'll sit behind the counter and let Wilson do the heavy stuff."

"So you still have a store after leaving Wilson in charge?"

"Yeah. He did a good job. Only managed to upset one customer, and he got it squared away, so it's all good."

"I'm glad to hear it."

"So, we're on for Friday?"

"We are." She felt a tingle of excitement at the prospect.

"Great. I'll make reservations, and I'll pick you up at seven. Okay?"

"More than okay." She hung up, smiling at the thought of going on a real date.

Both Jenna and Gracie were anxious to know all the details of Vivian's hospital visit, and both were happy to hear that everything had gone well for Hal.

"We're going out to dinner on Friday to celebrate," Vivian told them, feeling a bit self-conscious when her assistants exchanged knowing looks.

"Where's he taking you?" Jenna asked as she deftly poured tea into three cups.

"I don't know yet. He just said he'd make reservations."

"Well, we might bump into each other." Jenna handed a cup and saucer over to Vivian. "I'm going out to dinner with Tony on Friday."

"No kidding!" Gracie almost dropped her cup. "When did this happen?"

Jenna shrugged. "He called and invited me, and I figured, why not? Might as well have someone else pay for my dinner for a change."

Vivian laughed. "Go on. You're excited about it. Admit it."

A smile flickered across Jenna's face. "Yeah, maybe I am."

"Well good for you both." Gracie stared down at her cup. "You're both dating and I don't have anyone. That sucks."

Jenna stared at her. "What are you talking about? You're always going on dates."

"Yeah, but I never get past that first one. Either they don't call again, or they're losers and I want them to get lost."

"You'll find the right one eventually," Vivian said, picking up her cup. "You're still young. You've got plenty of time."

"I'm twenty-four." Gracie looked up with soulful eyes. "Most of my friends are married now. Alyssa's already been married and divorced, and she's only three years older than me."

"That's the problem," Jenna said, seating herself at the table. "They get married too young and for the wrong reasons. You don't really know what you want until you're at least in your thirties. Right, Vivian?"

"I'd say older than that." Vivian smiled. "But not all early marriages fail. I think it depends on the kind of person you are, and luck has a lot to do with it. You know, meeting the right person at the right time."

"Yeah." Jenna pursed her lips. "I sure met the wrong person at the wrong time."

"But you learn from your mistakes, and the second time around, you know what you don't want."

Jenna smiled into her cup. "That's for sure."

"Well, I hope you both have a great time." Gracie finished drinking her tea and stood up. "I've got cartons to unpack." With that, she took off for the storeroom.

"She sounds upset," Vivian said, gazing after her. "I hope everything's okay with her."

"I think she's getting a bit tired of Alyssa." Jenna put her cup down on the saucer. "I can see her throwing the woman out before too long."

"You never did tell me what's going on there." Vivian leaned back on her chair. "What's the problem there?"

"I don't really know. I don't think Gracie really knows. Apparently, Alyssa is entertaining a whole bunch of people in her room."

Vivian raised her eyebrows. "She's holding private parties?"

"No, not like that. They come in one at a time, stay for a while, then leave."

Vivian stared at Jenna for a several seconds. "Just men?"

"No. I asked her that. She said mostly women, though she does have men too."

"So, what are you thinking?"

Jenna sighed. "I'm thinking that maybe Gracie's roomie is dealing drugs."

"Oh, Lord."

"I know. That could get Gracie in a lot of trouble. The apartment is in her name."

"Well, she needs to get her out of there."

"I agree. I said as much to Gracie, but she gets on well with Alyssa and doesn't want to have to look for another roomie. She can't afford that apartment on her own."

"I'll have a word with her." Vivian picked up her cup and swallowed the rest of her tea. "I don't want her getting into that kind of trouble."

"She'll be mad at me for telling you." Jenna got up and collected the empty cups and saucers.

"I'll tell her we're worried about her." Vivian got up too. "We have to find a solution to this."

"Well, let me know how it goes and what I can do to help."

"I will." Vivian crossed over to the fridge and opened it. "I'd better start on these sandwich fillings. We've got a full house this afternoon."

"Your scones look great." Jenna nodded at the shelves. "I love the orange icing and the chocolate witch's hats."

"Not very British," Vivian said as she carried a bowl of hard-boiled eggs over to the table, "but I had to give a nod to Halloween."

"The customers will love them." Jenna pulled an apron out of a drawer and tied it on. "They always love everything."

Vivian smiled. "I hope so. That's what makes all the hard work worthwhile."

Jenna was right. The compliments poured in from the customers that afternoon, and Vivian was feeling pretty pleased with herself by the time she finally turned the "Closed" sign on the tearoom door.

She'd hoped to have a chat with Gracie before she left, but the assistant took off while Vivian was in the kitchen, cleaning up the shelves. Normally, Gracie would take home leftover scones or other pastries that she liked, but she'd left without asking for any, making Vivian worry about her even more.

"She's probably getting ready for hordes of trick-or-treaters," Jenna said when Vivian remarked on Gracie's abrupt exit. "She told me they had over a hundred last year."

"Well, I'm going to talk to her tomorrow and find out what's going on with her."

"Don't be surprised if she gets upset." Jenna headed for the door. "Enjoy your evening."

The door closed behind her, leaving Vivian alone.

When she went upstairs to her apartment a few minutes later, she endured yet another boisterous welcome from Felix. "I think you and I should go for a ride after dinner," she told him as she whisked up eggs for an omelet.

Felix responded by bouncing on and off the couch, sending cushions flying.

Pouring the eggs into her skillet, Vivian gave him a stern look. "Felix! You need to settle down, or I'll leave you at home."

Felix obediently sat, his steady gaze on her face as she sprinkled pieces of ham, cheese, and tomato on one half of the omelet and deftly flipped the other half over the mix.

He sat by her side as she ate her dinner, waiting patiently for a crumb to drop, until she felt sorry for him and deliberately dropped a small piece of her omelet. Watching him gobble it up, she murmured, "Don't get used to it, pal, or you'll be fighting a weight problem like the rest of us."

Felix licked his lips in appreciation, and she smiled. "Okay, let's go get the car and take a ride into Newport." She got up, with Felix circling her legs in his excitement.

After taking her plate and empty wineglass into the kitchen, she pulled on her coat, then walked over to the side table to pick up her purse.

Except her purse wasn't sitting where she usually left it.

Not again.

She fought the rising tide of dread and tried to think. She remembered stepping into the apartment and being met by thirty pounds of fur and tongue. Had she dropped the purse when she'd greeted Felix?

One glance across the room told her the purse was not on the floor. She must have put it somewhere else. But where?

Maybe she took it into the kitchen. A quick survey assured her the purse wasn't in there. Nor was it in the bathroom. Or the bedroom. There was only one other possibility. She must have left it in the car.

Now she was feeling really nervous. Had she locked the car? She couldn't remember. She grabbed Felix's leash from the nail and clipped it to his collar. "Come on, boy. We've got to get to that car before someone breaks in and steals my purse."

How could she have left it in the car? She never went anywhere without her purse. It was an automatic action to sling the strap over her shoulder any time she moved. And why couldn't she remember if she'd locked the car? Wasn't that automatic too?

There was no doubt about it. She was losing her mind. She needed to get checked out. She'd call her doctor tomorrow.

Felix was already trying to drag her across to the door. She started to follow him when something caught her eye. The edge of a black strap poking out from under the couch. *What in the world?*

She bent over and hooked a finger inside the strap to pull out her purse. For several seconds she stared at it, as if it could tell her how it became stuffed under the couch. Why had she done that?

Hugging the purse to her, she stared down at Felix. The dog seemed to sense that she was upset about something, as he looked up at her with anxious eyes and a soft whine.

The mournful sound helped clear her mind. She probably dropped the purse when Felix attacked her with his welcome home, and it somehow got kicked under the couch. That had to be the explanation.

Minutes later, she was still trying to convince herself of that as she drove into Newport.

Chapter Ten

The GPS on Vivian's Toyota took her into a quiet, tree-lined street of modest homes that looked like they'd been there for centuries. A rickety fence surrounded the house at the address Connie had given her, and dim light glowed behind curtains at the windows.

Felix whined when she shut off the engine.

"No," she told him. "I'm sorry. buddy, but you'll have to stay in the car. Be a good boy. I won't be long." With that, she climbed out and slammed the car door shut. Farther down the street, a group of kids, dressed in various flamboyant costumes, chattered with excitement as they streamed up a pathway.

Three women stood watching them, and Vivian relaxed her tense muscles. She wasn't exactly alone. That was reassuring.

A street lamp nearby shed just enough light for her to see her way up the uneven path in front of her. Spotting a doorbell on one side of the door, she gave it a jab and waited.

Seconds later a porch light flashed on, the door opened, and a small boy looked up at her from the doorway.

This, Vivian assumed, was Connie's grandson. She gave him her best smile. "Hi. You must be Noah. I met your grandmother. She told me about you."

Noah's blond hair fell into his eyes, and he swept it back with a grimy hand. "What did she say?"

"Well, she was telling me about a gift she gave to you. It's a—"

She broke off as a man appeared behind the boy. "Go inside," he told Noah, his harsh voice daring the boy to disobey.

Noah took one look at his face and fled back inside the house.

"I'm sorry," Vivian said, beginning to wish she had chosen to visit in daylight. "I met your mother, and she told me about Noah. I was just—"

"What do you want?"

Looking at the man's unshaven jaw, his straggly hair, badly in need of a trim, and his fierce eyes, Vivian felt intensely sorry for Noah. "My name is Vivian Wainwright, and I own a tearoom in Misty Bay. I met Noah's grandmother, Connie, and she told me she'd given Noah a model of Big Ben."

The man continued to glare at her without saying a word.

Thoroughly unsettled, Vivian cleared her throat. "To make a long story short, I sold the Big Ben to a woman a month ago, and it ended up in a thrift store. I'm trying to find out how it got there."

The man folded his arms in a way that somehow felt threatening. "I don't know how it got there. Noah took it down on the beach and left it on a rock while he was playing with his friend. When he went back for it, it was gone. That's all I know. I'm sick of hearing about the damn thing, so do us both a favor and forget about it. Goodbye."

The door closed abruptly in Vivian's face, and she wondered what kind of desperate woman had allowed that man to father her child.

Back inside the car, she fended off Felix's sloppy kisses as she got comfortable behind the wheel. Of course. Why hadn't it occurred to her before now? It seemed pretty obvious to her now that Lewis found the Big Ben on the beach while beachcombing and took it home.

So, there was no friend to mourn him after all. No one to care that his life had ended, leaving little behind except for a few treasures and a single diamond that he probably had no idea was hidden in his precious keepsake. So sad.

Heading home, she tried to shake off her melancholy. After all, she had never met Lewis. She didn't even know why she cared so much. Maybe it was the enigma of the whole thing, rather than the man behind it. She never could resist a good mystery.

After parking her car on the dimly lit side street, she took Felix for a short walk, which helped to lighten her spirits, then returned home to relax in front of the TV before going to bed. She was sorely tempted to call Hal again, but decided against it. He was probably asleep, and the last thing she wanted to do was disturb him.

Instead, she fixed herself a cup of hot cocoa, settled down on the couch, and reached for the remote. The local news had already started, and the meteorologist was halfway through the weather forecast: more rain and cooler temperatures—typical for fall weather at the Oregon coast.

Felix was snoozing at her feet, and her own eyelids felt heavy. She needed to go to bed, she told herself, before she fell asleep in front of the TV. Reaching for her mug, she paused as she heard a familiar name.

"Lewis Trenton," the anchor said, sounding totally bored, "an impoverished beachcomber, was found shot to death in front of his cabin. Trenton, an alleged fence for jewel thieves, is thought to have been killed while attempting to keep the stolen jewels."

Leaving her mug on the table, Vivian sat up. "He was not a fence!" she yelled at the TV. "How stupid can you be?"

Felix shot up with a growl.

Making an effort to calm down, Vivian bent over to pet him. "Sorry, buddy. I'm just so frustrated. How can they accuse that poor man of being a criminal when all he did was find a treasure on the beach?"

Felix whined.

Vivian stared down at the dog without seeing him. It was so unfair. Having lived with a prosecutor, she knew all about justice and how sometimes it can be misused or manipulated. Sometimes innocent people went to jail or had their good names destroyed by false accusations.

Although she'd never had reason to believe that of Martin, she knew there were prosecutors who would do anything to win a case. Little enraged her more than injustice toward an innocent person.

"That settles it," she told Felix. "I have to find out the truth. Somehow, I have to clear Lewis's name."

Felix licked her nose in agreement.

She slept badly that night, waking up between dreams of hunting for something on the beach and nightmares of drowning in the ocean.

She woke up before the alarm sounded, and lay in bed for a while, waiting for it to go off. Questions about what to do next whirled around in her mind.

The most sensible thing to do was talk to Messina and tell him everything she'd learned about the case so far. Then again, what did she really know except for how Lewis came into possession of the Big Ben model? She didn't even know that for certain. Noah's father could have been lying about losing the model on the beach.

Or what if he was the fence? He could have hidden the jewels in there for safekeeping. After all, how could he know his son would take the model to show it to his friend? Apparently, the beachcomber's hunt for treasure was a common sight on the beach. Maybe Noah's father suspected Lewis of picking up the model, tracked him down to get his jewels back, and shot him. In fact, any one of the people she'd spoken to could have done that. They all had motive, means, and opportunity. Any one of them could be the fence.

No, she needed more evidence before she went to Messina.

Knowing Jenna and Gracie, once they realized she was diving into another investigation, they would both insist on helping her. A big part of her would feel bad about getting them involved again in something that could possibly be dangerous, while another part of her welcomed their participation. It was a lot less daunting when the three of them were hot on the trail of a villain.

Questions were still swirling around in her mind later as she cut circles of dough for the lemon curd tarts and tucked them into the tart pans. She had just slipped them into the oven when her phone buzzed.

Seeing Hal's name on the screen, she snatched up the phone. "Hi! How are you doing?"

His husky voice made her smile. "I'm doing fine. How about you?"

"Same. I've just stuck some lemon tarts in the oven."

"I'll be right over."

She laughed. "They're not cooked yet."

"Then I'll take Felix for a walk. You can repay me with one when we get back."

"Deal." She dropped her phone back on the table and hurried over to the fridge to get the eggs, lemons, and butter for the lemon curd. Minutes later she had the baked tart shells filled and cooling in the fridge.

Hal arrived just as she was mixing the dough for the scones. He looked so much better that she had to fight the urge to hug him. "You're looking well," she told him as he followed her into the kitchen.

"I feel well." He sniffed the air. "I'll feel even better when I've sampled whatever you're baking."

"Banbury cakes. You can have one when you get back from walking Felix."

"Well, I don't know what they are, but they smell like something from heaven."

"They're like an Eccles cake, but instead of just currants, they also have brown sugar, mixed peel, nutmeg, and rum."

Hal raised his eyebrows. "Is that even legal?"

Vivian laughed. "Completely. There's not that much alcohol in each pastry, and most of it evaporates while baking."

"Well, I can't wait to taste one of those. Forget the lemon curd tart. Felix might get his walk cut short this morning." He headed for the door leading to her apartment. Pausing in the doorway, he added, "By the way, I made reservations for tomorrow night. We're having dinner at The Coastal Kitchen. It's a little restaurant farther down the coast. Very small, very private, and very romantic."

He was gone before she could recover her composure.

His words danced in her head as she sprinkled flour onto the cutting board and placed a lump of dough on top of it. After flattening out the dough, she cut circles with a serrated cutter and placed the scones on a baking sheet.

A quick glance in the ovens assured her the Banbury cakes were done, and she pulled out the trays to let them cool off, then slid the trays of scones into the ovens and closed the doors.

Just then, the shop doorbell rang, announcing the arrival of Jenna or Gracie, or both. She remembered, then, that they had offered to come in early that morning, to give them time to take down the Halloween decorations.

Vivian slapped her forehead with her fingers as she hurried across the tearoom to open the door. For more than two years she'd been meaning to get extra keys made for both her assistants. There had to be a Freudian slip going on with her—some reason she didn't want to give keys to the women.

Either that, or her worst fears were being realized and she really was losing her mind.

Jenna had arrived first and sailed into the tearoom with a grin that was totally unusual for her that early in the day.

"What's going on?" Vivian demanded as she followed her assistant into the kitchen. "You look like you've won the lottery."

Jenna shrugged off her jacket and threw her purse into the closet. "Tony called. He said he's been really busy with a new case that came in, but he's looking forward to our date. You'll never guess where he's taking me tomorrow night."

Hoping fervently that it wasn't The Coastal Kitchen, Vivian smiled. "So, tell me!"

Jenna folded her arms in a gesture of triumph. "He's taking me to The Bellemer!"

Vivian stared at her. "Wow. He's really trying to impress you."

"He's succeeding." Jenna's face dissolved into a frown. "What am I going to wear?"

Vivian reached out and patted her arm. "Relax. You'll find something. Keep it simple. That's the epitome of class."

"I have to buy something." Jenna looked at the clock. "I don't have time to go into Newport now. Would it be okay with you if I left early this afternoon?"

"Of course. We won't be that busy today. Everybody's at home finishing up the Halloween candy."

"Great. I haven't bought any new clothes since my divorce." She hurried over to the drawers and dragged out an apron. "I'm really nervous about this whole thing. I can't believe I'm actually dating a cop."

Vivian laughed. "Don't think of him as a cop. He'll be off duty. Just see him as a charming dreamboat who wants to get to know you."

Jenna raised her eyebrows. "Dreamboat?"

"One of my mother's favorite words."

"It'll be tough to forget what he is when he pretty much arrested me for murder."

"He also saved your life."

Jenna's frown faded. "Yeah, he did. I just wish I could remember him doing that."

"Ask him about it. It'll make for interesting conversation."

The doorbell rang again, and Jenna headed for the tearoom. "That's probably Gracie. I'll let her in."

Minutes later the three of them were seated around the table, enjoying a cup of hot tea while the scones were cooling on the shelves, alongside the Banbury cakes.

All except one, which had ended up in front of Gracie. "I like these even better than the scones," she said before taking a bite, her face crinkled with pleasure.

"You haven't made those before," Jenna said, leaning back on her chair. "At least, I don't remember them." She leaned toward Gracie and sniffed. "I think I would have remembered that smell."

"You're right." Vivian reached for her cup. "I was going through my mother's recipe box the other day and found this one. It dates back to the early 1800s, when they used to add brandy and rum to the mix. I wanted to try them out before making them a staple. I thought they would be good to serve at Christmastime."

"At any time," Gracie declared, spitting out crumbs in her enthusiasm. "These are awesome!"

"Thanks." Vivian glanced at her watch. "There's something I wanted to run by you both before we open up." She proceeded to tell them about her visit with Noah and his father.

When she was done, Jenna gave her an anxious look. "You think the kid's father is the fence?"

"I think any one of the people I visited could be." Vivian sipped her tea and put down the cup. "Which is why I need to look into it further before saying anything to Messina."

Jenna sighed. "That's what's worrying me. You're going to investigate another murder."

Gracie made a muffled sound of approval, her mouth still full of cake.

"How can I not?" Vivian looked at each of them. "They pretty much announced on TV last night that Lewis was the fence and had been killed by the thieves when he stole the jewels from them."

"And you don't believe that," Jenna said.

"Not for a minute. I believe that one of the people who had the Big Ben in their possession is the real fence. I think someone hid the jewels in there for safekeeping, and before they could retrieve them, the model got passed along to someone else. So they tracked it down to Lewis and then went after him to get the jewels back."

"They must have put a false base on that thing to keep them inside it," Gracie remarked, having successfully disposed of the cake.

"It did look like something had been screwed into the base." Vivian paused. "Anyway, I'm going to find that person and clear Lewis's name."

Jenna nodded. "You have a thing for that."

"A thing?"

"You know, a passion, a quest, a mission." She drained her cup and stood up. "Whatever you want to call it, because of it you saved me from going to prison for something I didn't do."

Vivian smiled. "I would have gone to bat for you even if you had killed your ex."

"I know." Jenna looked serious. "This time is different. You never met Lewis. You're putting yourself in danger for someone you never knew."

"Did I hear you say 'danger'?"

The voice had come from the doorway. Vivian swiveled her head around to see Hal standing just inside the kitchen, a look of concern clouding his face.

Feeling guilty for going back on her promise, Vivian got up from her chair. "Jenna's exaggerating," she said, hoping her smile would convince him. "I'm just talking to people, that's all."

"Yeah. I've heard that before." Hal moved toward her. "You promised me."

"I know. And I intend to keep that promise, but—" She paused, unwilling to have this conversation in front of her assistants.

Jenna caught on at once and shot up. "I've got to get out there," she said, striding over to the tearoom door. "Our customers will be here soon."

"Me too." Gracie jumped to her feet. "I've got shelves to stock."

They both disappeared into the tearoom, leaving Vivian alone.

She was beginning to feel nervous. Hal looked upset, and he had every right to be, she acknowledged. "I have to do this, Hal," she told him, praying he would understand. "I'm in a position to help an innocent man who will forever be branded a criminal if this case isn't solved. There's no one else who will help him. If I don't do everything in my power to find the real fence, I'll never be able to look myself in the face again."

"So, why can't you just tell Messina what you know and let them handle it?"

"Because I don't have any evidence yet. Just hunches, and that's not going to get Messina's attention. I need to talk to the suspects again."

"Suspects?"

"Stacey, Brita, Connie, and Noah's father. I never did get his name."

Hal pulled out a chair and slumped down on it. "Noah's father? You haven't told me about that one yet."

She sat down, too, and repeated her whole conversation with Noah's father. When she got to the part where the man slammed the door in her face, Hal winced.

"Nice character," he said, shaking his head. "I hope you're not planning on going back there."

"I may not have to." Vivian frowned, thinking hard. "I think we can rule out Stacey. Why would she give the model to Brita if the diamonds were inside it?"

Hal rested his elbows on the table. "If you want me to use some brain power, you'll have to fuel it with some carbs."

She looked at him. "You want a Banbury cake?"

"I thought you'd never ask."

Smiling, she got up and walked over to the cabinet to get a plate for him.

When she placed the pastry in front of him, he looked up at her. "What if Stacey is a courier for the robbers? You told me Messina said that they usually use a fence in another town. What if she brought the diamonds down to a fence, couldn't connect with him for some reason, and had to stash the jewels rather than risk taking them back to Portland. She could have left them with her friend—what's her name?"

"Brita." Vivian felt a twinge of excitement. "Of course. She couldn't take the model back to Portland, so she left it with Brita until she could come back, take out the jewels, and meet the fence again. Brita wouldn't have known there were diamonds in the model when she got rid of it."

Hal grinned. "I should write mysteries."

Vivian's smile faded. "You don't think any of that is feasible?"

"It's possible, of course, but right now it's all conjecture."

"I know. Which is why I have to talk to Stacey again. She would know where to find the fence." She paused as a thought struck her. "No, wait. I have an idea. If Stacey is a member of a robbery gang, she's not going to let me know that. But if someone else went there and asked to use her services, and told her she came highly recommended, she might give something away."

"Someone else?"

"Stacey has never met Gracie."

Hal choked on a mouthful of cake. He swallowed, then said hoarsely, "Gracie doesn't exactly look like a hardened criminal."

"Maybe not. But she's a great actor. And she's done this before, when we were looking for the creep who killed Jenna's ex. It's an old trick, but it works. Gracie came up with some important information that day."

Hal finished his cake, plucked a napkin from a holder on the table, and scrubbed his mouth. "Well, it all sounds risky to me. I'm beginning to wish I'd kept my mouth shut."

"No, I'm glad you didn't." Vivian gave him a reassuring smile. "You were a great help. There's safety in numbers, remember? Jenna and I will be right outside Stacey's apartment. Gracie will just be talking to her, that's all."

"And if Stacey says something incriminating?"

"We go to Messina with it. I promise."

"Okay. Wait. How do you know Gracie will go along with this? You haven't asked her yet."

Vivian leaned back on her chair. "Gracie will beg me to let her do it."

"And Jenna?"

"She won't want to be left out. We're the three rookies."

Hal gave her one of his warm looks. "Three rookies, hmm? Sounds to me like you're getting a little too much experience in this detective stuff."

Vivian laughed. "Don't worry, Hal. I learned my lesson from the last time. We almost lost Jenna. I'm not about to let that happen again."

"Glad to hear it." Hal looked at his watch. "I'd better get back to the store and make sure Wilson isn't insulting any customers."

"Thanks for taking Felix. I know how much he enjoys getting out with you."

"I enjoy it too. He's a great dog." He walked over to the tearoom door and looked back at her. "By the way, those Banbury cakes should be registered as hazardous material. I could eat a dozen of them at one sitting."

His approval gave her a warm glow. "I'm so glad you like them."

"See you at seven tomorrow."

"I'm looking forward to it."

"Me too." He lifted his hand in a farewell salute and left.

Seconds later, Jenna appeared in the doorway. "Is everything okay with you guys?"

Smiling, Vivian nodded at her. "Great. I told him we were going to talk to the suspects in the case, and he was a bit concerned, but I told him—"

"Wait. You said 'we'?"

"Yes." Vivian gave her an anxious look. "I hope that's okay? I mean, I wouldn't ask you to do something you're not comfortable with—or Gracie, for that matter."

"Oh, quit." Jenna walked into the kitchen. "You know very well we'll help you. Gracie is champing at the bit to jump into another crime hunt."

"I'm chomping what?" Gracie stood in the doorway, her eyes wide with anticipation.

"Champing," Vivian explained. "It's an expression from horse racing, when the horses are eager to begin the race."

"Kind of how you look now," Jenna told her.

Gracie gave Jenna a withering look, then turned to Vivian. "Are we going after the jewel thieves?"

"No, of course not," Vivian said, anxious to shoot that idea down. "We're just going to try to find out who they were using as a fence. Remember when you pretended you were interviewing for a job at the hotel?"

Gracie grinned. "Yeah. That was fun."

"How would you like to do something like that again?"

"Okay." Gracie walked over to the table and sat down. "Where am I getting a job this time?"

"Not a job." Vivian crossed the kitchen to the fridge. "It will mean going back to Portland to see Stacey Patel again. We can go on Sunday."

Gracie frowned. "So what do you want me to do?"

"She's never met you. I want you to go to her and pretend you want to hire her services."

"What are her services?"

"That's exactly what we need to find out. You tell her someone recommended her to you, and you're anxious to hire her. If she's involved in something illegal, she may say something that we can take to Messina."

Gracie thought about it for a moment. "Okay. I can do that."

"I'll drive this time," Jenna offered. "And Felix is welcome to ride with us."

Vivian smiled at her. "Thanks, Jenna. Felix will love that. I'll sit in the back with him. Gracie can sit up front."

"I don't mind sitting with Felix," Gracie said, getting up again. "He's a sweetheart."

"Even when he's trampling all over you to look out the window?"

Gracie grinned. "Yeah, he does love to do that."

"Well, okay, if that's what you want. We'll meet here at ten on Sunday." Vivian looked at Jenna. "Is that okay with you guys?"

"Sure." Jenna looked up as the shop doorbell rang. "Customers. It's showtime." With that, she strode out of the kitchen.

"Now I can't wait for Sunday." Gracie bounced over to the door. "The three rookies are hot on the trail again. Yahoo!"

Vivian shook her head as Gracie disappeared into the tearoom. The young woman might think this was all a fun adventure, but Hal was right. There was an element of danger in poking around a possible gang of robbers.

She would just have to play this with caution and consideration, and hope that it wouldn't land them all in trouble, like the last time.

Chapter Eleven

As Friday evening approached, Vivian's nerves tightened to the point where she twice dropped a knife on the floor and almost spilled an entire tray of custard tarts.

It didn't help that Jenna was apparently having the same jitters: she spilled a jug of milk in the tearoom and had to replace the tablecloth and everything else on the table before the customers could continue to enjoy their afternoon tea.

What was it about men, Vivian thought, that they could have this kind of effect on women, just by asking them out on a date? It was ridiculous. Understandable for Jenna, though. She'd barely met the man.

As for herself, she'd known Hal for over two years. They were friends, for heaven's sake. She knew everything about him: his likes and dislikes, what made him laugh, what made him angry, what he cared about the most.

It wasn't as if this was the first time they had dinner together. In the last month or so, they had fixed a meal for each other in their apartments, and gone out to a restaurant, although technically that wasn't an actual date. It was more a matter of convenience.

They were going to meet Felix for the first time and stopped to eat on the way.

This evening was an actual date. It wasn't just the thought of having dinner with him that had her dithering about what to wear, how much makeup to use, or what to do with her hair. It was that kiss in the parking lot of the hospital. That had changed everything, and now they had taken that first step, she was excited to see what would follow.

As she watched Jenna fly out the door shortly after six that evening, Vivian didn't know whether to feel sorry for her or envious that her friend was embarking on a completely unknown adventure. That could be exciting and terrifying at the same time.

She was glad, Vivian told herself, that her own adventure would begin with someone she already knew and loved. After tonight, they might get to the point where they could consider themselves a couple. She liked the sound of that.

After hunting through her wardrobe, she finally decided on a simple maroon sheath dress with a matching jacket, and dressed it up with a gold chain necklace. Studying the effect in the mirror, she wondered what Martin would say if he could see her now. She hoped he would approve and be happy for her.

"I will never forget you, Martin," she said aloud, "but it's time to move on. I hope you understand."

A soft whine answered her, and she looked down at Felix. "Yes," she told him. "I'm going out. You will have to be a good boy. I'll leave you a treat, and I'll take you for a walk when I get back. Okay?"

Hearing his favorite word, Felix pricked up his ears.

Vivian walked out into the living room and switched on the TV. "There. You have something to watch until I get back."

Felix barked, then turned his back on the TV.

Shaking her head, Vivian moved over to the table next to the couch, where she'd left her reading glasses. To her dismay, there was nothing on the table except for the table lamp, a coaster, and a half-read mystery novel.

Staring at the empty space where her glasses should be, Vivian felt the panic rising again. In an effort to keep it at bay, she concentrated on when she'd last worn the glasses.

It was less than an hour ago. After she'd come up from the tearoom, she'd sat on the couch to read her mail. She remembered taking her glasses out of her purse and slipping them on to read the electricity bill, her credit card bill, and a brochure offering her a discount on window cleaning.

She distinctly remembered taking off her glasses and putting them right down there on the table next to the coaster.

Or had she?

Had she put them back in her purse?

She snatched up her purse from the couch and scrabbled through the stuff inside it. No glasses. Where in great heaven had she left them?

The doorbell rang at that moment, sending her into fresh panic. Hal was here. She needed her glasses to read the menu. She tore into the kitchen to open Felix's bag of treats and threw a couple of them down in front of him. "Be a good boy," she told him, then flew out of the apartment.

Hurrying down the stairs to the tearoom, she made a desperate effort to calm down. It wasn't the end of the world. Her glasses were somewhere in the apartment, and she would find them. Just not now. She arranged a welcoming smile on her face and opened the door.

Hal beamed at her from the street. "You look wonderful," he told her, "but it's in the forties out here. Will you be warm enough without a coat?"

She stared at him, unable to believe she'd actually forgotten to put on a coat. She was losing her mind. She was really losing her mind.

Hal's smile began to waver. "Are you okay? I'll wait while you get your coat. Or I could get it for you?"

"No," she said quickly. "It's okay. I'll be in the car and then the restaurant. It's not like it's freezing out there."

"Pretty darn near." Hal held out his arm. "Come on, I'll keep you warm."

Pushing her anxiety away, Vivian stepped out into the street. She would not worry about her mind right now, she told herself. She was just going to forget everything and enjoy this time with her man.

Hal slipped his arm around her and pulled her close to him. "The car's right over there."

Right then she wouldn't have cared if the car had been six blocks down. Snuggling into him, she murmured, "This is nice."

"Yeah." In the glow from the street lamp, his eyes twinkled down at her through his glasses. "Real cozy." For a breathless second or two, she thought he might kiss her again, but they had reached the car and he let her go.

She climbed in, and tried not to shiver as she waited for him to join her. "So," she said, as he started up the engine, "how are you feeling?"

"Like a million dollars." He pulled out into the street. "Better than I've felt in years."

"Oh, I'm so glad." She touched his arm. "I've been so worried about you."

"Well, you don't need to worry about me anymore. I'm good."

More than good, she thought, settling back with a sigh of contentment. She couldn't ask for a better man to love.

"How was your day?" Hal reached out and turned up the heat. "Are you warm enough?"

She didn't think she would ever be cold again with this man at her side. "I'm fine, thanks. And the day went well. Except for when Jenna spilled milk all over a table and we had to scramble to clean it all up."

"Jenna did that? She always seems so competent and sure of herself."

"She usually is, but she has a date with Tony Messina tonight, and she's been on edge all day."

"With Messina?" Hal sounded shocked. "When did that happen? I thought she hated the guy. After all, he did try to arrest her for murder."

"Oh, she got over that. Messina is quite a charmer, and it doesn't hurt that he's easy on the eyes. I can see why she fell for the man."

Hal grunted. "Are you trying to make me jealous?"

She sent him a sidelong glance. "Is it working?"

He laughed, making her relax even more. "I can't compete with that six-foot-two Adonis."

Now it was her turn to laugh. "You don't have to compete. Looks aren't everything. Besides, I happen to prefer your looks."

"Yeah?" He shot her a quick glance. "Then I guess we're good."

"We are."

He didn't have to say anything. The look he sent her said it all.

The restaurant was everything she'd hoped for, and more. With just a dozen small tables covered in dark red tablecloths, flickering candles, and blazing logs in the fireplace, the room felt cozy and intimate.

There were just three other couples dining there when they arrived, giving them a measure of privacy at their table in the window. It was too dark to see the ocean, but they were close enough for Vivian to hear the waves washing the shore. In her opinion, Hal couldn't have picked a better place for their first real date.

Seated opposite her, he looked relaxed and comfortable in a gray sweater over a dark blue shirt. Her wave of tenderness took her by surprise, and she snatched up the menu. She was about to reach for her purse when she remembered she had no glasses with her.

Determined not to let her worry over her problem spoil the evening, she put down the menu and smiled at Hal. "I forgot to bring my reading glasses. What looks good to you?"

He answered promptly. "You do."

"I meant on the menu."

"I know."

Their gazes locked and she couldn't look away. "I think salmon would be good," she said, hoping it was on the menu.

"Yeah? I fancy steak myself."

They were speaking mundane words, but the vibes humming between them were saying so much more.

"Good evening. Welcome to the Coastal Kitchen. Can I get you a drink?"

Startled out of the trance, Vivian looked up at the pretty young server hovering at the table. "I'd love a glass of chardonnay, please," she said, relieved to hear her voice sounding normal.

"Make that a bottle," Hal said.

The server gave him a wide smile. "I'll be right back with it. Have you had a chance to look at the menu? We have two specials tonight." She reeled off a detailed description of two dishes so fast Vivian had trouble following her. "I'll let you decide while I get your wine," she said at last, and took off across the restaurant to the kitchen.

"Okay, let's see that they have." Hal picked up the menu and read down the list of entrees. "I still like steak," he said when he was done, making Vivian laugh for some reason.

"And I still like salmon."

"That's settled then. Now, tell me some more about your life before you came to Misty Bay."

"You already know most of it."

"I know you were married for almost forty years to a prosecuting attorney and that you have two daughters and two grandchildren. I know that your mother was English, which is why you always wanted to open an English-style tearoom. I know that you're passionate about mystery novels and you love dogs. But what was your life like before Misty Bay? Did you always have a dream to open your own tearoom, or did you have other dreams that never materialized?"

"Well, I wanted to be a ballet dancer, but my feet wouldn't fit into those tiny little shoes."

He grinned. "Funny."

She relaxed. "Okay. I wanted to write mystery novels, but I soon found out that reading them was a lot easier that writing them."

"I can relate to that. I wanted to be an astronaut until I found out I have a fear of heights."

She looked at him. "You do? Seriously?"

"Seriously."

"Then what made you go into firefighting? Didn't you have to climb up ladders and on roofs?"

"Yeah, and that terrified me more than the fires."

"But you did it anyway."

"You have to face your fears to conquer them."

She thought about that. Had she conquered her reservations enough to dive headfirst into a relationship with this man?

Hal leaned toward her. "What are you frowning about?"

She smiled. "I was just thinking of all the time we wasted getting to this point."

His expression softened. "Then we'll have to make up for lost time."

"We sure do." If she'd had any lingering doubts, they were swept away in that moment.

The server returned just then with the wine and took their order, and the rest of the evening flew by as they exchanged stories about their lives before moving to Misty Bay. The more Vivian learned about Hal, the more secure she felt in her decision to let go of her qualms and just enjoy what this man had to offer.

Hal was quiet on the way home, however, and she began to worry again. Now that he'd learned more about her, was he having second thoughts?

That question was swept away, too, when he parked the car, pulled her toward him, and kissed her full on the mouth. This was a lot more satisfying than the swift kiss in the hospital parking lot, and Vivian gave it everything she had.

When Hal finally let her go, she was out of breath.

"Wow," Hal muttered. "If I'd known kissing you was going to feel that good, I'd have done it a long time ago."

Vivian's laugh sounded a little shaky. "Well, like you said, we have to make up for lost time."

"Yeah." His smile seemed to warm the whole car. "I'm really going to enjoy that."

"Me too."

For a long moment they gazed at each other, until Hal cleared his throat. "I'd better let you go. Felix is probably tearing up the kitchen by now."

"He wouldn't dare." Vivian slowly opened the door, reluctant for this night to end. "Thank you for a lovely dinner and the stimulating conversation."

"Entirely my pleasure. Let's do it again. Soon."

"I'd love that. Goodnight, Hal."

"Sweet dreams."

She closed the door and watched him drive off before opening the door to the tearoom.

Felix greeted her with his usual bounce and lunge routine, and it took a minute or two to calm him down. Finally, she sank onto the couch, exhausted from all the excitement of the evening.

Her purse sat next to her, and she reached for it to grab a tissue. As she did so, a glint of metal caught her eye. Frowning, she dug down the side of the cushion and pulled out her reading glasses.

She must have left them on the seat earlier. Shaking her head, she laid them on the table beside her. She was usually so careful about leaving them in a safe place.

Once more she could feel the fear beginning to spread its cold fingers. She couldn't be losing her mind. Not now, when she was on the brink of true happiness.

She needed to calm herself down, she thought, when Felix collapsed at her feet with a contented sigh. A walk in the dark outside should help with that. Much to Felix's delight, she fastened his leash, giving him renewed energy as she opened the door. She let him run down the stairs ahead of her, then followed him out into the quiet street.

Walking along behind the dog, she shut her mind off to the possibility of dementia and instead relived the entire evening, smiling at the memory of Hal's jokes, his compliments, and his comments about her past life. She felt now as if she'd known him all her life and that fate was just waiting for the right time for them to be together.

She couldn't be happier right now, unless it was to solve the riddle of Lewis Trenton's death. That would have to wait until Sunday, however. Right now, and for the next few hours, she wanted to forget everything except this new stage in her life and what it meant for her future.

* * *

Saturday morning, Jenna arrived at the tearoom with a dreamy look in her eyes that told Vivian the evening before had gone well for her friend. She decided not to ask her about it until they were settled at the table with their usual cup of tea.

Gracie, however, had other ideas. The moment she flew into the kitchen, she looked at Jenna, who stood at the counter pouring tea into a cup. "So, how did it go? Was he super cool? Are you going to go out again with him? Did he kiss you?"

Vivian swallowed hard, then held her breath, waiting for Jenna to yell at Gracie to mind her own business.

Instead, Jenna's face lit up with a rare smile. "Yes, yes, and yes," she said, "and that's all I'm going to say about it, so don't ask."

"Awesome!" Gracie rushed over to Jenna and gave her a hug, then turned to Vivian. "How about you? Did you have a good time too?"

"I had a wonderful time." Vivian smiled at the memory. "And I can answer yes to all three questions too."

Gracie stared at her. "Hal kissed you?"

Vivian nodded, then grunted as Gracie threw herself at her with a bear hug.

"This calls for a celebration," Vivian said when she caught her breath again. "How about a large slice of Victoria sponge cake?"

Gracie answered with a squeal of delight. "I'll get the knife." She darted over to the cutlery drawer and pulled it open.

Jenna smiled at Vivian. "I'm happy for you. You two deserve to be together."

"Thanks. And the same to you. It sounds promising."

Jenna shrugged. "Who knows? We're going to take it slowly. We've both been through some bad times, and we're not in any hurry to rush into things."

Vivian nodded. "Very wise."

Gracie came back with the knife. "Now, where's that sponge cake? I can't wait to sink my teeth into it."

While Jenna finished pouring the tea, Vivian took down the light, fluffy cake filled with strawberry jam and whipped cream, and laid it on the table. "Here's to future relationships," she said, as she picked up the knife. "May they be satisfying and enjoyable for all of us."

"Amen to that." Gracie raised her cup. "Now, if I can just find my one and only, we can all celebrate the future."

*   *   *

Jenna arrived promptly at ten on Sunday morning, while Gracie, as usual, arrived ten minutes later, panting apologies.

"Alyssa was hogging the bathroom this morning," she explained, after gulping down half of her tea. "I don't think she went to bed all night."

Vivian exchanged a meaningful look with Jenna. "Is she sick?"

"What? No!" Gracie frowned. "I don't think so. I woke up in the night and heard her talking to someone like she was on her phone." She paused, then added, "She sounded pissed."

"Are you worried about her?"

Gracie put down her cup. "I guess. When she lost her job last month, she said she'd be okay because she could work from home. But what kind of work does she do in the middle of the night?"

"She could've been talking in her sleep," Jenna said.

Gracie shook her head. "Nah. She was definitely talking to someone."

"Did you ask her about it?" Vivian picked up the empty cups and took them over to the sink.

Gracie got up from her chair. "No, but I guess I'm gonna have to ask her." She looked at Jenna. "I know you think she's into, like, something bad, but I still can't believe that."

"Then don't." Jenna picked up her jacket from the back of her chair. "Just come right out and ask her what's going on. It's your apartment. You have a right to know what she's doing."

Gracie looked unconvinced. "Okay. I'll do that."

"Good." Vivian stacked the cups and saucers in the dish-washer. "Right now, we need to get going. I'll go up and get Felix and meet you at the car."

Jenna marched over to the door. "Come on, shrimp. I'm driving, remember?"

"I wish you wouldn't call me that," Gracie grumbled as she followed Jenna out into the tearoom. "Just because you're six feet tall doesn't mean I'm short."

"I'm not six feet; I'm not quite five feet ten. And I didn't mean you're short. It's just—"

Vivian rolled her eyes as the door closed behind them, shutting off Jenna's last words. Those two were always sparring, yet they remained the best of friends, she reminded herself as she climbed the stairs to her apartment.

Felix was quivering with excitement when she attached his leash to his collar. "You'd better behave in the back seat with Gracie," she told him. "I'll be keeping an eye on you."

Felix reassured her with a wet lick to her chin.

Minutes later they were in the car, heading into the mountains once again. The heavy rain forced Jenna to drive more slowly around the twists and turns of the highway, much to Vivian's relief. Jenna tended to treat every open road like a race track, creating some hairy rides at times.

They arrived safely in a wet Portland and parked in the garage of Stacey's apartment building. With a stern word of warning to Felix to behave, they locked him in the car and headed for the elevator.

"We'll be waiting just down the hallway," Vivian said as they paused a few feet from Stacey's door. "If there's any sign of trouble, just yell."

Gracie sent an anxious look down the hallway. "What kind of trouble?"

"I'm not expecting anything bad to happen," Vivian assured her. "I'm just letting you know you're not alone in this. You remember everything I told you to ask?"

"Yeah." Gracie drew in a deep breath. "I tell her I need help with a certain project, and I need someone who can, like, keep it confidential. I tell her she comes highly recommended."

"Good." Vivian pressed her arm. "You'll be fine. We'll be right outside."

As she watched Gracie saunter down to Stacey's apartment, Vivian silently prayed she wasn't making trouble for the young woman. She motioned to Jenna to draw back out of sight as the door opened.

She heard Gracie announce her name and then lower her voice, apparently adding the words she'd rehearsed. Seconds later she stepped forward and disappeared inside the apartment.

It seemed like an eternity but could only have been a few uneasy minutes or two before Gracie stepped out into the hallway. "Thanks for your time," she sang out as she started back to where Vivian and Jenna waited.

"Well?" Jenna demanded as Gracie reached them.

"Wait." Vivian pressed the button on the elevator. "Let's get back to the car."

"She's not a fence," Gracie said, as they rode down to the parking lot. "She's a nurse. She thought I had a medical problem and wanted a diagnosis."

"Oh, wow." Vivian shrugged off her disappointment. "What did you tell her?"

"I made up a bunch of symptoms."

The elevator door opened, and Vivian followed Gracie outside, with Jenna right behind her.

"I think I might have laid it on a bit too much," Gracie said as the three of them walked over to the car. "She looked real worried and said she didn't know why I wanted to keep all that secret from everyone, but told me I really needed to see my doctor right away. She acted like I was dying already."

"Did she ask you where you live?" Jenna opened the car door. "I bet she'll want to check up on you."

"Actually, she did ask." Gracie opened the rear door and poked her head inside. "I'm here, Felix! Good boy!"

"You didn't tell her, did you?" Vivian asked as Gracie scrambled into the back seat.

"Tell her what?" Gracie's voice was muffled by Felix's enthusiastic welcome.

"Your address, dope." Jenna looked at Vivian. "Are you going to get in?"

"Yes, of course." Vivian hurried around to the other side and crawled into the front seat, twisting her head to stare at Gracie. "Tell me you didn't tell that woman where you live."

Gracie gently pushed Felix down next to her. "No, I didn't. But I don't see what all the fuss is about. I don't think she's going to come all the way down to Misty Bay to check on a complete stranger."

"Unless she was lying about being a nurse and is really the jewelry fence." Jenna switched on the engine.

"She wasn't lying," Gracie assured her. "I saw pics on a table of her in a nurse's uniform."

Vivian sighed. "Well, I guess that's one down."

"We still have three to go," Jenna reminded her.

"Yes, and the next one to talk to is Brita."

"The one with the fancy apartment?" Gracie sounded excited. "I'll go! I want to see that place."

"I think Jenna should go to see Brita." Vivian looked back at Gracie. "I think it's safer if we take turns with this. Just in case someone is watching us."

Gracie's eyes widened. "You think we're being followed?" She sent a concerned glance out the window.

Vivian hurried to reassure her. "No, not really. But it doesn't hurt to be cautious."

"Vivian's right." Jenna backed out of her space and shifted into forward. "We don't want to stir up trouble. I'll talk to Brita. Meanwhile, I'm starving. How about lunch?"

"Okay." Vivian thought for a moment. "There's a nice restaurant right before we get onto the freeway. Just take a right when you get out of here, and I'll guide you the rest of the way."

"Sounds good. After that we'll still have time to stop off in Newport on the way home to talk to Brita."

"Good idea." Vivian leaned back to get comfortable. "Maybe this time we'll get lucky, and she will give us a clue to the fence." And just maybe, she added to herself, they could finally clear Lewis Trenton's name and allow him to rest in peace.

Chapter Twelve

"You don't think Brita is the fence?" Jenna asked as she drove out of the garage and onto the street.

Vivian thought about it for a moment. "I don't know. She didn't seem at all like a criminal, but there's that fancy condo that must have cost a fortune, and she could have been lying about her parents leaving it to her in their will."

"Yeah," Jenna said as she pulled up at a light. "She could have hidden the jewels in the Big Ben to hide them from her boyfriend."

"But then why would she take it to the thrift store with the jewels still inside?" Vivian frowned. "No, that doesn't make sense."

"Maybe she forgot they were there," Gracie suggested.

Jenna snorted. "Forget where you stashed a fortune in jewels? I don't think so."

Vivian concentrated on the problem as they drove through the city streets to the restaurant. "What if," she said at last, "the fence was supposed to pick up the Big Ben at the thrift store, but Connie happened to be there and bought it before he could get there?"

"Wow," Jenna uttered softly. "You really are a mastermind."

Vivian grinned. "No, just an avid reader of mystery novels."

"Well, now I can't wait to talk to Brita."

"Are you sure you don't want me to come with you?" Gracie said, practically bursting with hope.

"I'm sorry, Gracie." Vivian turned to look at her. "It's better that she does this alone."

"Okay." Gracie hugged Felix, who rewarded her with a lick to her cheek.

After enjoying a delicious salad at the restaurant, Vivian was feeling more hopeful as they returned to the car. There was a good possibility that even if Brita wasn't the fence, she could know his identity. Jenna was shrewd—she'd pick up on any clues that the woman might spill.

Daylight was beginning to fade when Jenna pulled up outside Brita's condo later. "You weren't kidding," she said as she peered up at the building. "This is what I call luxury."

"Wait until you see inside." Vivian nodded at the door. "There's a receptionist who'll ask you for your name. She looks like the models on the cover of Vogue. The elevators have artwork on the walls, and Brita has a white couch. Can you imagine Felix jumping all over that?"

Gracie laughed. "He'd have the best time messing that up."

"Well, I won't be looking at the furniture." Jenna unbuckled her seat belt. "I'll be watching Brita's face, trying to figure out if she's lying."

"What are you going to ask her?" Gracie grunted as Felix jumped on her lap to look out the window.

"Same as you did with Stacey." Jenna looked at Vivian for confirmation. "Right?"

"Right." Vivian let out her breath. "Just be careful, okay?"

"Don't worry. I'll be on guard the whole time." Jenna opened the door. "I'll be right back."

"I certainly hope so," Vivian muttered as she watched Jenna vanish through the ornate door of the building.

"She's going to be okay, right?"

Hearing the anxiety in Gracie's voice, Vivian quickly turned to her. "She'll be fine. She's just asking questions, that's all. Just like you've done."

"Can't we go up there with her and wait outside the door?"

"The elevator opens up into the condo. There's nowhere to wait without being seen."

"Okay." Gracie buried her face in Felix's soft fur.

Vivian sighed. "Why don't you take Felix for a short walk? He probably needs to pee by now. That grass verge on the street is calling out to him."

Felix barked in agreement, and Gracie lifted her head. "Would you like that, Felix?"

The dog barked again and leapt up with excitement.

Laughing, Gracie buckled his leash to his collar. "Alrighty, then. Let's go!" She opened the door, gasping as Felix leapt over her out onto the sidewalk. "He's going to break a leg doing that," she said as she scrambled out of the car.

Vivian watched as they walked a few yards, with Felix tugging at the leash, until he stopped, sniffed, then lifted his leg against a tree. Gracie waited for him to finish, then walked farther down the street, pausing now and then for Felix to investigate the next odor.

Vivian smiled, picturing Hal with the dog. A sudden longing to see him took her by surprise, and she caught her breath. She was actually missing the man, and she'd seen him just two days ago.

She was still reliving her magical evening with him when Jenna appeared in the doorway to the condos.

Gracie must have caught sight of her too, as she came racing back to the car, Felix bounding along at her side. They reached the car together, and both doors opened at once. Felix leapt into the back seat, with Gracie jumping in after him.

Jenna climbed in her seat and leaned back with a sigh. "Well, that was a waste of time."

Vivian's spirits sank. "What happened?"

"She wasn't there?" Gracie asked, sounding just as disappointed.

"Oh, she was there." Jenna fastened her seat belt. "I don't think she's the fence. She said she's a hairdresser. Or she used to be. She wanted to know who recommended her."

"Oops." Vivian frowned. "What did you tell her?"

"I made up a name." Jenna switched on the engine. "She said she'd never heard of the woman, which wasn't really surprising, since she doesn't exist."

"Awkward," Gracie said.

"Then she said the woman must have been one of her previous customers. I asked her what she was doing now if she was no longer cutting hair. She said she was selling cosmetics. She took me into another room where she had boxes of hair products and makeup. I think she wanted me to buy something, but just then her boyfriend came in and interrupted her sales pitch, so I left."

"That was Chris," Vivian said. "I met him when I spoke to Brita."

"Yeah, he seemed like a friendly guy. He wanted to chat, but I figured if Brita was selling cosmetics, she wasn't making money as a fence, so I left."

"That leaves Connie and Noah's father." Vivian winced as Jenna shot out of the parking lot and took off down the street.

"We're narrowing it down," Gracie said, hanging onto Felix as they rounded a corner. "Are you hungry, Jenna—or do you have to pee?"

"What?" Jenna glanced at her in the rearview mirror. "Why?"

"You're in a real hurry to get home."

"Sorry." Jenna slowed the car down, and Vivian relaxed. She often wondered how her friend avoided an accident, with her habit of treating the roads like a racetrack.

"So," Jenna said, "do you really think Connie could be a fence for a gang of robbers?"

Vivian smiled. "No, not really. But what about Curtis? He really didn't want Connie talking about the Big Ben. Remember, he said he'd heard enough about it and practically dragged her away from us."

"Yeah, I remember that." Jenna pulled a face. "Like I said, what in the world does she see in him?"

"There's no accounting for taste." Vivian glanced out the window as they drove past Hal's pet store. "One man's meat is another man's poison, as they say."

"Well, that man is closer to poison than meat."

Jenna sounded disgusted, and Gracie laughed. "I wish I could have met this guy. He sounds like a real loser."

"He's a jerk." Jenna parked the car and switched off the engine.

"Thanks for driving today," Vivian said as she loosened her seat belt. "And thanks to both of you for giving up your day off and indulging me in this frustrating venture."

"We're the three rookies, remember? All for one and one for all." Gracie opened the door to let Felix jump out before following him onto the sidewalk.

Vivian smiled, remembering when Gracie had transformed The Three Musketeers name. "How can I possibly forget?"

Jenna shook her head. "I wish I had her energy."

"I wish I had yours." Vivian eased out of the car. "Goodnight, Jenna. Drive carefully."

She was rewarded with a grin from her friend. "Don't I always?" With that, she roared off down the street.

"Thanks for letting me take care of Felix today." Gracie handed over the dog's leash. "I had a ball."

"So did Felix." Vivian looked down at the dog, who was peering at her with his tongue hanging out of his mouth. "Are you hungry, buddy?"

Felix barked, and Gracie laughed. "He knows what you're saying."

"Every word." Vivian paused, then added carefully, "Gracie, I know you're anxious about asking Alyssa what kind of work she's doing, but you need to get some answers. You're responsible for what goes on in your apartment."

"I know." Gracie looked down at her feet. "I just worry about what to do if she tells me she's, like, doing something bad."

"You come to me," Vivian said firmly, "and we'll figure out what to do together."

Gracie's worried frown faded. "Thanks, Vivian. You're always there for me. You're like a substitute mom." She stepped forward and gave Vivian a brief hug, then darted off down the street, calling out, "See you tomorrow!"

Vivian blinked back tears as she unlocked the door to the tearoom. She missed her two daughters. Carrie was in California, and Rachel was in Seattle with Vivian's granddaughters, whom she hadn't seen in months. Almost a year.

It was time she paid them a visit, she told herself. Maybe she could close down the tearoom for a week. It made her sad to think of all the time she was losing with her grandchildren. Not to mention her two daughters.

Opening the tearoom had been the culmination of a lifelong dream, and she enjoyed every minute of it. But she wasn't getting any younger, and she was missing out on so much of her family's lives. Maybe it was time to make some tough decisions.

But not tonight. She sighed as she climbed the stairs to her apartment. Right now, she had an obligation to fulfill, and she wasn't going to let anything get in the way of that. A man's reputation was at stake. Any life-changing decisions on her part would have to wait.

* * *

"I think I'll talk to Curtis myself," Vivian announced as she sat enjoying a cup of tea with her assistants the next day.

Jenna looked at her. "You want me to come with you?"

"No, thanks. I'll get more out of him if I go alone."

"You'd better wear a suit of armor." Jenna leaned forward to pick up the sweetener jug. "That man is a womanizer."

Vivian laughed. "I don't think I'm his type."

"Any woman is his type. Connie isn't exactly a beauty queen." Jenna frowned. "He knows you're looking for the Big Ben. If he put those jewels in there, things could get dicey."

"I'll be fine." Vivian reached for her cup. "I'll be in a retirement home surrounded by watchful people. What could go wrong?"

"Famous last words," Jenna muttered, pouring a spoonful of sugar into her tea.

"I could talk to him," Gracie said, waving a half-eaten scone at Vivian. "I'm getting good at this."

"You are," Vivian agreed. "But I think we'll all be less visible if we spread our interviews out among us. Less chance of someone noticing us."

"She could go with you as backup," Jenna said.

"Yeah! I'm dying to meet Curtis the Charmer."

"You'd be too much of a distraction," Vivian told her. "He definitely does have an eye for pretty faces."

Gracie grinned. "Thanks for the compliment."

"Don't let it go to your head, shrimp." Jenna took a sip of her tea and put down the cup. "By the way, did you talk to Alyssa last night?"

Gracie's grin vanished. "I did. I found out what she's been doing."

Vivian's empty cup clattered as she dropped it onto the saucer. "Oh no. Is it bad?"

Gracie sighed. "Not as bad as I thought. She's body piercing."

Jenna choked on her tea, while Vivian stared at her. "What?"

"Body piercing. You know," Gracie tugged at her ear, "poking holes in your ears or nose or belly button so you can put rings in them."

Vivian swallowed. "I know what it is. But that can't be legal. Don't you need a license? It can't be sanitary to do that in an apartment. Don't you have to have inspections or something?"

"All of that." Gracie took another bite out of her scone and chewed it down before adding, "I told Alyssa she either has to quit the business or get a license. She said she couldn't afford to do either one. So I asked her to leave."

"Oh, Gracie, I'm sorry." Vivian exchanged a worried look with Jenna. "What did she say? When is she leaving?"

"She's already gone." Gracie finished eating her scone and wiped her mouth with the back of her hand. "She packed up and left before I got up this morning."

"So, what are you going to do now?" Jenna asked, looking as concerned as Vivian felt.

"I don't know." Gracie leaned back on her chair. "I really don't want to go looking for another roomie. I don't seem to have much luck with them. If I don't, though, I'll have to find a cheaper apartment, I guess. That'll take a while. There's not much out there that I can afford."

Jenna stared down at her cup. "You could move in with me until you find something. I have a spare bedroom."

Vivian had to smother a gasp of surprise. Jenna had always been a lone wolf, very independent, withdrawn at times. Gracie was the complete opposite. Although the two were close friends, living together could prove to be challenging.

Then again, Jenna had changed a lot in the last few weeks. Whether it was her brush with death a month ago or her new relationship with Tony Messina, the experience had brought her out of her shell. Maybe having Gracie around full time was just what she needed.

Gracie seemed at a loss for words. She stared at Jenna, as if trying to figure out if she'd heard right.

"It was just a suggestion," Jenna said. "I won't be offended if you'd rather not stay with me."

"No! I mean yes!" Gracie looked as if she was about to cry. "I'd love to stay with you and Misty. I can help take care of her, and I'll, like, split the rent and help with the housework, and . . ." Her voice broke, and she swallowed. "Thanks, Jenna. I won't stay longer than I need to, I promise. I'll look for an apartment every day, and—"

"Oh, shush." Jenna cut her off with a flip of her hand. "I'll enjoy the company, and Misty will love having you fuss over her. Cats thrive on attention."

Vivian cleared her throat. "That's settled then. Now we'd better get moving, or our customers will be here before we're ready."

Gracie jumped to her feet. "I have to unpack those cartons that came in on Saturday." With that, she rushed off to the storeroom.

"That was nice of you," Vivian said as Jenna got up from the table. "Gracie is a lucky woman to have a friend like you."

Jenna brushed it off with a shrug. "I'm glad to help out. You would have done the same if you'd had the room."

"I don't know if I could put up with Gracie's high energy full time."

"What she needs is a good man." Jenna picked up the empty cups and took them to the counter. "That would keep her occupied."

Vivian laughed. "Great idea. We'll work on it."

"Actually, I was thinking of introducing her to Ken Brady."

Vivian's smile vanished. "Messina's Brady?"

"Yes." Jenna's gaze slid across Vivian's face. "He seems like a good guy, and that time he came into the tearoom, he was staring at Gracie like he wanted to get to know her."

"Really? I never noticed that." Vivian was still trying to get used to the idea of Gracie dating a cop.

"Well, anyway, Tony was talking about him the other night, and he said that Ken had broken up with his long-time girlfriend months ago. He's single and looking. So is Gracie."

"He's quite a bit older than her, isn't he?"

"Thirty-one. That's only seven years."

Vivian nodded. "But would he appeal to Gracie? Her last boyfriend had tattoos, a beard, and a man bun."

Jenna looked at her, and they both grinned.

"She's lacking stability in her life," Jenna said. "Ken Brady might not be cool or mod or whatever word they use now for 'with it,' but he could be just what she needs."

"I'm not so sure he can keep up with her, but I guess it won't hurt for them to meet. After that, it'll be up to them."

Jenna gave her a satisfied nod. "That's what I think. I'll let you know how it goes."

"Do. I'll be panting with anticipation."

"Me too!" Jenna pulled an apron from the drawer. "Now I'd better go and unlock the door."

Vivian watched her leave, then hurried over to the fridge. The day's work was about to begin. Tonight, she would visit the Cozy Nest Retirement Home and play cat and mouse with Curtis. She needed to get to the bottom of this mystery, and time was running out. She'd checked with the coroner's office and learned that Lewis was to be buried in about a week. That didn't give her much time to get at the truth.

During a lull that afternoon, she called Hal, anxious to know how he was doing.

"I'm fine," he told her. "I'm sitting here behind the counter, watching Wilson try to answer questions about dog treats."

Vivian laughed. "I take it he's having a hard time?"

"Considering he's a computer genius, he's remarkably clueless about anything else in the world. I sometimes wonder if he's an alien from outer space."

"That would explain a lot." Vivian paused, then added, "I really enjoyed our date the other night."

"Me too. In fact, I've been thinking about it a lot. How about doing it again this weekend?"

Her day suddenly got a whole lot better. "I'd love that."

"Great. I'll make reservations." He was silent for a moment, and when he spoke again, he sounded a little cautious. "How would you like to go to The Bellemer?"

She gasped with excitement. "I'd love that! I've heard so much about it, but I've never been there. Jenna was there last week, and she couldn't stop talking about the food."

"Then it's settled." He grunted with exasperation, then added, "I've gotta go. I think Wilson's customer is reaching the boiling point."

"Oh no. Good luck with that."

"Yeah. I'll be over tomorrow to take Felix for a walk."

"He'll love that." Happy that she wouldn't have to wait the rest of the week before seeing him again, she slipped the phone back in her pocket.

For most of the afternoon the customers kept her busy, and she was thankful when the last one left and she could close up shop.

Gracie was in a hurry to leave. "I have to give a month's notice to move out," she explained as she tugged on her jacket. "I paid for two months up front, so I should be okay to move out in a couple of weeks, right?"

"I don't see why not," Jenna said, taking her own jacket out of the closet. "You can move in with me any time."

"I can't wait to get out of there now." Gracie zipped up her jacket. "I've got some, like, decluttering to do, but I should be ready to go in two weeks." She snatched up her purse. "I'll have to put my stuff in storage."

"I'll help you with that. I could come over later tonight, and we'll see what will fit in my house."

"Awesome!" Gracie beamed with excitement. "This is so cool."

Jenna followed Gracie to the door, turning her head to look at Vivian. "Be careful, tonight, Viv. Watch out for that creep."

"Don't worry. I'll be fine." Vivian waited for them to leave and locked the door behind them. First thing tomorrow, she told herself, she'd take her keys to a locksmith and get extra ones cut.

Checking the internet later, however, she discovered there were no locksmiths in Misty Bay. She would either have to drive to Newport, or she could call and have one come out to the tearoom, which would be expensive. The keys would have to wait until she had more time to go get them.

After taking Felix for a walk, she piled the dog into the car and climbed in behind the wheel. It was almost nine. Hopefully, Connie would be on her way to bed soon. Somehow, Vivian told herself, she'd have to find a way to get Curtis alone.

She was dismayed when the receptionist at the retirement home told her that visiting hours were over. That was something she hadn't thought about. "It's vitally important that I talk to Curtis," Vivian told her, giving the stern-looking woman her best smile.

"Is it a life-or-death emergency?" The woman's rigid features warned Vivian that gaining access to Curtis was out of the question.

Vivian was tempted to lie, but there was a chance the receptionist would call in a superior, and the last thing she needed was to bring that much attention to herself. "There's something important that I forgot to tell Curtis the other night when I was here. I really need to speak with him again. I won't be more than a minute or two. Please?"

The woman stared at her for a long moment, then sighed. "Very well. But make it quick."

"I will. I promise." Vivian turned to head for the lounge, but paused when the receptionist called out to her.

"If he's not in the lounge, he'll be in his room. Third floor. Number 312."

"Thank you so much!" Hurrying to the lounge, Vivian hoped she'd find him in there. She didn't relish the thought of confronting him in his room.

She spotted him the moment she entered the lounge. He was leaning back in an armchair, chatting to two women who hovered over him like robins over a bird feeder. They were both giggling like teenagers, and Curtis was obviously basking in their adoration.

There was no sign of Connie. Either that liaison was over, or Curtis was taking advantage of her absence. Vivian hurried forward, wishing she'd worn something a little more glamorous than black pants and a purple sweater under her coat. Much as she hated the idea, she needed the man's full attention.

Curtis caught sight of her just as she reached him, and his eyes widened. "You're the afternoon tea lady. Vera, isn't it?"

"Vivian." She looked at the other two women, who were both giving her hostile looks. "Please excuse me for interrupting, but I really need to talk to Curtis."

One of the women glared at her in silence while the other murmured, "Goodnight, Curtis. We'll see you at bingo tomorrow." She tugged her friend's arm, and the two of them stalked off.

Curtis shook his head as she watched them leave. "Nice women, but they talk too much." He looked back at Vivian with watery blue eyes. "What can I do for you, dear lady?"

Vivian summoned a smile. "I have a proposition for you." She looked around the lounge, where several of the residents still lingered. "Is there somewhere more private we can talk?"

Interest flared in Curtis's eyes. "Why don't we retire to my room?"

Vivian swallowed. "I don't think that would be appropriate. Maybe we could go outside?"

His disappointment was evident in his face. "Too cold. We could try the library. It's usually uninhabited this time of night."

"Perfect." Vivian waved a hand at the door. "Lead the way."

He got up slowly, as if anticipating pain. "I have to admit, I'm immensely curious about this proposition."

"I'll tell you once we have some privacy."

She followed him out the door, beginning to have serious doubts about his possible connection to a gang of jewel thieves. He just didn't fit the bill. Then again, as she'd reminded herself so often, one could never judge people by their appearance. The most seemingly harmless, gentle soul could be a cold-blooded killer without remorse. She just couldn't take anything for granted.

Arriving at the library, she was relieved to see that they would be alone. She chose a comfortable, gray velvet armchair to sit on, and waited for Curtis to get settled. She wasn't entirely surprised when he dragged a small chair over to be closer to her.

"Now, then," he said, positively drooling with anticipation, "tell me what this proposition is all about."

She made herself think like a crook, glancing around the empty room as if suspecting someone to be hiding in the corner. Leaning forward, she lowered her voice. "I have a project that needs someone with your special expertise. Someone—I won't say who—gave me your name and impressed me with his glowing recommendation. I'm asking for your help."

Curtis narrowed his eyes. "I see." He appeared to be considering the matter. "I may be able to help you. What exactly do you want me to do?"

She hesitated, not sure how to answer that. "I want you to help me solve a problem."

"What kind of problem?"

"It involves the model of the Big Ben."

He made a guttural sound of disgust in his throat. "I've heard quite enough about that pesky model. I'm not going to waste my talent on something so trivial."

She raised her eyebrows. "Trivial?"

"Yes. When I work on something, it has to have meaning, a depth to it that will bring tears to your eyes and an ache to your heart."

Vivian sighed. It was becoming abundantly clear to her that Curtis was not the jewelry fence.

"I cannot," Curtis said, raising his voice for emphasis, "waste my time on frivolous froth. I must dig into my subject and bring out the hidden strengths and weaknesses, the tragic truth behind the face of farce." He flung out his arm in a wild gesture of emphasis. "I must enthrall my audience, holding them captive until they are saturated with my work."

Vivian slumped back on her chair. "You're an actor?"

"What? No." Curtis sounded offended. "I'm a writer. I thought you knew that." He frowned. "Didn't you say someone recommended me?"

Vivian pushed herself up from the chair. "I'm sorry, Curtis. I seem to have made a mistake. "I'll say goodnight now. Give my regards to Connie."

190

Curtis rose too. "Are you sure you wouldn't like a nightcap in my room? I have an excellent brandy—"

"Thank you, no." Vivian headed for the door. "It's been a pleasure, but now I must leave." She was beginning to sound like him, she thought as she hurried out of the building.

Felix greeted her with his usual joyful abandon when he returned to the car. She petted him until he quieted down, then drove back to Misty Bay, her mind turning over the past few days. There was only one suspect left now—Noah's father. She hated the thought of that little boy finding out that his daddy was a criminal and was on his way to jail.

It bothered her so much that she considered dropping the whole thing and letting the police finish the investigation. Sooner or later, they would arrive at the truth. Maybe.

What if they didn't? Or what if they did, but not before Lewis was buried? It seemed desperately important to her that justice prevail before Lewis went to meet his Maker. And if Noah's father deserved to go to prison, then his son was better off without him.

No, she was going to see this through. At least as far as she could get before she went to Messina. Otherwise, it would prey on her conscience for the rest of her life.

* * *

Messina eased back in his armchair and heaved a sigh of relief. It felt good to be home after another long day. It had been a stressful, though successful, week. He'd wrapped up his latest case in record time. Just a few days ago the report came in of drug dealers operating in town. It took hours of surveillance and an undercover cop, but he'd finally apprehended the culprits, and they were safely locked up.

Now he had time to search for Lewis Trenton's killer and uncover the truth. He reached for the beer at his side and refreshed his memory of what he knew so far. It wasn't a lot. The Portland detective seemed convinced that Trenton was a fence who'd tried to double-cross the robbers and gotten himself killed for his trouble. He maintained the theory that the cabin was a cover.

Messina had to admit that was possible. Trenton could have easily made an appearance there now and then, making it look like he lived there, and spent the rest of his time living it up in a luxury hotel.

Messina frowned in concentration. Maybe if he checked all the hotels in the area, he might come up with something. Then again, if the Portland cop was wrong, that would be a total waste of time.

He took a gulp of beer. He'd had doubts about Trenton's involvement in the robbery from the beginning, but it was Vivian's words that kept playing through his mind. *"Why would he spend his time combing the beach for items to sell?"*

She had a good point. That was a helluva lot of trouble to go to for a cover.

No, it was much more likely that Trenton picked up that model on the beach and kept it, not realizing he had a fortune in diamonds hidden inside it. The fence traced the model back to him, went after the jewels, and killed Trenton in the attempt.

Messina took another gulp of beer. If he was right about that, then he needed to find out how the model ended up on the beach. In other words, he was back to square one. He needed to get the name of the customer who bought the thing from Vivian in the first place. That meant another visit to the Willow Pattern Tearoom and another chance to see Jenna.

The thought conjured up her face in his mind. She had the most beautiful eyes—dark green with gold flecks. He loved her laugh, deep in her throat, warming his insides. He couldn't wait to see her again.

So then, why wait? He could ask her out to dinner again, though it would be hard to find somewhere more spectacular than The Bellemer. What he needed was somewhere quiet and inti-mate, where they could have a significant conversation without being overheard.

Like his home. That was quiet and intimate and had a really nice view of the ocean. The more he thought about it, the more he liked it. He was a pretty decent cook. He'd broil a couple of steaks, add a salad, a French baguette from the bakery, and a bottle of wine. Maybe a shrimp cocktail to start.

Smiling, he picked up his phone.

Chapter Thirteen

Jenna arrived early the next morning, carrying a large grocery bag in her arms. "I thought we could put these on the tables," she said as she dumped the bag on the kitchen table.

Vivian peeked into the bag and exclaimed with delight at the sight of the pumpkin candleholders adorned with red, yellow, orange, and brown foliage. "Beautiful! They're perfect for Thanksgiving. But I can't let you guys keep paying for decorations. How much did they cost? I'll reimburse you."

"No, you won't." Jenna slipped out of her jacket and hung it in the closet. "Besides, I made them. A long time ago. I've had them for ages, but I'd forgotten about them until I was clearing some stuff out of the spare bedroom for Gracie last night and found them in the closet."

"You made these?" Vivian pulled one of the holders out of the bag to take a closer look. "They're beautiful. I had no idea you were so talented."

Jenna laughed. "Don't look too closely. They're not perfect."

"You made eight of them?"

"Actually, there's ten. I made them for a high school project years ago. I don't know why I kept them. They took me hours and hours to make, and I guess I just didn't want to throw out all that hard work."

"I'm very glad you didn't throw them out. These will look wonderful on the tables." Vivian placed the holder back in the bag. "We still have Thanksgiving decorations left from last year. If you're not in a hurry to leave tonight, we can put them up after we close."

"I was hoping you'd say that." Jenna's face lit up. "I'm so looking forward to the holiday season." She picked up the bag. "I'll put these in the closet for now."

Vivian had to smile. She couldn't remember Jenna ever being excited about anything until now. It was amazing what the promise of romance could do for people. She wondered if Messina had mellowed now that he'd finally taken that first step toward a possible relationship with Jenna. She hoped and prayed that it would all work out for the two of them.

"So, how did your little fling with Casanova go last night?" Jenna asked as she headed for the cabinets. She took down a kettle and began filling it with water.

Vivian was about to answer when the doorbell announced Gracie's arrival.

"I'll get it." Jenna stood the kettle on the stove and hurried out of the kitchen. Seconds later, Vivian could hear Gracie's voice, high with excitement, though she couldn't understand what she was saying.

"Well," Jenna said as she reached the kitchen door, "I'm glad you got that settled." She walked in, followed by Gracie, whose eyes sparkled with glee.

"I gave my notice," she said when Vivian looked at her in anticipation. "And I don't have to pay them any more rent. I can leave when I want."

"I'm happy for you." Vivian glanced at Jenna. "So, when are you moving?"

"As soon as I can get rid of some stuff." Gracie tore off her jacket. "Jenna and I figured out what I can bring to her house, and the rest will go in storage." She looked at Jenna. "How about a week from Sunday?"

"Sure." Jenna walked over to the cabinets and pulled out a teapot. "I'll come over and help you load up."

"So will I." Vivian gave Gracie a hug. "I'm really happy for you two. I think this will be a wonderful experience for you both."

"Yeah, I can keep Misty company while Jenna goes out with Messina."

Jenna coughed and turned her back on them to take down cups and saucers from the cabinet.

"You're going out with Messina again?" Vivian stared at her friend in delight. "When were you going to tell me?"

"He just called last night while I was at Gracie's place." Jenna's cheeks were warm when she turned around. "I'm going over to his place tomorrow night. He's going to cook me dinner."

Vivian gasped. "He can cook? Hang onto that man."

Jenna laughed. "Let's wait and see how well he can cook before we get too excited about it."

"If a man made me dinner," Gracie said, taking a carton of milk from the fridge, "I wouldn't care how it tasted."

"Ditto." Vivian took the two of the cups and saucers over to the table. "You're a lucky woman, Jenna."

"Yeah, I know. So, you were going to tell me how things went at the retirement home last night."

"Oh, right!" Gracie put the milk on the table. "Did Curtis flirt with you?"

"He tried, but he didn't get very far." The kettle began singing, and Vivian hurried over to the stove. "He invited me up to his room. Twice."

Gracie giggled, while Jenna made a sound of disgust. "That man thinks he's George Clooney."

"I wish." Vivian filled the teapot with boiling water. "I would have enjoyed last night a lot more."

Jenna carried the last cup and saucer to the table and sat down. "So, what did you find out?"

"I found out he's not the fence." Vivian brought the teapot to the table and set it down. "He's a writer, and judging from what he said about it, he's not very good at it."

"Is he published?" Jenna sat down. "What does he write?"

"I don't know." Vivian sat down. "I didn't ask. Once I realized he wasn't a criminal, I just wanted to get out of there."

Jenna wrinkled her nose. "I don't blame you. I wouldn't want to be anywhere near that guy again."

Gracie raised her eyebrows. "That bad, huh?"

"Well," Vivian said as she poured a small amount of milk into her cup, "that leaves only one suspect: Noah's father. The more I think about him, the more convinced I am that he's the fence. I think he put the jewels in the model to hide them until he could sell them. Can you imagine how horrified he must have been when his son took them down to the beach and left them there?"

Gracie giggled. "He must have gone nuts."

Vivian reached for the teapot. "He might have seen Lewis beachcombing and figured he might have taken the model. Somehow, I have to make him say something incriminating or at least give me a clue we can follow."

Jenna's eyes widened. "You're not going to tackle him alone, I hope?"

"I'll be fine." Vivian wished she felt as secure as she sounded.

"Vivian!" Jenna leaned forward. "He's your last suspect. Which means he's probably the fence. And most likely dangerous. You can't go poking into his business. Something real bad could happen to you."

"She's right, Vivian." Gracie looked anxious now. "It just isn't safe for you."

"Let's just go tell Tony what you know so far and let him handle it." Jenna's eyes pleaded with her. "Please."

"But I don't know anything." Vivian's frustration made her voice rise. "All I have is gut feelings and guesswork. You know Messina won't listen to that. He needs hard evidence."

"Then all three of us will go talk to Noah's father." Jenna looked at Gracie. "Are you in?"

"You bet I'm in." Gracie raised her teacup. "To the three rookies. One for all and all for one."

Vivian sighed. It was doubtful they'd get anything out of Noah's father other than some really bad language. She would just go on her own and not tell them until it was over.

She was still trying to decide when and how she would handle it when Hal arrived to take Felix for a walk.

Jenna and Gracie were out in the tearoom when he walked into the kitchen. At the sight of him, she dropped the knife she was holding, and went into his arms for a swift hug. "You're looking good," she said when he let her go. "Are you feeling better?"

"I'm feeling on top of the world." The look in his eyes warmed her as he added, "Thanks to you."

"Me?" She laughed. "I didn't do anything."

"You don't have to. You just have to be you."

He might not think that if he knew she was on the verge of dementia, she thought, her smile fading. To hide her sudden depression, she turned back to the table, where egg and cress sandwiches waited for her attention. "Well, I'm glad you're feeling good."

He must have sensed something wrong, as he drew closer. "What's the matter? Are you okay?"

"I'm fine." She spread mayonnaise over a slice of bread.

"No, you're not." He sounded worried now. "Are you having second thoughts?"

His question surprised her, and she looked up at him. "About what?"

"About us."

Seeing the anxiety on his face chased away her own worries. "Oh no! Of course not! You're the best thing that has happened to me in years. I could never have doubts about that."

He still looked worried. "Then what's bothering you? I can tell something is up."

She put down the knife and turned to him. "I'm just frustrated about this thing with Lewis Trenton. We've talked to all these people, and I'm no closer to finding something conclusive to clear his name."

Hal's face cleared. "So, you had no luck talking to Stacey?"

"According to Gracie, Stacey is a nurse. Jenna talked to Brita—that's the woman Stacey gave the model to—and she sells cosmetics. I talked to Curtis, Connie's friend, and he's a writer. None of them are the fence."

"Unless one of them is lying."

"That's a possibility, I guess. Though I really think that it could be Noah's father, much as I hate the idea. If I'm responsible for putting that little boy's father in jail . . ." She let her voice trail off, too upset at the thought to finish the sentence.

"Hey! You're not responsible for anything other than trying to find justice for a man you believe is innocent."

"I do believe it."

"Then you're justified in doing what you're doing."

She smiled at him. "Thank you. I'm going to talk to Noah's father again, and I hope he'll say something incriminating."

"No."

She widened her eyes. "No what?"

Hal's jaw set in a firm line. "You're not going to talk to that man. From what you've told me, he's unpleasant at best and could well be dangerous."

"So, I'm just supposed to sit back and let him get away with murder?"

"You don't know that he killed Lewis. And if he did, he's not going to let you tell anyone about it."

"He won't know that I know. All he knows is that I'm looking for the Big Ben. I could be working for the jewel thieves for all he knows."

She could see the apprehension on Hal's face and felt bad that she was giving him so much worry. "I'll be careful," she said, knowing that wouldn't satisfy him.

She was right. Hal took his phone from his pocket. "Give me the address," he said. "I'll go talk to the guy."

Alarm bells rang in her head. "No! I can't let you do that."

"Then you'll drop the whole thing?"

Her gaze clashed with his for several seconds before she finally relented. "How about we both go talk to him?"

"On two conditions. I drive and you wait in the car."

She struggled with that one, torn between the compromise and her worry about getting him involved in something possibly dangerous.

"Or we take what you have to Messina and let him take care of it."

That settled it. "I'll wait in the car." She managed a smile. "And if you're not back in five minutes, I'll call the cops."

"Deal."

He reached out for her and pulled her close. "This is better than a handshake," he said as he gave her a warm hug.

She looked up at him. "Can we go tonight?"

"Tonight it is." He looked down at her, his face inches from hers.

For a breathtaking second, she thought he was about to kiss her, but just then Gracie's voice sang out from the doorway.

"Oops, sorry! I didn't mean to disturb you guys, but I need to get to the storeroom. We're out of Liquorice Allsorts."

Hal dropped his arms and stepped back. "I'd better go get Felix," he muttered as he headed for the back door.

Vivian cleared her throat and looked at Gracie. "It's okay," she said, trying to sound mature. "Hal's just taking Felix for a walk. You're not disturbing anything."

"Yeah, I can see that." Gracie practically skipped across to the storeroom and disappeared inside.

Shaking her head, Vivian picked up her knife again. Much as she cherished those stolen moments, she thought, she would have to be a little more discreet in the kitchen, to save everyone embarrassment.

She had a hard time hiding her excitement at the thought of the visit with Noah's father that evening. Not only was Hal going to be there to help her hunt for the truth, but they might actually find out something useful they could take to Messina, and Lewis could rest in peace.

It would be a terrific ending to the whole episode, and she could put it behind her and enjoy a peaceful holiday season with Hal and Felix. She couldn't think of anything she wanted more.

* * *

Later that evening, as Hal drove down Noah's street, all Vivian's apprehensions returned. Lewis had been shot. What if Noah's father had killed him? He could shoot Hal too. The thought of that terrified her so much, she turned to Hal as he parked the car.

"Maybe we shouldn't do this," she said, grasping his arm. "Let's just go home."

She couldn't see his eyes behind his glasses in the dark, but she could hear the resolution in his voice. "You've come this far, and I know how much it means to you. I'm going to talk to this guy and see what I can find out. I'm much more convincing as a crook than you are."

If she hadn't been so worried, she would have laughed out loud. Hal looked the least like a crook of anyone she'd ever met. She refrained from telling him that, however. The last thing she needed to do was undermine his confidence. "Just be careful," she said instead. "I meant what I said this afternoon. If you're not back in five minutes, I call 911."

"Give me ten, and I'll be fine." He leaned over to her and gave her a quick kiss. "That's to last until I get back."

Before she could gather enough breath to answer, he was out of the car and closing the door.

Heart hammering, she watched him march up the garden path to the door. She couldn't see inside the porch from where she sat. She was tempted to get out of the car and move closer so she could see what was going on, but then Noah's father might see her and realize that they were on to him. That wouldn't be good for either of them.

Instead, she turned the key in the ignition just enough to power the windows, and rolled down the one next to her. She could hear a rough voice raised in anger and felt sick. What had she done? Her voracious thirst for solving a mystery might cost Hal his life.

She unbuckled her seat belt, ears straining to hear Hal, but all she could hear was Noah's father, still yelling. She just couldn't sit there while Hal was being abused by that man. She pushed open the door and climbed out. Maybe she should just call the cops.

Sticking her head back inside the car, she reached for her purse. She had her phone in her hand when a voice spoke behind her, making her jump.

"What are you doing?"

She straightened so fast she hit her head on the rim of the doorway. "Ouch." She turned to see Hal staring at her in dismay. "Oh, thank God. I was just about to call the cops."

Hal shook his head. "Are you okay? You hit that pretty hard."

"I'm okay." She explored the top of her head with her fingers. It felt sore, but no bump. She peered at Hal, trying to gauge his expression in the dim light from the street lamp. "Are you okay? I heard him yelling at you."

"I'm good. Get back in the car and let's go home." He glanced over his shoulder, as if half expecting Noah's father to appear behind him.

She needed no further bidding. Scrambling back into her seat, she sent up a prayer of thanks. It was one thing to risk her own life, she told herself, but to drag people she loved into danger was incredibly selfish, and she should be ashamed of herself.

"That," Hal said as he drove away from Noah's house, "is one mean dude."

"I know." Vivian gave him an unhappy glance. "I'm sorry. I should never have involved you in this. I'm just glad he didn't hurt you." She peered at him. "He didn't, did he?"

"No, but I wouldn't have been surprised if he had." Hal slowed down to turn onto the main street. "I did my best to sound tough when I spoke to him. I told him word was out that he had skills that I could use."

"Oh, good one." Impressed, Vivian leaned closer to him. "What did he say?"

"He said he was good with a gun, if that's what I meant."

Shocked, she drew back. "Whoa. He doesn't mince words."

"Then I said that I needed someone to handle a delicate trans-action for me, and I'd like to discuss it with him."

"Good. What then?"

"He got really irritated. He said he'd had enough of people who couldn't mind their own business. He suggested, forcibly, with language I won't repeat, that I leave before he lost his temper and did something we'd both regret."

"Oh my." Vivian slumped back on her seat. "Well, at least you got out of there unscathed."

"Yeah, but I didn't get anything useful out of him."

"I think you did." Vivian chewed on her lip. "He acts like he's got something to hide. I believe he's involved in this somehow. I just wish I could prove it."

"Isn't that a job for the cops?"

She didn't answer him right away. He was right. She just didn't want to admit it. After everything she'd done, tracking the progress of the model as it changed hands, and talking to everyone who had any connection with it, she still had no proof that any of them were involved in the robbery or Lewis Trenton's death. The trail had ended, and she had nothing to show for her efforts.

"You're right," she said at last. "I need to talk to Messina and tell him everything I know. Maybe there's something there I'm missing that he will be able to pick up."

"I think that's the best idea you've had yet."

Hearing the relief in his voice, she smiled. "I just hate to give up."

"I know. It's what I admire most about you."

"Some people would call it being extremely stubborn."

He sent her a quick glance. "I call it a determination to see justice done, no matter what it costs you. I respect that."

"Thank you." It gave her an incredibly warm feeling to know that he understood her motivation. "I just feel so bad that Lewis has no one to stand up for his rights. I wonder what turned him into a hermit. There must have been some tragedy in his life for him to turn his back on everyone and live like a pauper. Chris told me that Lewis didn't even have indoor plumbing. He said he used a shack out back."

"No kidding. I didn't know that. Poor guy. It must have been hell to go out in the rain every time you had to use the bathroom."

"Can you imagine the smell? How do people live like that?"

"I guess some people don't have any choice." Hal pulled up in front of the tearoom. "Which is why I'm always thankful for what I have."

"Me too." Vivian unfastened her seat belt. "We live like royalty compared to some people."

"Well, at least Lewis had a roof over his head. There are too many people who don't even have that."

"I know." She sighed. "It's so sad to think about."

"I'm sorry. I didn't mean to bring you down."

She smiled at him. "You didn't. I could never be depressed when I'm with you."

"I'm glad to hear it." He put his arm around her and drew her close. "I feel the same way."

His kiss lifted her spirits as nothing else could, and she was still smiling as she opened the door of her apartment, bracing for Felix's excited onslaught.

After taking him for a short walk, she made herself a cup of hot chocolate and sat down to watch the news. The anchor made no mention of Lewis. Apparently, any interest in his death had waned. She wondered if the Portland police were still pursuing the case, or if they, too, had put it on the back burner in favor of more noteworthy crimes.

Was this how it was going to end? With an innocent man buried alone, his name forever vilified? If so, it would haunt her forever. Tomorrow she would leave her assistants in charge of the tearoom, and she would talk to Messina.

She really didn't have much hope for a resolution. The cops might never know the identity of the fence or who killed Lewis. But she had to make one last bid to clear Lewis's name.

She had trouble falling asleep that night but finally dozed off with Felix's warm body at her feet. Hours later she awoke with a start, aware that a sound somewhere had disturbed her. She realized at once that Felix was not on the bed. Had he gone to investigate the noise?

Alarmed now, she slid out of bed and felt for her slippers. A glance at the alarm clock told her it was a little past three AM. She stood for a moment, ears straining for any sound, but could hear nothing.

Creeping silently out of the bedroom, she paused, her nerves screaming at her to be careful. Surely, she told herself, if there was an intruder, Felix would be all over him in a second. Unless something bad had happened to the dog.

She felt sick. The urge to call out Felix's name was strong, but caution kept her silent. She wished she had a weapon. Her late husband's walking stick lay in the closet, and she thought about going back to get it. A baseball bat would feel good right now. She needed to buy one.

A soft sound stopped her breath. It came from the kitchen. She'd left her cell phone in the bedroom. She should go back and call the cops. Common sense kicked in, and she let out her breath. It was probably Felix, looking for food.

She crept forward the few steps until she could peek into the kitchen. The glow in the window from the street lamp outside gave her enough light to see Felix. He stood by the counter, staring up at her scarf dangling over the edge. She'd thrown it there last night and hadn't bothered to put it away.

As she watched, she saw the dog reach up and take the edge of the scarf in his teeth. He pulled it down to the floor, then dragged it over to his bed, where he gently tucked it in.

Relief flooded Vivian as realization dawned. She hadn't misplaced anything after all. It was Felix all along. He must have been taking her things and leaving them somewhere else.

Her soft gasp had alerted him. He stood staring at her as if expecting a reprimand.

Still disbelieving what she'd seen, Vivian reached for the light switch and turned it on. "What in the world are you doing?"

Felix lowered his haunches to the floor and stared back at her with innocent eyes.

She didn't know whether to scold him or hug him in her relief. She wasn't losing her mind after all. She felt an urge to dance around the kitchen. "It was you all this time." She wagged a finger at him. "You've been taking my things and hiding them."

Felix pricked up his ears and tilted his head to one side, as if trying to decipher her words.

"Do you have any idea what you put me through?" She marched over to his bed and picked up her scarf. "You made me think I was heading for dementia."

Felix hung his head.

In spite of her exasperation, her heart melted, and she crouched down beside him. "Am I not giving you enough attention? Is that the problem? You're so lonely while I'm working that you need to hide my things?"

Felix licked her face.

She put her arms around him and gave him a gentle hug. "I'm sorry, baby. I wish I could spend more time with you—I really do. But the tearoom keeps me so busy, and I'm tired when I get home. Maybe it was wrong to adopt you. You need a family who's around all the time and can play with you."

She felt like crying now. She couldn't give him up. That would break her heart. Yet she was breaking his heart by leaving him alone so much. She had to think of him and what he needed. Sadly, she led him back to bed, and finally fell asleep with his comforting presence warm against her feet.

Chapter Fourteen

"I'm going to talk to Messina," Vivian said as she filled a tea-kettle with water the following morning.

Jenna had arrived minutes before and had just hung her jacket in the closet. She snapped the door shut, her voice rising in surprise. "You've found the fence?"

"Maybe. I just can't prove anything."

"So you're giving up."

Vivian set the kettle on the stove. "I don't know what else to do. I've run out of suspects."

The doorbell alerted them to Gracie's arrival. "We'll talk about this," Jenna said, walking over to the door.

Vivian shook her head as she took down a teapot from the cabinet. Maybe now that she had stopped chasing after criminals, she'd have time to get the keys cut.

Gracie bounced into the kitchen with her usual big grin. "I sold my bed last night," she said as she dragged off her jacket. "I've been wanting to get rid of that thing for months."

"That's great," Vivian murmured, her mind still on her failure to finish what she had started.

Jenna followed her in, her face creased in a frown. "What are you going to sleep on?"

"My couch." Gracie slung her jacket on a hanger and closed the closet door. "I'm so tired by the time I've finished sorting and packing, I won't have trouble falling asleep."

Jenna shook her head. "Look, why don't you just bring your clothes over to my place. You can do what you have to do at your apartment in the evenings and crash with me."

Gracie smiled. "Thanks, but it'll go faster if I stay there. I want to be ready to move out by next week."

"Well, okay, but if you change your mind . . ."

Vivian smiled. It was good to hear her friends making plans together. After making the tea and placing a plate of fresh scones on the table, she sat down to enjoy a cup of her favorite brew.

"So," Jenna asked, picking up her cup, "Do you think Noah's father is the fence?"

Vivian took a moment to answer. "I'm pretty sure he is," she said at last. "I just wish I could prove it."

Jenna's eyes widened. "What happened last night? Did Hal talk to him?"

"Yes." Vivian shivered at the memory. "He told Hal he was good with a gun."

Gracie uttered a squeak of dismay. "He didn't point one at him, did he?"

"No, thank God." Vivian cradled her cup in both hands. "But he was pretty belligerent. I could hear him shouting while I was in the car."

"So, you're going to tell Tony you think he's the fence?" Jenna looked doubtful. "He's going to take some convincing."

"I know." Vivian sighed. "I just wish I had something more solid to give him. After all that talking and questioning all those people, we have nothing to show for it."

"We did get to go to Portland," Gracie said. "That was fun."

Jenna tipped sugar into her cup and began to stir. "You know what's weird? No one said anything about someone else asking them about the model."

Vivian stared at her. "What do you mean?"

"Well, you said that whoever was the fence must have hidden the jewels inside the model, which then got passed along to someone else before he could get the jewels out again, right?"

"Right, but I don't see—"

"Well, what would you do if you were the fence and thousands of dollars of your jewels went missing?"

"I'd try to find them before the robbers found out and came after me," Gracie said.

Vivian's pulse quickened. "He would have to track down the model, just like I did."

Jenna nodded. "Right. Yet no one said anything about someone else asking about the model. You'd think they would have mentioned that."

Vivian's brain went into high gear. "Let's think about that. If Stacey was the fence, she would have asked Brita where the model had gone."

"And Connie and Noah's father." Jenna picked up her cup. "Brita would have asked Connie and Noah's father—"

"And Curtis would have asked Noah's father," Vivian finished for her. "So, assuming I was the only one asking questions about the Big Ben, that could mean the fence is Noah's father."

"Yep." Jenna grinned. "We're getting good at this."

"We still don't have proof." Vivian took a sip of tea and put down the cup. "It's still all assumptions. I just wish we had one solid clue that would confirm our suspicions. I keep thinking about Lewis. He lived all alone, scratched out a living as well as he could, and bothered no one. He didn't deserve to die that way." She looked up at Jenna. "Did you know he didn't even have a bathroom in the cabin? Chris said he used a shack out back." She shivered. "I just can't imagine that."

Jenna raised her eyebrows. "No kidding?"

"Wow, really?" Gracie sounded shocked. "That must have been a bummer. Especially if you had to go in the middle of the night. What if there were bears or wolves out there?"

"I'd have to have a commode," Jenna said. "Like they did in Victorian times."

Something clicked in Vivian's mind. She stared at Jenna, trying to absorb what she'd just heard. "Did you know that before now?"

Jenna looked confused. "Know what?"

"That Lewis had no indoor plumbing."

"No, you just told us now."

Vivian looked at Gracie. "And you never heard it from anywhere else?"

"Nope." Gracie grinned. "I would have remembered if I had."

"Hal hadn't heard about that either." Vivian stared at her cup, her mind replaying her visit to Brita's condo. "I think I need to go into Newport again. Can you two take care of things for an hour or so?"

"Of course." Jenna frowned at her. "Is everything okay?"

Vivian made an effort to smile. "Yes, of course. I just have an important errand to run. It shouldn't take too long. An hour at most."

"No problem." Jenna pushed her chair back. "Did you make all the fillings for the sandwiches?"

"I did." Vivian got to her feet. "Everything's ready in the fridge. We don't have a full house this afternoon, so there should be plenty. In any case, I'll be back before you run out."

"I can make more." Gracie got up and picked up her cup and saucer. "I know how from watching you."

Vivian smiled at her. "Thanks, but I'm sure it won't be necessary. Thanks to both of you. I don't know what I'd do without you two."

"You'd close up shop and marry Hal," Jenna said as she carried her own cup and saucer over to the sink.

Vivian laughed. "That's not likely to happen."

She had to admit, though, as she climbed the stairs to her apartment, the idea had merit. Marriage to Hal would be very different from her marriage to Martin.

Although she had considered herself happily married, she and her late husband lived their own lives, sometimes not being together more than a few hours a week. They went out to dinner every Friday night unless Martin had an important case that needed a lot of preparation, in which case he would spend half the night pouring over evidence and scenarios that would hopefully lead to a conviction.

The rest of the time, Vivian took care of her two daughters until they no longer needed her constant supervision. She took a job as a teacher's aide and enjoyed it until Martin died suddenly, leaving her alone.

Remembering those dark days, Vivian shuddered. She didn't know why she was reliving it all now, but one thing was certain. She never wanted to go through something like that again.

She opened the door to the apartment, endured Felix's greeting, then hurried over to her computer. There was one thing she needed to check before leaving for Newport.

Entering Lewis's name in the search engine, she quickly scanned the few lines that came up. Most of it was news of the shooting, and robbery of the jewels. Vivian was shocked to see the total value of the diamonds was over half a million dollars. No wonder whoever hid those gems was desperate enough to kill to get them back.

One article mentioned the fact that Lewis was a beachcomber and scraped out a living selling what he found, but she couldn't find a single word about Lewis's lack of a bathroom. Even more convinced now that the end of her quest lay in Newport, she pulled on her coat.

There was no point in worrying Jenna or Gracie now. It could all end the way all her other endeavors had ended, with nothing to show for it. If, on the other hand, she got the slightest hint that her suspicions were on target, she would go immediately from there to Messina and tell him everything she knew.

She looked down at Felix, who stared up at her, his eyes brimming with hope. "You want to go for a ride?"

The second she said "go," he was at the door, jumping up and down in his excitement.

Shaking her head, she grabbed his leash off the nail and snapped it onto his collar. "Okay, buddy. Let's go nail this lowlife."

Felix barked in complete agreement.

Driving along the coast road to Newport, Vivian went over everything in her mind: all her conversations with Stacey, Brita, Connie, and Noah's father. They'd all had an interest in the Big

Ben at some point. She'd been so focused on all of them, she'd missed the obvious until now.

She recalled Jenna commenting on the fact that no one had mentioned anyone else asking about the model. But now that she was thinking about it, she remembered Curtis saying he'd heard enough of it, and Noah's father being a little more aggressive, saying he was sick of hearing about it.

So, it was possible that both he and Connie had been questioned about the Big Ben. And Vivian thought she knew who had been looking for the model.

Brita's boyfriend, Chris, had mentioned that Lewis had no indoor bathroom, yet she had found no mention of that anywhere in the media reports. Neither Jenna, Gracie, nor Hal had heard about that. So how would Chris know unless he had actually been inside the cabin?

She needed to talk to Brita and get just a little more information she could take to Messina.

Minutes later she pulled up in front of Brita's condo. Praying that she'd find the woman home, she rode the elevator to the third floor.

To her relief, Brita opened the door, her eyes widening in surprise when she recognized her visitor. She stood back, gesturing with her hand for Vivian to enter.

The condo seemed even more elegant than Vivian had remembered. She hadn't noticed the expensive artwork on the walls the last time she was there, nor the gleaming gold handles on the white sideboard. Brita's parents must have been wealthy.

Brita beckoned her over to the couch. "Can I get you a glass of water? Wine?"

Vivian smiled. "Thanks, but I'm good. I just noticed your sideboard. It's beautiful."

"Thanks. Chris bought it. He didn't like the furniture that was in the condo, so he got rid of it and bought a ton of new stuff." Brita glanced at a door across the room. "Don't tell him I said so, but I really don't like all this white furniture. It's not at all cozy."

So, Chris had plenty of money to spend. Now Vivian was even more certain she was on the right track. Still, he could have earned his money anywhere. She needed more information, but she needed to be careful. Brita could be a willing partner in crime.

"Are you here about the Big Ben model? Did you find it?"

Vivian looked up at her. "Actually, I came to buy some cosmetics. I heard that you sell some excellent makeup."

Brita's face lit up. "Oh, great! I'll get my sample case. Wait there. I'll be right back."

Vivian did her best to relax and leaned back against the soft cushion. So this is what it was like to live in luxury. Not that she would want it. The apartment was beautiful, but Brita was right. All that white made it look cold. She preferred something cozy, warm, and less sterile. She could just see Felix's hairs all over the white couch.

Her disturbing vision of spilling red wine on the creamy fabric vanished when Brita walked back into the room, carrying a purple case.

"I think you will love this brand," Brita said, laying the case on the coffee table. "It's designed for the older woman."

Vivian wasn't sure how she felt about being referred to as an older woman, but decided she was being a little too sensitive.

"I don't normally use much makeup," she said, "but I thought I might try something different for a change."

Brita peered at her. "You have a warm skin tone, hazel eyes, light brown hair. Do you dye it?"

"No, I don't," Vivian assured her.

Brita peered closer. "You have very few gray hairs for your age."

Vivian was beginning to get a little resentful about the inference that she was old. Lately, since things had developed between her and Hal, she'd been feeling remarkably younger. She didn't need the constant reminder that she was no longer in her prime. "Thank you," she said, hoping her irony didn't show up in her tone.

"I think this shade would be perfect for your skin." Brita held up a small bottle. "This foundation is thick with moisturizer, to help disguise wrinkles."

Vivian clenched her fingers. "That's nice."

Brita shook out a miniature cotton ball and dabbed some of the moisturizer onto it. Leaning forward, she patted it all over Vivian's face, then smoothed it in with the tips of her fingers. Finally, she sat back to study her handiwork. "Yes, I thought so. It's perfect for you. It takes years off your face."

When she heard that, Vivian snapped to attention. There might be something to this stuff after all. "Really?"

"Really." Brita lifted a small mirror from the case and handed it to her. "See for yourself."

Studying her face in the mirror, Vivian had to admit, the foundation did make her skin look smoother, more polished. It wasn't a look she was used to, but she could maybe get acquainted with it.

"You need a dab of blush, eye shadow, and lots of mascara." Brita dug into the case again. "Your eyelashes have thinned out."

She didn't say "with your age" but Vivian could hear it in her voice. This was crazy, she told herself. She would never pile all this makeup on her face. She preferred the natural look. She could just see Hal's expression if she waltzed up to him made up like a clown.

"I think I'll just stick with the foundation," she said, feeling compelled to buy something after making Brita go through all that selling spiel.

"Just a little blush," Brita said, ignoring her words. Again, she leaned forward, this time with a cotton ball covered in blush. She puffed Vivian's cheeks and leaned back. "There. That's better. It brings out the color of your eyes."

Looking at her image in the mirror, Vivian thought she looked like she was coming down with a fever. "Very nice," she said, trying to muster some enthusiasm. "I'll take some of that too."

"Good. Now, let's take a look at the lipsticks." Brita picked out a golden tube of lipstick. "I think this will tone in perfectly with that foundation."

"Thanks, but I have a ton of lipstick at home," Vivian lied. "I'm sure I have something that will work."

"Wouldn't you just like to try this?" Brita uncapped the lipstick. "Here. I'll just put a light coating on."

Before Vivian could protest, the young woman leaned over and dabbed the lipstick on her mouth. "There. Now don't you think that looks glamorous?"

Once more Vivian glanced at the mirror. No, it didn't look glamorous. It looked like an *older* lady trying to shed a few years. "Just the foundation and blush," she said, toughening her tone.

Brita looked disappointed. "Okay. But I think that lipstick is perfect for you. If you change your mind, you know where to find me." She picked up the foundation and blush. "I'll pack these up for you. That'll be forty-eight dollars. I'll take cash or a check."

Vivian swallowed. Twice what she'd expected to pay. This visit had better turn out the way she hoped. "I'll write a check." She dug in her purse for her checkbook. Drawing it out, she added casually, "So, how long have you lived here?"

Brita took a small paper bag, decorated with roses and violets, out of her case. "Almost a year."

"Oh, really? Where did you live before that?"

"I grew up in Salem. I was a hair stylist there, but when my parents died, I quit my job and moved into this." She waved a hand at the room.

"Is that when you met Chris?"

For a moment, Brita seemed startled by the question, and Vivian held her breath. Had she been too abrupt?

She relaxed again when Brita answered. "I met Chris a couple of years ago in Salem. When I moved down here, he moved in with me. He helps with the mortgage and the upkeep." She stared down at her cosmetics case. "I'm not exactly making a fortune with this."

Vivian nodded. "I know what you mean. It's hard to make money in business these days. So, does Chris work here in Newport, or does he have to commute?"

"He works for a consulting company in town. I don't know which one. He never talks about his work. He always says he leaves his work behind when he comes home."

"He goes on business trips, then?"

Brita sighed. "Now and then. He was supposed to go on one a month ago, but he sprained his ankle and had to stay home. He was in a foul mood about that for a while."

Vivian's pulse quickened. She remembered seeing Chris limping when she was there before. That could be why he had to hide the jewels. He couldn't get to the seller, so he hid them in the model until he could rearrange another meeting. "I can understand him being upset," she said. "It's frustrating when you need to work and can't get there."

She glanced at the sideboard. "Those vases are beautiful. So elegant. I can see why you wanted to get rid of the Big Ben model."

"It didn't exactly go with my decor."

"What did Chris have to say about it? He must have been relieved when you gave it to the thrift store."

"Actually, he wasn't." Brita frowned. "He was really acting weird about it. He yelled at me for not consulting him before I got rid of it. Then, the other day, after you left, he called the thrift store and told them not to tell you who bought it. I asked him why he did that, but he wouldn't say. Just went off in a huff and—"

"I don't know why you couldn't just mind your own business."

The harsh voice had come from the hallway, and Vivian jumped. She watched with nerves tightening as Chris walked into the room. Obviously, his ankle had healed. Judging from the look on his face, however, he was in no mood for congratulations.

"I'm sorry." Vivian strove to keep her expression casual. "I didn't mean to disturb you."

"Oh, I think you did." Chris walked over to the couch and stood over Brita. "And you talk too much."

Brita glared up at him. "What's your problem?"

Chris nodded at Vivian. "Ask your friend. Ask her what she's really doing here."

"She's buying my cosmetics." Brita waved the bag at him. "What's wrong with you? Have you been drinking?"

"He's been doing a lot more than that," Vivian murmured. She could tell that Chris knew she was on to him. Apparently, Brita didn't know about his criminal activities, or she would never have admitted he'd called the thrift store.

Brita frowned up at him, obviously confused. "What does she mean?"

"I think she means that she knows about the diamonds." Chris looked at Vivian with hostile eyes. "Isn't that right?"

There was no point in denying anything. Vivian figured there were two of them, and Brita looked like a strong woman, whereas Chris was not exactly robust. "Yes," she said quietly. "I assume you're a fence for a gang of robbers."

Now Brita's eyes widened in alarm. "A fence?" She stared at Vivian. "You're accusing him of being a criminal?"

Chris uttered an unpleasant laugh. "That's because I am one."

"No!" Brita shot to her feet, the bag of cosmetics falling to the floor. "This is all a big joke, right? You're just trying to get back at me for getting rid of the Big Ben."

Chris narrowed his eyes. "No joke, honey. You almost had me killed by that dumb move."

Brita uttered a soft whimper of disbelief. "What have you done?"

"I believe he hid over half a million dollars of diamonds in the Big Ben model," Vivian said quietly, "and killed Lewis Trenton while getting them back."

The last part was guesswork, but she knew by Chris's face that she had scored.

"That stupid nutcase," he muttered. "If he'd just stayed out of my way, he'd still be alive. He heard me breaking into his cabin and came at me with a shotgun. I had to bring him down before he shot me."

Brita stared at Chris as if he'd turned into an alien monster.

Deciding it was time to leave, Vivian got to her feet. Both Chris and Brita stood between her and the door. Even if she could get past them, she wouldn't get far. This was a time for diplomacy. "Well, like you pointed out, this is none of my business, so I'll just butt out and leave you two to sort things out between you."

"I don't think so." To Vivian's utter dismay, Chris put his hand behind his back and drew out a gun. "I can't let you go telling stories to the cops."

Brita cried out, "No! Chris, no!"

Chris turned on her. "Sit down!" He pointed the gun at Vivian. "You too."

Vivian sat, cursing herself for her stupidity. Hadn't she learned her lesson from the last time she went investigating criminals? She was in real danger this time. She thought about Felix, waiting for her in the car. And Hal. He would be heartbroken. At least, she hoped he would be.

Then there were the girls, waiting for her to get back to the tearoom. She should have told them where she was going. She and her stupid pride. She hadn't wanted to tell them until she had positive proof.

Now she had it, and she might never be able to tell anyone about it. More than likely, she had just made her last mistake.

Chapter Fifteen

"What are you going to do?" Brita remained on her feet; her face ashen and her voice shrill with fear.

Vivian prayed that the young woman wouldn't do anything crazy, like lunging for the gun. Mustering all her self-control, she forced herself to speak calmly. "He's going to be sensible. He's not going to shoot us. That would be stupid, considering that someone is bound to hear the shots and call the cops."

"She's right," Chris said, "I'm not going to shoot you. I'll leave that for the gang to do."

Brita whimpered. "No, Chris! Why?"

"Because you could put me in jail for the rest of my life, that's why."

"But we won't." Brita turned to Vivian. "Tell him you won't tell the police." Before Vivian could answer, Brita looked back at Chris. "I love you! I could never turn you in to the cops. I thought you loved me."

Chris stared at her for several seconds, then said softly, "I do love you, hon. It's okay. I'm not going to let anything bad happen to you." He pointed the gun at Vivian. "But we have to get rid of her."

Brita cried out again. "Why? She won't say anything."

Vivian spoke up. "I won't talk to the cops. I promise." That was one promise she'd be happy to break, she thought as she looked hopefully at Chris.

For a long, tense moment, Chris stared at her while she did her best not to flinch. Then, finally, he nodded. "Okay. I guess I'll have to trust you. But I need to lock you up for a bit. Until I get some things settled. Then I'll come and let you out."

Vivian seriously doubted that, but at least if he left her alone for a while, she might have a chance to escape.

"Where are you going to lock her up?" Brita's voice still wobbled. "There's nowhere in here."

"I know a place." He gave Brita a smile of pure evil. "You'll have to drive, hon, while I keep an eye on this meddling bitch."

Brita shook her head. "No, I don't like this. Why can't we just let her go? She's promised not to tell anyone."

"I have to make sure to cover my tracks before we let her go. You don't want me to go to jail, right?"

"No, I don't."

"Then you have to go along with what I say." He waved the gun at Vivian. "Okay, let's move."

Vivian got to her feet and smiled at Brita. "I'll be fine. Just do what he says."

Brita's face looked white and drawn. "How are we going to get past Melinda? She watches everyone coming and going."

Vivian figured she meant the receptionist. If she could just attract the woman's attention on the way out, she told herself, she might be able to send some kind of message.

"We won't be going past Melinda," Chris said, dashing Vivian's hopes. "We're going out the back door." He turned back to Vivian. "We're taking your car. Where did you park it?"

"Right out front."

"Give me the keys."

She hesitated just a little too long. He leaned forward and snatched up her purse from the couch. Turning it upside down, he shook the contents onto the coffee table. The keys fell with a clatter, and he picked them up, then grabbed her phone. "I'll take this too. Just in case you're tempted to call the cops."

Vivian's lips tightened. This was not looking good. The thought occurred to her that Chris might shoot Felix or shove him out onto the street. She struggled to sound calm. "You might want to think twice about taking my car. My dog is in there. He's not friendly toward strangers."

Chris stared at her for a second or two, making her squirm. She flinched as he brought the gun closer to her head. "You are one big pain," he snarled. "I should just shoot you here and be done with it."

Brita uttered a cry of protest, and he turned to her. "It's okay. She won't get hurt as long as she does what she's told. We'll take my car. Now let's get moving before I change my mind."

He didn't exactly say what he meant by that last comment, but Brita apparently took it as a warning. She started toward the door, then paused. "I have to get my purse first."

"You don't need your purse, hon. We're just gonna drop your friend off and we'll be right back here."

"But—"

Seeing Chris's face darken, Vivian broke in. "Do as he says, Brita. The sooner we get this over with, the better."

Chris's eyes were cold when he looked at her. "Just keep your mouth shut from now on, okay?"

Vivian shrugged. "Okay."

Brita looked at her. "Yeah. Quit telling me what to do."

Vivian's spirits sank even further. She'd been hoping she could rely on Brita to be an ally, but apparently the silly woman was in love with the creep and was determined to help him. Even if it meant involving herself in murder. Vivian had no illusions about Chris's intent. He couldn't afford to let her live, knowing what she knew. Her only hope was to attract someone's attention on the way out of the complex.

Those hopes were dashed as Chris punched the elevator button that would take them to the parking garage below the lobby. They passed no one as they walked past parked cars, SUVs, and a pickup, with Chris practically breathing down Vivian's neck. Acutely aware that he had one hand on his gun, she gauged her chances of escape. Maybe she could make a run for it, or scream and yell.

"Don't even think about it," Chris warned, apparently reading her mind. He dug his fist into her back, shoving her forward. "Here's the car. Get into the back seat." He looked at Brita. "You're driving."

Brita halted. "Why me?"

"Because I have to keep the gun trained on this bitch, to make sure she doesn't do anything stupid."

"Oh, okay." Brita waited for Chris to pop the locks, then opened the driver's door. "So, where are we going?"

"I'll tell you when we're on the road." He gave Vivian another shove. "Get in."

Vivian had to restrain herself from taking a shot at his jaw. Her stomach churned as she climbed into the back seat of the car. She couldn't even write in the dust on the window with Chris sitting next to her, the gun pointed at her.

"Okay," he said as Brita pulled out into the street, "take a left up there."

Vivian stared frantically out the window as the car turned onto the coast road. Her only chance of attracting someone's attention was now. Once they left the town, her chances would be nil.

A few visitors strolled along the seafront, but no one even glanced at the car as it sailed past them. Vivian forced herself to relax. She didn't know if Chris meant what he said about locking her up. He could just drive to the highest point of the cliffs and dump her over.

A flashback of a devious monster holding an unconscious Jenna on the edge of the cliffs turned her insides to ice. Now it was her turn. *I'm sorry, Felix. I'm sorry, Hal. I love you both.*

At the thought of Felix, her misery deepened. The poor dog was trapped inside the car. Surely someone would notice him being left alone for so long? She'd told Jenna she was going to Newport. Jenna was smart. She'd figure out that she was going to talk to one of the suspects again. Maybe she'd tell Hal. *Please.*

She envisioned Hal finding Felix and taking him back home. Maybe he'd keep him. But then Felix would be left alone again all day. It would be better if Hal found a good home for him.

She decided right then and there that if she survived this, she would find that home for Felix. He deserved to have company, maybe kids to play with, people to give him the attention he needed. She wasn't being fair to him, leaving him alone all day.

She fought the tears at the thought, but they escaped anyway, running down her cheeks as she fumbled in her pocket for a tissue. It didn't matter. She was probably never going home again.

The car sped along the shoreline, but for once, Vivian wasn't gazing at the ocean or the stretch of sandy beaches. Her mind was on Hal and how he'd take the news that she had been killed by the robbers. He had warned her so many times. He would be angry with her for taking so many dangerous chances.

She closed her eyes, envisioning his face. He would be the last thing she thought of in her final moments.

"Park the car up ahead," Chris ordered, snapping Vivian out of her reverie. "There's a spot to park right up there."

Vivian's stomach heaved, and she took a few deep breaths. He was going to throw her over. At least it would be quick. Better than dying from a gunshot wound.

Brita brought the car to a bumpy stop. Vivian noticed a house a short distance from the road but could see no signs of life. Her last faint hope faded. Too bad it wasn't summertime. They might have run into someone.

Brita's voice was tight with anxiety when she asked, "What are you going to do?"

"There's an abandoned beach hut down there. We'll take her down and lock her up."

Vivian's relief was short lived when Brita twisted around to look at him. "Then what?"

"I'll figure that out later."

"Okay." Brita cut the engine.

Chris jerked the gun at Vivian. "Get out."

All hope was rapidly fading as Vivian stumbled down the rocky path to the beach below. The wind cut through her coat, making her shiver with the cold. Dark clouds hovered over the ocean, where whitecaps signaled yet another storm approaching.

The sand was soft under her feet, and she could hear the cries of the seagulls as they swooped and circled over the water. If she had to die, she thought, this would be her last memories: the sights, sounds, and smells of her beloved seashore.

For a moment she wondered if he planned to shoot her there on the beach after all, leaving her body to wash out to sea, but then she saw a broken-down shack nestled below the cliffs. Hope flickered again. If he left her locked up in there, surely she could find a way to escape.

Stumbling across the sand, she finally reached the hut. It looked weather-beaten, its cedar shakes bleached by the sun and roughened by the salty winds. The door seemed fragile, secured by a rusted padlock.

Chris handed Brita a key. "Unlock it," he ordered.

"What is this place?" Brita took the key and studied the hut with a frown. "Do you own it?"

"No, but I use it sometimes." Chris jerked his head at the cliffs. "I think it belongs to the people who own the house up there, but they never use it anymore. I don't think they live here. The house is rented out to visitors."

"How did you get the key to it?" Brita turned the key in the padlock.

"I bought the padlock so I could use the hut."

"What do you use it for?" She unhooked it, and the door swung open with a loud creak.

"Storage."

"Storage of what?"

Chris's tone warned he was getting impatient. "Enough of the questions. I'll tell you everything later. Right now, we need to tie the bitch up. There's rope inside." He pointed the gun at Vivian. "Get in there."

Sending up a prayer, Vivian stepped inside the damp, bleak shack, closely followed by Brita. The place smelled of dead fish and something she didn't want to analyze. The hut had no window, and it took her a moment or two to adjust to the gloom. In the daylight spilling in from the doorway, she saw nothing but a pair of oars, a couple of fishnets, an oil lamp, a pile of ropes and a wooden crate.

At least she'd have something to sit on, Vivian told herself, bracing for whatever came next.

Chris still had the gun leveled at her as he snapped another order at Brita. "Tie her up. Wind the rope around her arms tight so she can't wriggle free."

Brita stared at the pile of ropes. "I . . . don't want to tie her up. Can't we just leave her locked up in here?"

"Or I could just shoot her now." Chris raised the gun, and Vivian sat down on the crate and closed her eyes.

"No! Wait! I'll do it." Brita rushed over to the pile of ropes and pulled out a long strand. She carried it over to Vivian and began winding the rope around her body, trapping her arms against her sides.

For a brief instant their eyes met, and Brita, with her back toward Chris, mouthed, "I'm sorry."

Vivian gave her a slight nod. Maybe there was hope after all. Seconds later, that was swept away by Chris's next order.

"Tie it around her ankles. Make sure she can't walk."

Vivian winced as the rope bit into her flesh. She couldn't move now. She was completely helpless, trussed up like a Christmas turkey. Her odds of escaping appeared to be nil.

"That's good," Chris said when Brita stepped back. "Except you don't have enough on there." He tucked his gun into his waistband and walked over to the ropes. After dragging a length from the pile, he walked back to Brita. "Sorry, hon, but now it's your turn."

Brita backed up against the wall. "My turn for what?"

"I can't take any chances. I'm gonna have to leave you here too."

"No!" Panic made Brita's voice rise. "I love you! I thought you loved me!"

Chris's smile made Vivian feel sick. "Yeah. About that. You were useful, hon. Thanks for the help." He grabbed Brita, who struggled violently to get away, making him swear. "Hold still or I'll shoot you right now."

Brita went limp, allowing Chris to shove her down on the crate next to Vivian and bind her up too. Then he dug into Brita's pocket and took out her phone.

Vivian closed her eyes. This was the final blow. Until now there had been a glimmer of hope that Brita would feel remorse and somehow help rescue her. Now that miniscule hope was gone too. She was going to die.

Chris stood back to assess his work. Then, seemingly satisfied, he walked over to the door. Turning his head to look back at Brita, he raised his hand. "You'll be getting some company soon. They'll take care of you. Bye. It was fun while it lasted." With that, he stepped outside and slammed the door shut, leaving them in darkness. Vivian heard the rattle of the padlock as he secured it, then nothing but silence.

So, he was going to send gang members to finish them off. Her disgust left a bad taste in her mouth. For all his bravado, Chris was nothing but a sniveling coward. He'd killed Lewis in self-defense. He'd had no other choice. But obviously, killing someone in cold blood was something he couldn't stomach. He wouldn't last long in the criminal world.

"At least he didn't gag us," Brita said, sounding near tears.

"He probably figured we were too far away for anyone to hear us if we yelled." Vivian shifted her body as the hard crate dug in behind her knees. Remembering Brita's silent apology to her earlier, she added, "I'm sorry. That man is evil. I know you love him but—"

Brita's bitter laugh interrupted her. "Not anymore. Not after this. I was pretending, going along with him so he wouldn't shoot us both. I was hoping to call the cops once I got the chance. If I hadn't helped him, you could be dead by now." She uttered a trembling sigh. "Now it looks like we're both going to die."

"Not if I can help it." Immensely relieved that Brita wasn't the enemy after all, Vivian tested the ropes. Her arms were trapped, but she could move her hands. "He made one mistake. They usually do."

"Who's 'they'?"

"Criminals." Vivian smiled in the dark. "It's the mistakes they make that bring them down. And this was a big one. We're going to get out of here."

Brita sounded unconvinced as she muttered, "How?"

"Chris should have made sure we couldn't reach each other. Sit closer to me."

"What?"

"Closer." Vivian wriggled her fingers. "If we get close enough, I should be able to untie you."

"Seriously?" The crate creaked as Brita thumped her way closer. Her shoulder collided with Vivian. "How's this?"

"Okay, I think." Her fingers searched for Brita's rope but could feel only bare arm. "You have to get lower, or I have to get higher," she said, struggling to raise her hand.

"Wait." Brita grunted, and the crate creaked again. Vivian's eyes were beginning to adjust to the darkness now. Faint light seeped in through cracks in the siding, enough for her to see outlines. Brita was on the floor at her feet.

Vivian strained forward as far as she could, hope rising when she touched the rope binding Brita's arms. It took a lot more prodding and poking before she finally located the knots. Many minutes later, with fingers stinging and raw, she managed at last to loosen the rope enough for Brita to wriggle out of her shackles.

As she watched the woman fumbling with the ropes around her ankles, Vivian wondered for a tense moment if Brita would simply break her way out of the shack and leave her behind.

Once she had freed herself, however, Brita turned to Vivian and quickly untied her. "Now," she said, as the ropes fell to the floor, "maybe we can get out of here."

That possibility was quickly eliminated as they both heaved their shoulders at the door. All that accomplished was what would undoubtedly be spectacular bruises by the next day.

If they made it to the next day.

After several more frantic assaults on the door, Brita finally gave up. "We're going to die," she said, slumping back down on the crate. "Chris is going to get someone to kill us. I know it. He'll be here soon." She burst into tears, wailing, "I don't want to die. I'm too young!"

Vivian felt like crying too, but she managed to pull herself together. "From what I've heard, the gang is situated in Portland. It will take someone at least a couple of hours to make it down here. That's if Chris even called them. He could have simply taken off, figuring on getting out of town and leaving us to die of starvation."

Brita stopped crying. "You think?" She sniffed and swiped her hand across her nose. "That could be worse than being shot. At least that would be quick."

"We're not going to die." Vivian wished she felt as confident as she sounded. She eyed the walls of the shack, squinting at the thin strips of light filtering through. "These walls are not soundproof. I think if we both yell loud enough for long enough, eventually someone will hear us."

Brita's face was in shadow, but Vivian could hear the hope rising in her voice. "Then let's do it." She raised her voice and yelled, "Help!"

Vivian took a deep breath, opened her mouth, and started shouting, "Help us!"

Their screams echoed around the empty shack, bouncing off the walls and hopefully, seeping through the cracks. Vivian tried not to dwell on the fact that eventually their voices would give out. In spite of her assurances to Brita, she was well aware that their chances of being heard were slim to none. This was the off season for visitors, and it was doubtful that anyone would be walking along the beach this late in the day.

Soon it would be dark, destroying any chance of someone hearing them. Her voice faltered, leaving Brita to yell alone.

In the next instant, she scolded herself. She was a survivor. She wasn't going down without a fight. She had no doubt that once Jenna and Gracie realized she was missing, they would alert the authorities. They would also probably call Hal. People would be looking for her. They might even come this far along the coast looking for her.

With renewed hope, she opened her mouth again and bellowed, "Anyone out there! Help us!"

* * *

Messina checked his watch, irritated to see only half an hour had passed since he'd last looked at it. He couldn't ever remember time passing so slowly. He was anxious to get out of the office with its ringing phones, raised voices, and the constant coming and going of the officers.

He wanted to be home, showered and dressed, making the salad for his visitor. He made an effort to curb his impatience. He had to wait for Brady to come in with his latest report, and then he could call it a day. After that, he'd have the entire evening to enjoy being with Jenna.

He didn't know where their date would lead them. Jenna had made it clear she wanted to take things slowly, and he was fine with that. Neither one of them could be certain of their feelings at this stage, but he was sure looking forward to finding out if what they had was real, or whether it was just two lonely people connecting.

Tomorrow he would visit the tearoom and talk to Vivian again about the customer who bought the Big Ben model. Or maybe he would just call her. It depended on how things went that evening. Right then, all he wanted to do was concentrate on that.

He looked up to see Brady ambling toward him, a bottle of water in his hand. Pausing at Messina's desk, he took a swig of water. "So, did you get my report?"

Messina glanced at his computer. He'd been so deep in thought he hadn't noticed the message come in. He opened the email and scanned the report. A missing dog, two fender benders, and a noise complaint. "Not much here."

"Nope." Brady rested his hip on the corner of the desk. "Nice to have a quiet day after the last couple of weeks. This is more normal for us."

"Thank the good Lord." Messina shut down his computer and got up from his chair. "I get to go home and relax again."

"Yeah, me too." Brady raised the bottle at him. "Have a nice night."

Messina smiled. "You too."

He watched Brady saunter across the room to the door, nodding at another officer as he passed by him. Jenna had suggested that they double-date with Brady and Gracie. Messina had grave concerns about that. For one thing, he wasn't sure he wanted to share his private life with his sergeant. He was sure, however, that he didn't want company during his time with Jenna.

He'd managed to evade the idea that evening, but if Jenna brought it up again, he'd have to have a discussion about it. He shoved his chair under his desk and picked up his keys. Now he could go home and get ready for his date.

At that moment, the phone on his desk rang. He glared at it, his heart sinking. Usually, if a call came through to his desk, it meant a delay of some sort. Probably the chief, wanting to know more about the drug bust. *Not now.* Not when he was on the brink of an adventure that could change his life.

For a second or two, he considered ignoring it. If the call had come in five minutes later, he would have left already. But he would have to go by the chief's office to leave, in clear view through the windows. He would have to answer the call.

He dragged out his chair and slumped down on it, then reached for the phone. Slapping it to his ear, he uttered a terse "Messina."

When Jenna's voice answered him, for a crushing moment he thought she was calling to cancel their date. But then he realized by her frantic tone that something was wrong. She talked so fast he couldn't understand her. "Whoa there! Slow down. Take a deep breath and tell me what happened."

"It's Vivian," Jenna said, her voice breaking now. "She's missing. I'm afraid something bad has happened to her."

"What do you mean, she's missing?"

"She left the tearoom around one this afternoon and said she'd be back in an hour or so. She didn't come back, and she's not answering her phone. She's in trouble. I know it."

Messina let out his breath. For a while there he'd thought he had another tragedy on his hands. "Okay, calm down. There could be a dozen reasons why she's not answering her phone. Maybe she lost it. Or she could be somewhere where she doesn't want to answer it. It's only been five hours. That's not long enough for someone to be counted as missing."

Jenna's voice rose. "Don't tell me to calm down. You don't understand. She's been investigating Lewis Trenton's murder. She left this afternoon to go on an errand. She didn't say where she was going, but I'm pretty sure she was going to question one of the suspects."

Messina closed his eyes, propped an elbow up on his desk, and buried his face in his hand. "I should have known. What the hell was she doing going after a killer on her own?"

"Well, she wasn't on her own all the time." Now Jenna sounded uncomfortable. "Gracie and I have been helping her question people."

Of course they had. "Uh-huh. So who was she going to talk to this afternoon?"

"That's the problem. We don't know. All Vivian said was that she was going into Newport. There are three people she's been talking to in Newport. I don't know which one she was going to see."

"I see. Well, give me the names of the three people, and I'll check them out."

"You will?" Jenna's voice was weak with relief. "Thank you, Tony. Can I come with you?"

There was nothing he'd like more, but common sense prevailed. "I can't take you on an official investigation, Jenna. Where are you?"

"I'm still at the tearoom. Gracie and I have been waiting for Vivian to come back. I know she would have been back long before this. She would never leave us alone all afternoon unless she couldn't come back. I know something bad has happened to her."

"Alright, give me the names and addresses."

"I don't know the addresses. Vivian has them on her phone."

He sighed. "Okay. I can look them up. Just give me the names." He scribbled them down as she gave them to him.

"Brita Stewart—she has a condo on the beach. Then there's Connie. I don't know her last name, but she lives in the Cozy Nest Retirement Home. Then Noah's father." Again, her voice rose to a wail. "I don't his name!"

Messina pinched his lips together. "So, who is Noah?"

"He's Connie's grandson. She gave him the Big Ben, but Vivian talked to his father about it, and he was so mean to her."

"Okay, so this Connie can give me his name and address."

"Yes, she gave it to us. I can't remember . . . Oh, wait—I remember the street. I think it was Larch Street. I don't remember the number."

"Okay. Just sit tight, and I'll call you as soon as—"

"Russell! That's Noah's last name."

Messina nodded, impressed by her recall. "Russell. Got it. I'll call as soon as I know something."

"I'm sorry, Tony. I was looking forward to seeing you tonight."

"Wait, don't cancel on me just yet. If I can get this wrapped up in an hour or so, we can still have dinner at my place."

She sounded doubtful when she answered. "Okay. Just find her, Tony. That's all I want right now."

She hung up, and he slammed the phone down. If he found that woman alive and well, he'd have a stern word with her about chasing after killers. Not only did she put herself in danger, but her actions threatened the lives of her two assistants. Jenna had almost died the last time Vivian had gone hunting for a murderer.

That had to stop. Now. That is, if the woman survived this mess.

Chapter Sixteen

The pale light no longer crept through the cracks of the shack. Vivian stared into the darkness, cursing herself for having messed up things so badly. Now that the daylight had gone, their chances of being rescued had sunk to zero.

Brita's voice had given out first, and Vivian's soon after. That was hours ago.

Vivian cleared her throat. It still stung but didn't feel quite so raw. She hadn't heard from Brita since they quit yelling. It was time to test their voices. "I'm sorry," she started to say, but the words came out like a rasping buzz saw. Once more, she cleared her throat. "I'm sorry," she said again. "This is all my fault."

Brita's hoarse words drifted out of the darkness. "No, it's not. It's mine. I should never have gotten involved with Chris. I always had a feeling he was hiding something from me."

"You saved my life. I'll never be able to thank you enough for that."

"Don't thank me yet. Someone could be here any minute to wipe us both out."

The same thought was terrifying Vivian, but she wasn't going to admit it. "I don't think anyone will come until the middle of the night, when there's less chance of being seen."

"I hope you're right. Though it's dark outside now. No one will be walking on the beach in the dark."

"Sometimes people light bonfires on the beach at night."

"Not when it's this cold. My teeth are chattering."

Vivian had to agree. The cold, damp air crept into her bones, making her shiver. She needed to talk, to take her mind off her misery. "You had no idea Chris was fencing for a gang of thieves?"

"None. If I'd known that, I would have dumped him in a second." Brita uttered a shuddering sigh that echoed around the room. "The saddest thing about all this is that no one will know I'm missing. I have friends, but even if they called, Chris has my phone. He'll probably tell them some story and they won't know anything until our dead bodies are found."

"Well, I do have people who will miss me. My two assistants are probably frantic by now. I'm sure they would have called the police to let them know I'm missing." And Hal, she added silently. Maybe he was searching for her too. The thought gave her just a tiny flicker of hope.

"If we ever get out of this," Brita said, "I'm going to sell the condo and go back to Salem. I don't want to ever see Newport again."

"I can understand that." If she ever got out of this, Vivian promised herself, she would never chase criminals again. All she seemed to do was get other people into trouble along with herself. First Jenna, now Brita. Next time it could be Hal. She couldn't bear the thought of that.

She stirred, strengthened by a new resolve. She *was* going to get them out of there. Some way, somehow. "Let's give the door another try," she said, getting to her feet. "If we both throw our bodies at it, we may be able to break it down. It didn't look that strong. At the very least, it will warm us up a bit."

"You're right." Brita jumped up from the crate. "Let's do it. Anything's better than sitting here waiting to be killed."

"Okay." Vivian squared her shoulders. "On the count of three. And if you have any voice left at all, scream as loudly as you can. If we have to die, at least we'll go down fighting. Ready?"

"Ready."

"Give it everything you've got," Vivian ordered, then took a deep breath. "One, two, *three*!" She hurled herself at the door, screaming as loud as her voice would allow.

Brita landed against the door with her. It creaked, groaned and held solid.

Vivian rubbed her bruised shoulder, braced herself and called out, "Again! One, two, *three*!"

They both crashed against the door, and this time Brita's scream came out more as a croak. Still the door held, and she fell back, clutching her throat. "It's no use. It's dark out there. No one will be around to hear us."

Vivian shook her head. Part of her knew Brita was right, but she wasn't about to give up until she dropped to the floor. "One more time?"

"Okay, but I can't yell anymore."

Vivian shook off the panic rising in her chest. "That's okay. I think I can give one more shout." Her throat felt raw, and her lungs ached. She thought about Hal and what she would be missing if she died. Her own voice sounded weaker as she called out, "One, two—"

She paused, wondering if she'd really heard what she thought she'd heard.

"Three?" Brita's voice was high with concern.

"No, wait." Her heart beginning to pound even more, Vivian strained her ears. Hope leapt as she heard it again. A faint, but distinctive barking of a dog. *Felix?*

She couldn't be sure it was Felix, but she summoned every bit of breath she had left, prayed her vocal chords would hold out one more time, leaned against the door and screamed, "Help! Felix, help!"

An answering bark brought tears gushing from her eyes. He was closer now. She turned to Brita. "It's okay. I think my dog is here. Which means someone is probably with him." Her words came out gruff and broken, but Brita's hand came out of the dark, groping for hers.

"Please, God, you're right. "

The dog barked again, and Vivian started crashing her fists on the door, her voice reduced to a squeak.

Brita joined her until the heavenly sound of Hal's deep voice answered her. "Hold on—I'll get you out of there."

Vivian was crying now, deep sobs that came from way down inside her. The sound of breaking, tearing wood was music to her ears, and then suddenly, magically, the door flew open.

Felix bounded forward, leaping and whimpering in his joy. Holding back her sobs, she hugged him, murmuring, "Good boy," over and over, then looked beyond him to the most beautiful sight she'd ever laid eyes upon.

Hal stood holding Felix's leash in one hand, with moonlight flashing off the vicious-looking hunting knife in the other. "Thank God," he said, his own voice breaking.

"You found Felix." Vivian rose to her feet.

"I did. I went looking for you when Jenna called me to say you were missing. She told me about the condo and I spotted your car outside. I had to call the cops to come open it so I could get Felix out."

Regardless of the weapon in his hand, Vivian flung herself forward and fell into his arms. "You saved us! Thank you, thank you, thank you!"

He held her, murmuring soft words of comfort, until she heard him say, "Hi. I'm Hal. Are you okay?"

She finally remembered Brita and pulled herself away from him. She barely recognized her own voice as she croaked, "I'm sorry. This is Brita. She saved my life too. That's twice in one day."

"Thank you so much for rescuing us." Brita rushed over to Hal and hugged him.

Hal looked confused as Brita stepped back. "I want to hear the whole story. But first I have to call Jenna." He pulled his phone from his pocket. "She's going nuts worrying about you."

Vivian nodded, thankful that she didn't have to say anything else just then.

Hal spoke rapidly into the phone at his ear. "She's okay," he said. "Felix found her. I'm bringing her home."

Those words brought more tears to Vivian's eyes. She couldn't see her new friend's face clearly, but she could tell Brita was also silently crying. She grabbed her hand and gave it a squeeze before letting it go again.

"No," Hal said into the phone. "She was locked up in a shack on the beach. I was driving along the coast road with the windows down. I was going slow, hoping to see some sign of her, but then Felix started barking so I pulled over. He must have heard her yelling and pounding on the door."

He paused to listen to Jenna, then said, "Yes. I let him out of the car, and he led me down here. Call Messina for me, will you?

Let him know she and her friend are okay." He paused again. "Yes, Brita's with her." Again, the pause. "No, I don't know. We'll get the whole story when we get home. Right now, I need to get them out of here."

"Yes, you do," Vivian wheezed. "Chris said he was sending gang members down to kill us."

She couldn't tell his expression, but she could hear the tension in his voice when he asked, "And where does this Chris guy fit in to all this?"

"He's been living with Brita in her condo. She didn't know until now that he's the fence for the robbery gang. He killed Lewis Trenton."

Hal's tone grew even more assertive. "You and I are going to have a long talk when this is over."

She wasn't sure if that was good or bad news. What she did know was that she loved this man. And that was enough for now. Except she was dying for a cup of tea.

By the time she'd struggled up the path to Hal's car, she was out of breath and exhausted. She couldn't remember ever feeling so weak. It had to be the stress, and all that pounding on the door had taken a toll.

"I can't go back to the condo," Brita said as she climbed into the back of Hal's car with an excited Felix. "Chris could still be there."

"Not if he's got any sense." Hal made sure Vivian was settled on the front seat before taking his place behind the wheel. "He's probably hotfooted it out of town by now."

"You can stay with me tonight, Brita." Vivian cleared her throat. "Though you'll have to share the bed with me. We can decide what to do tomorrow."

"Neither of you is going to stay there tonight," Hal said firmly. "We can't take any chances until that lowlife has been apprehended."

"What about the robbers?" Brita asked, sounding scared.

"That was probably just a threat to scare you. You can't identify any of the gang members, so they would have no reason to get rid of you. I can't see any of them committing a double murder just to keep a fence safe. If anything, they're more likely to go after him so he can't tip off the cops."

"I hope you're right." Vivian slumped back on her seat. "So, what do you suggest?"

"The first thing we have to do is talk to Messina. He'll most likely be waiting for you at the tearoom. Then we have to find somewhere for you both to stay until we know it's safe for you to go home."

"It will have to be somewhere that will let me take Felix."

"I was going to suggest the Blue Surf, though I don't know if they allow pets."

Vivian felt a pang of dismay. The Blue Surf Hotel had been the scene of the crime when the body of Jenna's ex-husband had been thrown from one if its balconies. It was not a memory she wanted to resurrect. "It's a nice hotel, but I'm sure we can find something a little less pretentious."

"It's the safest place I can think of right now. Unless you want to go out of town?"

Vivian shook her head. "No, I can't do that. I have a business to run."

"I don't think Chris knows where Vivian lives," Brita said. "I never told him you owned the tearoom."

"He may have overheard me telling you that first day." Vivian closed her eyes, enjoying the luxury of sitting on something infinitely more comfortable than the hard crate she'd endured for hours. "He must have been listening to us. He heard me mention Lewis before he came into the room."

"Okay," Hal said, "we'll discuss all that later. Right now, the important thing is to tell Messina everything you know so they can go after this guy."

Vivian was half asleep by the time they arrived back at the tearoom. Jenna and Gracie were standing out on the sidewalk, talking to Messina and Brady. The moment they caught sight of Hal's car approaching, both women frantically waved while Gracie jumped up and down in her excitement.

Hal brought the car to a halt in front of them, and Jenna tugged on Vivian's door. Felix whined to be let out, and Vivian handed Brita his leash before struggling to get out of the car.

Jenna immediately engulfed her in a bear hug, then let her go so that Gracie could hug her too.

"We were so worried about you," Gracie said, holding onto Vivian as if she was afraid to let her go.

Seeing tears in the young woman's eyes, Vivian felt like crying again too. How lucky she was to have such loyal friends.

"I hate to break up this touching scene," Messina said, stepping closer, "but time is of the essence. I need every bit of information you can give me so we can catch the guy who did this to you."

"His name is Chris Bailey. I can give you his car's make and license plate," Brita said.

Messina pulled his phone from his pocket and treated her to one of his rare smiles. "Lady, you just made my day." He thrust the phone to his ear. "Put this out on alert," he ordered the unseen officer. He thrust the phone at Brita. "Here you go. Give him the information."

Brita took the phone and gave the cop the make and license plate of Chris's car. "I just want him behind bars," Brita said, handing the phone back to Messina. "Even that's too good for him. I'd like to throw him in the ocean and let the sharks get him."

"I second that." Vivian smiled at her, then stooped down to pet a happy Felix. "As for you, buddy, you deserve a whole plate of treats. If it hadn't been for you, we might have died in that horrible hut."

"I'm probably going to get a bill for the damage," Hal said, as he looked at Messina. "I pretty much destroyed the door getting them out. It was padlocked and I didn't have a key."

"Don't worry about it," Messina assured him. "Brady will take care of that, right?"

"Yes, sir." Brady tore his gaze away from Gracie. "I'll have to find out who owns that shack."

"Chris said it belongs to the owners of the house up above it," Brita said. "Then again, I wouldn't trust anything that jerk said."

"I hope they won't sue me." Hal looked worried.

Messina laid a hand on his shoulder. "Like I said, the Misty Bay Police Department will take care of it. Right Brady?"

"Right, sir."

Messina turned back to Hal. "You rescued these women, and that's all that matters. Great job."

"Most of the credit goes to Felix." Hal bent down to rub Felix's ear. "He led me right to them."

"He's a clever dog, that's for sure," Vivian said, smiling down at him.

"It's amazing that he heard you." Gracie stooped to pat the dog's head.

"I'm glad I had him with me." Hal shook his head. "I didn't hear a thing. Luckily, dogs can hear at least twice as well as humans. I kept the windows down in the car, just in case. It paid off."

"Well, we're so grateful to you both," Vivian said, and Brita nodded her head in agreement. "I don't know how long we could have survived in that hut, even if the robbers didn't come to finish us off. We had no food or water, and it was so cold in there." She shivered at the memory. "Let's go inside. I'm dying for a cup of tea."

Jenna laughed. "Are you sure you wouldn't rather have a glass of wine? A very large glass of wine?"

Vivian smiled. "Maybe later. But a cup of tea got the Brits through two world wars, and tea will get my nerves back in shape right now. They've taken quite a beating."

"Come." Hal put his arm around her. "You look exhausted. You need to sit down."

"Just what every woman loves to hear from her man," Vivian murmured, allowing him to guide her to the door.

"I'm going to need the whole story from you both," Messina said as he and Brady followed them inside.

The two cops sat down at one of the tables in the tearoom, where Messina took out his phone. "I'm going to record this," he said, laying it on the white tablecloth.

Vivian motioned to Brita to sit down with them, and took the last chair.

"I'll make the tea," Jenna said, heading for the kitchen.

"I'll help her." Gracie followed Jenna while Hal took a seat at the next table.

"Now then," Messina said, "tell me everything that happened, starting with when you arrived at Brita's condo."

Vivian cleared her throat again and began recounting the moments that led up to Chris brandishing a gun and admitting he killed Lewis Trenton. "That's when I knew I was in trouble."

She ignored Hal's faint groan as Brita said, "I couldn't believe it. I thought I knew Chris. I had no idea he was such a monster."

Messina looked at Vivian. "What made you focus on him out of all the people you suspected?"

Vivian covered a yawn with her hand before murmuring, "Excuse me. He mentioned that Lewis used an outhouse. I couldn't find any mention of it in the news, so I figured he must have been to the cabin. Also, I noticed he was limping the first time I visited Brita. It occurred to me that the fence must have had some kind of delay if he had to hide the diamonds."

"Yeah," Brita said, butting in. "I told Vivian that Chris had to postpone a business trip because he'd sprained his ankle." She slumped back on her chair. "I just can't believe I lived with that toad all this time and never knew that he was a murderer. What's wrong with me?"

"I'm sure he went to great pains to hide his profession from you," Messina assured her. "You can't blame yourself for someone else's misdeeds."

Vivian smiled. She liked the man for saying that. So did Jenna, judging from the way she gazed at the detective as if she'd just discovered gold.

"Well, I guess I have all I need for now." Messina got up from his chair. "Just sit tight, and I'll let you know how things go down."

Jenna and Gracie appeared in the doorway at that moment, both carrying trays loaded with teapots, cups and saucers, and leftover pastries.

"You're not leaving, are you?" Jenna laid her tray on the table. "I made enough tea for all of us."

"As a matter of fact," Messina said, giving her a long look, "I have a dinner date tonight."

Jenna's eyes widened. "But I thought . . . it's kind of late . . . I'm not dressed or anything."

Messina held his stern expression. "Have you eaten?"

"No." Jenna shot Vivian a quick glance. "I was too worried to eat."

Vivian felt a stab of guilt. "I'm sorry, Jenna."

"No, it's fine." Jenna looked back at Messina. "I'd love to have dinner with you, if you don't mind how I look."

"You look real good to me."

Vivian had to hide a smile. This was a side of Messina she hadn't seen before. She liked it.

Brady loudly cleared his throat as he got up from his chair. "How about you, Gracie?"

Still holding her tray, Gracie gave him a startled look. "Huh?"

Brady's face began to warm. "Uh, I was wondering, since none of us have eaten and all, if you'd like to grab a bite to eat with me?"

Gracie stared at him as if he'd just offered to take her on a rocket to Mars.

Vivian was beginning to feel sorry for him as Messina and Jenna murmured goodnight and took off into the night.

Hal stood up and took the tray out of Gracie's hands. "Go ahead," he said, and gave Vivian a meaningful glance. "We'll drink this in the kitchen."

"Of course." Vivian scrambled out of her chair and led the way, with Brita following behind. "I need to take Felix upstairs," Vivian said. "He's not supposed to be here in the kitchen."

Hal put the tray down on the kitchen table. "How about you both coming over to my place? Felix too. I can make tea there, and we can decide where you'll sleep tonight."

The front doorbell jingled, and Vivian exchanged a look with Hal. Brita looked surprised. "Did Gracie leave with Brady?"

Vivian walked over to the door and peeked into the tearoom. "Yep." She walked back to them, smiling. "This is all turning out very well."

"For everyone except me." Brita sank down on a chair. "I have to sell the condo and find somewhere else to live."

Vivian yawned again. "We'll talk about that in the morning." She looked at Hal. "I'm sorry, Hal, but I'm wiped out. Can we just go straight to the hotel? We can get room service there, and we'll both think better after a good night's sleep. I'll have to get up early tomorrow so I can get back here to get my baking done."

"You're right." Hal stooped to pat Felix. "Why don't you let me keep this guy tonight? I'll take you both to the hotel and pick you up tomorrow."

Vivian would rather have taken Felix with her, but she had to admit, leaving him with Hal was the best idea. "Well, okay. But I'm going to miss him."

Felix whined, as if he understood every word.

"I'll just run up and grab a few things." Vivian turned to Brita. "Do you want to stop by the condo before we go to the hotel?"

Brita shuddered. "I don't want to go anywhere near that place until I know Chris is gone."

"Well, I'll find something you can wear for now." Vivian sighed. "Though it won't be your size."

Brita uttered a wry laugh. "That's the least of my problems right now."

"Maybe we can get Messina to go along with you to the condo tomorrow," Hal suggested.

"That's a great idea." Vivian walked over to the door leading to her apartment. "Meanwhile, I'll see what I can find. I'll pick up some things for Felix too."

"I'll help you." Hal followed her to the door.

"I'll wait here," Brita said, eyeing the pastries.

"Help yourself to whatever you want," Vivian said, then headed for the stairs, with Hal following behind and Felix springing ahead of her.

Inside her apartment, Vivian breathed in a sigh of contentment. For hours that afternoon, she'd wondered if she'd ever see her home again. Or if she'd ever cuddle Felix again, or hug Hal. All of it had become so much more precious to her now that she had come so close to losing it all.

Watching Felix toss a ball around, she knew she could never let him go. He'd already lost one owner. She couldn't put him through that again. Somehow, she would have to work out some arrangement so that he wasn't left alone for much of the day.

"Are you okay?"

Startled out of her thoughts, she smiled at Hal. "I'm more than okay. I'm ecstatic. I thought I was never coming back here. I kept worrying about what would happen to Felix if that happened."

"And me," Hal said, his voice tightening. "I would have been devastated."

Guilt made her squirm. "I'm so sorry, Hal. It was stupid of me, I know. I should have gone straight to Messina. I just wanted to be sure about my suspicions first."

He stepped closer and grabbed her arms. "You promised me."

"Yes, I know." She gazed up at him, silently pleading with him to forgive her. "I swear I will never do something that stupid again."

"Until the next time."

She shook her head. "From now on, I'll leave catching criminals to the police."

He stared into her eyes, making her heart beat faster. "I hope so, because I don't know what I'd do if I lost you now."

His kiss was fierce and sweet, and banished everything from her mind except for that moment. She had found her man, and from now on, she was going to do everything she could to make him happy.

Chapter Seventeen

While Vivian packed a large travel bag with underwear, extra clothes, and toiletries, Hal kept Felix company in the living room. When she walked in there later, carrying the bag, Hal was on the floor with the dog, playfully boxing with him.

Vivian laughed as Felix reared up on his hind legs and pawed at Hal's face, narrowly missing his nose. "He's going to win," she said as she set the bag down on the floor.

"Only because I let him." Hal sat up and eyed the bag. "How long are you planning to stay at the hotel?"

"Just for the night." Vivian felt a pang of anxiety. "I have to come back here tomorrow. I have bookings for afternoon tea."

"It doesn't mean you have to spend the night here."

Vivian sank down on the couch. "I'm not going to hide in a hotel for the rest of my life."

Hal slowly stood up and sat down next to her. "You won't have to do that. The chances are good that Chris is somewhere in California, heading for the border. But at least for the next few days, you'll be safer in the hotel."

Vivian sighed. "I thought I was doing the right thing, trying to clear Lewis's name. All I've done is cause a lot of trouble for myself and others."

Hal put his arm around her and pulled her closer. "You exposed a dangerous criminal, and you did clear Trenton's name. You did everything you set out to do, and an innocent man will lie in peace because of you. I think that deserves nothing but praise and gratitude."

She looked at him through a haze of tears. "You really are the nicest man I've ever met."

He smiled. "Nicest? Not most handsome, most intelligent, or most entertaining?"

"All of those things." She leaned in to kiss him. "Thank you. And now we'd better get downstairs, or Brita will be getting nervous about being alone down there."

"Right." Hal got up and picked up the bag. "Let's go."

At the word "go," Felix leapt toward the door.

Hal shook his head. "That dog understands everything we say."

"Of course he does." Vivian picked up his leash from the couch. "He's a Wainwright now. We're exceptional."

"With that I can agree."

She laughed as she led him downstairs, although she didn't feel much like laughing. She didn't want to spend one night in the hotel, much less a few nights. If she'd had her way, she would have insisted on staying in her apartment and taking her chances with Chris and the jewel thieves. After all, Hal was probably right. Once Chris found out they had escaped, he would most likely leave town, and the robbers would have no reason to come after her or Brita.

But she knew Hal wouldn't sleep if she stayed at home. And Brita would be more comfortable in a hotel. She would just have to put up with it for a while, until they both felt safe enough to go on with their lives.

Brita still sat at the table when Vivian walked into the kitchen. "I ate one of these," she said, pointing at the plate of pastries. "It was delicious. I would have eaten all of them, except I know we're going to order room service at the hotel."

"We are," Vivian agreed. She looked at Hal. "Have you eaten? You could join us at the hotel."

"Thanks, but I grabbed a burger before I went hunting for you." Hal looked down at Felix. "I don't want to leave this guy alone tonight. I'll just drop you off at the hotel, okay?"

"Sure. That's fine." Vivian leaned down to pet Felix. "I'll miss you tonight, buddy. You be a good boy, okay?"

Felix whined and licked her hand.

"He's adorable." Brita leaned over to pet him too. "He was letting me hug him in the back of the car on the way here." She was also rewarded with a lick on her hand.

"Okay, then." Hal looked at his watch. "We'd better get going before it's too late for you to order room service."

Brita jumped up. "I'm ready."

"Me too." Vivian ushered everyone out ahead of her and locked the door of the tearoom before climbing into Hal's car. Minutes later they were parked outside the entrance of the Blue Surf Hotel.

"I'll come in with you," Hal said, cutting the engine. "Just to make sure you get settled okay."

It was on the tip of Vivian's tongue to inform him she'd stayed in hotels before, but she caught it just in time. She wasn't used to someone caring for her. Long before Martin died, she'd spent so much time alone she'd become used to doing everything for herself. Now she had someone eager to take care of her. It would take some getting used to, but she had to admit, she liked it.

Much to her surprise and relief, Hal had apparently called ahead to book a room for them. He must have done that while she was packing in her bedroom, she thought, grateful again for this man's consideration.

After checking in, Vivian gave Hal a hug. "Thanks for saving our lives. You'll always be my hero."

"I hope I'll be more than that." Hal's kiss was brief. "Have a good night's sleep and call me in the morning, okay?"

"I will. Though I'll get up at the crack of dawn. I have pastries to bake."

He winced. "Maybe I'll call you."

"Good idea. You'll have to call the tearoom phone. Chris took my cell phone." She frowned. "I wonder if the cops could trace him through that."

Hal shook his head. "If he's got any brains at all, he'll have tossed it."

"Mine too," Brita said, sounding worried. "I just hope he's far away by now."

Hal turned to her. "I'm sure he is. Try not to worry. You'll be safe with us."

Brita nodded. "I know. Thank you. For everything."

Hal smiled. "I don't need your thanks. I'm just happy Felix heard you, and I was able to help. See you both in the morning." He ambled off and disappeared through the door.

"He's a good man," Brita said as Vivian led the way to the elevators.

"He sure is. I'm discovering more of that every time I see him." Vivian yawned as the door slid silently to a close.

"Hang onto him. Good men are tough to find."

She sounded dejected, and Vivian reached for her hand and gave it a squeeze. "You'll find the right one. Probably when you least expect it."

Brita summoned a tired smile. "I hope so."

The elevator jerked to a halt at the third floor. Their room was halfway down the hallway, and Vivian yawned again as she slid the key card into the slot. Opening the door, she murmured a soft "Wow," as she stepped into the room.

Rose-pink comforters covered the twin beds, and across the room, a gray couch and armchair invited guests to enjoy the ocean view from the floor-to-ceiling windows. A flat screen TV adorned one wall, next to a large painting of Haystack Rock.

"This is really nice," Brita said as she followed Vivian into the room.

Remembering the luxurious condo Brita lived in, Vivian considered that high praise. Sinking onto the side of a bed, she reached for the menu. "Let's order room service, then I'll unpack."

Brita joined her on the bed, and they scrutinized the menu.

"I like the smoked salmon Caesar salad," Vivian said.

"Sounds good." Brita scanned the menu again. "How about adding the cheese board?"

"Wonderful." Vivian picked up the bedside phone. "I've been promising myself a vacation for months. This is a good substitute, though it will take months to pay it off my credit card."

"Well, I'll share the cost, of course," Brita said. "Though we should get the Misty Bay Police Department to pay for it."

Vivian laughed. "Don't hold your breath on that one." A voice on the phone interrupted her. "We'd like the Caesar salad and cheese board," she told the server. She hesitated for a moment, then added, "And a bottle of chardonnay."

"Good thinking," Brita murmured.

"We might as well go whole hog." Vivian replaced the phone. You only live once, right?"

Brita's smile faded. "We almost didn't. If it hadn't been for Hal and Felix . . ."

"Let's not think about that." Vivian got up from the bed. "I'm going to unpack. Not that there's a lot in here." She unzipped the bag. "I did find a pair of jammies for you." She shook out the primrose-and-daisy-covered fabric. "They're a bit dowdy for you, but comfortable."

"They're perfect." Brita took them with a smile. "Thank you."

"You're welcome." She unpacked the rest of the contents and stashed the bag in the closet while Brita wandered around the room, inspecting the pamphlets on the coffee table and the view from the window.

"It's too bad it's dark," she said as Vivian came out of the bathroom. "I can't see the ocean."

"It'll be dark when I get up tomorrow too." Vivian sat down on the couch and leaned back with a sigh.

Brita shuddered. "I can't imagine getting up every morning at six. I'd be a zombie by the middle of the day."

"You get used to it." Vivian yawned. "Though I must say, I don't have any trouble falling asleep at night."

"Well, I'll get up with you. I'd like to help in the tearoom tomorrow if you'll let me. I love to bake, and I have to know how you make those delicious pastries."

"I'd like that very much." Vivian gave her a tired smile. "I don't usually give away my recipes, but I might make an exception for you."

"That would be fantastic! I promise I won't give them to anyone else." Brita sat on the couch, slipped off her shoes, and curled up her legs. "This is nice. It was good of Hal to bring us here. How did you guys meet?"

Vivian smiled. "I'd just opened the Willow Pattern, more than two years ago now, and he came in for afternoon tea. I was in the kitchen, making up sandwiches, and he sent Gracie in with a note, telling me how much he enjoyed the scones. It was so sweet, I had to go meet the guy. We've been friends ever since."

"But you're more than friends now, right?"

"That's only recent." Vivian stared down at her hands. "Though I guess the feelings have been there a while. I think we were both trying to ignore them."

"Why? You guys were meant for each other. Anyone can see that."

"I think we were afraid to get too close to someone. We didn't want to go through the pain of losing again."

"You lost someone?"

"Yes. I was married to a prosecuting attorney for more than thirty-eight years. He died suddenly from a heart attack. It was the most painful period of my life."

"I'm sorry." Brita sighed. "That must have been hard."

"It was. But it was because of it that I opened the tearoom. My mother was from England, and she was a wonderful baker. I grew up devouring her pastries. She took me to afternoon tea in Victoria, Canada, when I was small, and I fell in love with the whole experience. Ever since then, I've wanted to own my own tearoom. After my mother died, I kept thinking about the recipes she'd left behind and how much people would enjoy her creations."

"They certainly are delicious." Brita closed her eyes. "I'll have to visit sometimes and have afternoon tea."

"Do that!" Vivian turned to her. "I'd love to keep in touch."

"Me too. So, what about Hal? Did he lose his wife?"

"Yes." Vivian sat back again. "He's had a couple of traumas in his life. He was a firefighter and got caught in a wildfire with two of his friends. He escaped, but they didn't. I think he still blames himself for that. He was injured and had to retire from the fire bureau. That was when he bought the pet supplies shop down the street from the Willow Pattern. His wife died of cancer shortly after that."

"Wow," Brita said softly. "You guys sure have had it rough."

"So have you. You lost both your parents. That must have been devastating."

"Yeah, it was." Brita started picking imaginary crumbs off her pants. "It took me a long time to accept the fact they weren't coming home. I still wake up sometimes and imagine I can hear them talking."

"I'm sorry." Vivian reached for her hand. "You are so young to have had to deal with that kind of ordeal. And what you went through today was devastating. I hope it doesn't have a lasting effect on you."

Brita shrugged. "It turned out okay. One good thing came out of it. I met you."

Warmed by the sentiment, Vivian squeezed her hand. "Aw, that's sweet."

"I don't have any older friends, and I miss my mom."

"Then I'll be happy to—" The tap on the door cut off her words.

"Room service." Brita jumped up from the couch. "I'll get it."

She hurried over to the door, and Vivian lazily stretched her feet out in front of her. This was luxury, she told herself. She could get used to it very quickly.

She heard the door open and Brita say, "Hi!" But then her greeting was immediately followed by a gasp, and the door flew wide open with a loud bump.

Startled, Vivian sat up, watching in horror as Brita backed slowly away from the door. The food cart soared into the room, followed by the server. All the blood seemed to drain out of Vivian's head when she saw Chris, a gun clasped firmly in his hand.

Obviously, they hadn't escaped him after all.

"Chris!" Brita had tried to sound happy to see him, but her voice was little more than a squeak.

Judging from the scowl on Chris's face, he wasn't exactly overjoyed to see her. "You gave me up to the cops," he snarled.

Brita shook her head, "No, I didn't—"

"Don't bother lying about it. I heard you."

Brita looked bewildered. "What?"

"I saw you all standing outside that tea place. I heard you give the cops the license plate of my car."

Brita's eyes widened. "You were there?"

"Yeah. I had second thoughts about leaving you in that shack. I thought we might make a go of it, so I went back to get you. I saw the door had been broken down and figured someone had got you out. So, I drove down here to find you. That's when I saw you on the street, talking to the cops."

Vivian let out the breath she'd been holding. Chris must have reached the shack right after they left. If he'd arrived there any earlier, all three of them might have been shot, as well as Felix.

Shuddering at the thought, she eyed the phone sitting on a table by the bed. If she could somehow get close enough to take it off the hook and press the service button, someone might hear what was going on in the room.

It was a slight hope, but all she had. She just had to pray they could keep Chris talking long enough for her to reach the phone. "We need to talk this out," she said, rising slowly to her feet. "I'm sure we can come to some agreement."

Chris swung the gun toward her with a snarl. "Shut your mouth. This is all your fault. If you hadn't butted into something that was none of your business, everything would have been fine. So keep your mouth shut or I'll shut it for you."

It was the first time Vivian had ever stared down the barrel of a gun. She had never felt so cold in her life.

Brita cried out. "Chris! It's not her fault. This is between you and me."

Vivian went limp and sank back on the couch as the gun swung away from her.

"You bet it is, hon. You betrayed me. You said you loved me but you betrayed me to *the cops*."

His voice had risen to a shout. Maybe, Vivian thought, someone would hear him and alert the management. She clung to that desperate hope, though her common sense told her it was unlikely.

"I'm sorry!" Brita was weeping now. "I do love you, Chris. I wanted you caught because I was afraid I'd never see you again."

"Yeah? Well, say your prayers, because you're never going to see anyone again." Chris raised the gun and pointed it at Brita's head.

Vivian closed her eyes. She felt suddenly calm, as if she were watching the scene from far away. *I'm sorry, Hal. Always remember that I loved you. Be a good boy, Felix. Hal will look after you. I love you too.*

It was over. Any second now, she and Brita would be dead, and Chris would be on his way to the border. She fiercely hoped Messina would eventually track him down and throw him in jail for the rest of his miserable life.

Keeping her eyes closed, she waited for the shot.

*   *   *

Messina looked across the table at Jenna, his heart warming at the sight of her. There was no doubt about it. He was falling for her. By the look on her face right now, she wasn't exactly repulsed by him. He hoped he was reading her right. He raised his glass of wine and smiled. "Thanks for coming tonight. I know it was a last-minute thing, but I hope you enjoyed your dinner."

"I enjoyed it very much." Jenna lifted her glass too. "Thank you. You're quite the chef."

He liked that. He liked everything about her. After his wife died, he hadn't thought he could ever feel this way about someone else, but dammit, he was going to enjoy it while he could. "Let's move to the living room. I'll get the dishes later."

"I'll clear the table." Jenna drained her glass and stood up.

"No!" Messina cleared his throat. That had sounded like an order. He softened his tone. "Leave them. You've done enough table clearing today."

To his relief, she laughed. "Okay. To the living room, then."

"Okay." He was looking forward to sitting on the couch with her and moving their relationship a step onward. "I'll refill the glasses." He reached for her glass, pausing as his cell phone buzzed.

Jenna gazed at him for a moment, then got up. "I'll let you get that," she said, and walked away from him to the couch.

"I just have to check it." Sighing, he pulled his phone from his pocket. The station never called him unless it was an emergency. If it was anyone else, he would have ignored the call.

The number on the screen alerted him at once. He pulled a face at Jenna. "Sorry. I have to get this." Putting the phone to his ear, he barked, "Messina."

Brady sounded tense. "Just got a call from Hal Douglass. There's a problem at the Blue Surf Hotel. Hal spotted Bailey's car in the parking lot. He thinks Bailey's tracked the women down and is on his way up to their room. Third floor. Number 315."

Messina narrowed his eyes. "I'll meet you there. Bring Johnson and Dexter." He clicked off his phone and jammed it back in his pocket.

Seated on the couch, Jenna looked at him. "Emergency?"

He hesitated, unsure how much he should tell her. Deciding he didn't want to worry her, he shrugged. "I'm not sure, but I have to check it out. Sorry, Jenna. This has been a messed-up evening."

"It's fine." She stood up and walked toward him, her smile lighting up her face. "I had a good time. Now let's go." She leaned in to kiss him, then picked up her purse and headed for the door.

He would have given anything to stay there with her and deepen their relationship, but duty called. *Later,* he promised himself, and followed her out the door.

* * *

It was as if she'd heard her mother's voice in her head. *"Vivian! Don't just sit there. You can't give up now. Do something!"*

Vivian opened her eyes. Brita was pleading with Chris, who still held the gun pointed at her head. *Do something. Now!* Vivian soared to her feet. "Wait!"

Chris swore and swung the gun around to her. "I told you to shut up."

"Just listen to me." Vivian softened her voice. "There was a shotgun lying next to Lewis Trenton's body. He was pointing it at you when you shot him, right?"

Chris's scowl darkened. "Yeah. So what?"

"So, you can claim you shot him in self-defense. You'll get a much lighter sentence for that. Maybe even probation. If you kill us, you'll be in prison for life."

Chris's grin was evil. "I don't plan on being caught. By the time the cleaners discover your bodies in the morning, I'll be across the border."

"She's right, Chris," Brita said, her voice breaking. "Listen to her."

Chris turned on her again. "You betrayed me, bitch. You gotta pay for that."

Brita closed her eyes, her face chalk white.

Vivian took a step toward them. "Wait, I—" She cut off as a loud rap on the door interrupted her.

The command that followed was loud and clear. "Bailey! This is the police. Open up the door. The hallway is lined with cops. You're not going anywhere."

The harsh voice brought tears to Vivian's eyes. She uttered a soft squeak, then snapped her lips shut. There was no way she was going to let Chris know that it wasn't the police outside the door.

It was her beloved Hal. She prayed he wouldn't do anything fool-ish. He wouldn't stand a chance against Chris's gun.

"He's got a gun!" Brita shouted out.

"Put the gun down," Hal ordered. "Open the door. As long as the women are not harmed, I can promise you a fair trial and a light sentence."

Vivian nodded. "Exactly what I said to you," she said. "Listen to him. I know you're hurt and angry, but is it really worth giving up your freedom for the rest of your life?"

Chris seemed to waver, and she held her breath. But then he raised the gun again. "I don't care what happens to me. I'm gonna—"

He didn't get a chance to finish the sentence.

Vivian heard some scuffling behind the door, then an almighty crash, and the door flew open. She caught a glimpse of Messina, gun in hand, with Brady close behind him. Chris swung around, and Vivian reached out and grabbed Brita, pulling her away from him.

Messina charged into the room, and to Vivian's immense relief, all the fight ebbed out of Chris. He dropped the gun and raised his hands in the air.

Vivian's legs gave way, and she dropped onto the couch. Her entire body shook, as if she sat on an iceberg. Brita started sobbing and sat down next to her.

A loud argument broke out in the hallway. Vivian could hear Hal demanding to be allowed into the room. Seconds later he charged in, pulled Vivian to her feet, and wrapped his arms around her in a bear hug. "Thank God, thank God, thank God," he murmured, his voice husky with emotion. "I was so afraid I was going to lose you after all."

She looked up at him, feeling the strength seep back into her body. "How did you know?"

She was vaguely aware of Messina leading Chris out of the room in handcuffs, and Brady disappearing with him as Hal answered.

"I saw Chris's car in the parking lot. I remembered the make and model Brita gave to Messina. I called him and came back up here."

"He got here pretty fast."

"Thank God. I didn't know how long I could keep Chris talking while I waited for him."

"That's twice you guys have saved my life." Brita held out her hands, then dropped them again. "I don't know how to thank you."

She was crying again, and Vivian's heart went out to her. "Come back to the tearoom with me. We don't have to stay here tonight."

"Thanks, but I'd like to go home to the condo." Brita wandered over to the closet and collected her coat. "I feel like I've been run over by a truck."

"But you haven't eaten dinner yet."

Hal burst out laughing. "Always the practical one, even in a crisis."

"What do you expect? I'm half British."

"You are, indeed." He gave her a swift kiss.

"I'm not hungry anyway," Brita said. "Why don't you two enjoy the dinner." She walked over to the door. "I'll visit the Willow Pattern before I leave town."

"Please do. I'd like to keep in touch." Vivian blinked back tears. The two of them had been through a lot together. They had a bond now that couldn't be broken.

Brita hesitated at the door. "You're always welcome at the condo. Until I sell it, anyway."

"I'll call you," Vivian promised.

Brita nodded. "Goodnight." She stepped out into the hallway and closed the door.

Vivian suddenly felt self-conscious. She was alone in a hotel room with Hal.

He seemed a little ill at ease as well. He gestured toward the food cart. "I'm not hungry, but if you want to eat?"

She shook her head. "I can grab something to eat later. I want to go home. I want to be in my apartment, in my own bed, with Felix curled up at my feet."

Hal smiled. "I think we can arrange that. Get your things. I'll drive you home."

It was the best offer she'd had all day.

Chapter Eighteen

"This is nice." Vivian gazed around the elegant restaurant in awe. From the gold drapes at the windows, to the miniature chandeliers hanging above each table and the silver candlesticks with their flickering gold candles, the entire place spelled luxury. It was the first time she had been inside The Bellemer, and she was enjoying every second of it.

She had ordered the coconut shrimp, and Hal had decided on the surf and turf. Until their meals arrived, she had a cool glass of chardonnay to sip on and a man she loved sitting opposite her.

She gave him a closer look. He looked sharp in a black sweater over a white shirt, and she marveled at how he was able to dress casually but still look classy. He did seem a little tense, however. That was unusual for him. Most of the time he was so laid back, she'd often wondered if anything upset him.

Of course, that question had been answered in the last couple of days, with her narrow escape from death. She had never seen Hal so distraught. Maybe that's why he looked so edgy now.

He looked up and met her gaze. "What?"

She smiled. "I was just thinking that this is turning out to be a perfect evening. Just what I needed after all the trauma."

His bleak expression warned her he wasn't comfortable talking about it. "You must have been terrified."

"I was. Both times. I can't even describe the relief I felt when I heard you yelling outside the shack, but even that paled in comparison to the joy I felt hearing you again outside the hotel room door. I really thought I was going to die."

"So did I." Hal's voice was grim. "My whole future seemed to vanish in front of my eyes when I heard that bastard's voice in the room."

"Mine too." Vivian sighed. "I still find it hard to believe that it's over."

"Well, you can relax now and put it out of your mind. Brady called me and told me the Portland police rounded up the jewel thieves. Apparently Chris helped identify them in exchange for a deal with his sentencing."

Vivian uttered a derisive laugh. "Of course he did. Now, I suppose he'll get off light for almost killing Brita and me. Let alone killing Lewis Trenton."

"Well, he'll spend time in jail, that's for sure."

"I guess that'll have to be enough." She raised her glass. "I'm glad that I don't have to worry about it anymore. Thanks to you, I have a future to look forward to now."

"Well, that's kind of what I wanted to talk to you about." Hal looked around the crowded room. "I'm not sure this is the best place to do this, but here goes. The thing is, I've been thinking a lot about my future. I'm going to retire soon—sell the pet store and buy a motor home. I want to travel the country, visit all the places I've read about and never seen. When I've seen enough to know where I want to live out the rest of my life, I'll buy a small house and settle down again."

Vivian felt as if a hole was growing in her heart. "You're leaving Misty Bay?"

Hal smiled. "Not yet. Not for a while. But when I do, I was kind of hoping you and Felix would come with me."

The hole closed up. Vivian realized her mouth hung open, and quickly closed it. For a second or two she was dizzy with delight. Then reality sunk in. "What about the Willow Pattern?"

Hal shrugged. "You have to retire sometime."

She thought about it. No more dragging herself out of bed at six in the morning. No more scrambling to satisfy demanding customers. No more slaving over a hot stove. No more Jenna or Gracie? That would be hard. Would she miss it? Of course she would. But to tour the country with Hal and Felix would be heaven. She wouldn't have to worry about leaving Felix all day. He'd love that.

Aware that Hal was gazing at her with anxiety written all over his face, she smiled. "It's a lot to think about."

"Maybe this will help you make up your mind." Hal dug into his coat pocket and pulled out a box.

Vivian caught her breath as she watched him open it. Surely he wasn't going to . . .

"We've known each other for more two years now," Hal said, his voice gruff with emotion. "I think that's long enough to know what we both want. Life is short and I don't want to waste any more time. I've loved you for so long now, I can't imagine life without you. I hope it's what you want too. So, Vivian Wainwright, would you consider becoming my wife?"

She gasped as she saw the sparkling diamond ring in the box he held out to her. For once she was speechless, unable to say the words tumbling around in her mind.

Hal looked worried. "I'd get down on one knee," he said, "but I'm afraid I'd need help getting up again."

That did it. Trust Hal to break the tension with a joke. "I would love nothing more than to marry you," she said, the tears threatening when she saw the joy on his face. She loved this man, and he loved her back. She had a whole new future ahead. What could possibly be more perfect than that?

Acknowledgments

To my agent, Paige Wheeler, for so many years of cooperation, support, and friendship. You are an exceptional agent, and I'm fortunate to be working with you.

To my editors, for all your hard work on my behalf and for having the patience to work with me.

To my readers. I have often said that you are the best fans in the world. This past year has proven that. I deeply appreciate your loyalty, your caring, and your love. As always, I write for you, and you never disappoint me. Bless you all.